Author's Note

When I wrote Anna and the domestic abuse, I wanted leaders, protectors, and car have to rely on adults to prot(discover their courage and in: world. The story is told through the eyes of Anna, aged 11, but I hoped adult readers would enjoy it too.

They told me they did and I then realised I would have to write a sequel. Domestic abusers are unlikely to relinquish power without a fight, regardless of what a court order might say.

I felt the wicked fairy-tale King, who had formerly turned his Queen into a Snake, would now attempt to 'shrivel' her, by turning her into a worm – but what sort of worm? I love the novels of Terry Pratchett and in his world a rigorous logic prevails. A vampire can only turn into a bat if the bat has the same body mass as the original. Pratchett's vampire becomes a swarm of little bats.

Please read on ...

Anna and the Shrivelling

by

Jill Clough

SWALLOW BOOKS

SWALLOW BOOKS

OF THE ENGLISH LAKES

matthew-connolly.com

Copyright © Jill Clough 2024
www.jillclough.live

Text design: Debbie Aitchison

This book was authored by Jill Clough and not generated by any machine or artificial intelligence. This statement serves as a legally binding guarantee of authenticity and can be used to establish the true creator of this work should any doubt arise.

All rights reserved. No part of this publication may be reproduced, stored in a retrieval system, transmitted in any form or by any means, electronic, mechanical, photocopying, recording or otherwise, without the prior written permission of the author.

This is a work of fiction. Names, characters, businesses, places, events and incidents are either the products of the author's imagination or used in a fictitious manner. Any resemblance to actual persons, living or dead, or actual events is purely coincidental.

This book is sold subject to the condition that it shall not, by way of trade or otherwise, be lent, re-sold, hired out, or otherwise circulated without the author's prior consent in any form of binding or cover other than that in which it is published and without a similar condition including this condition being imposed upon the subsequent purchaser.

ISBN 978-0-9575740-7-6

Also by Jill Clough

Morph, Lakeland Book of the Year Award for Fiction 2019

Anna and the Snake Queen, 2020

If Dreams Should Die, 2022. Longlisted for Lakeland Book of the Year Award 2023
The Making of Cassie Clearwater, 2024

Chapter One: Friday

Stalking

'Anna. Stop. I need to talk to you.' The voice was sharp. No, don't run. You know I can catch you. I'm faster. You know I'm much stronger than you. Don't be silly.'

Anna gripped the top of the stone wall so hard she scraped the skin on the inside of her wrist. Where was he? He shouldn't be talking to her. Mum kept saying Dad wasn't to see her or Mikey. She licked the scratch and tasted blood.

He was right, of course, he could run fast and if he caught her she'd not be able to get away. Maybe she could bite his hand or poke him in his eye. 'You are not to talk to me.' Her heart beat so fast her mouth dried up.

'Nobody can force me to ignore my own daughter. Nobody believes that court order is valid. It's laughable.'

How had he found her? Parents didn't wait outside secondary schools, unless they were driving four-by-fours and didn't want their kids to catch a bus or walk. Some of the older pupils at her school were as tall as Dad, taller. It was a huge school, hundreds of pupils wandering out at the end of the school day. At least she didn't have to listen to other people's mums saying Dad was *drop dead gorgeous* and nudging one another, like in her primary school playground.

'Anna, are you listening?' His voice changed to the soft, wheedling tone he'd used when he said Mum was poorly and he'd keep her in bed for the day so could Anna kindly take Mikey to school on her own.

She did not mean to look at him but somehow she had turned her head, and there he was, on the other side of the wall, under a tree. The walk through the park alongside the river was one of her favourite ways home from school. She wished she had not stayed late for the reading club. Her heart still thundered in her ears but she knew what to say. Karina had helped them to practise.

'I can't talk to you and you can't talk to me. It's the law.' It would have sounded better if her voice hadn't squeaked.

Dad threw back his head and laughed. His hair flew out. He hadn't fastened it into a pony tail today. It was still so fair, it seemed to catch the sun and hold it.

'Law?' Dad folded his arms and raised an eyebrow. 'Laws can be changed. Besides, what about your mother breaking the law? She's twice taken you out of the country without my permission, dragging you off to that Greek island without letting me know.'

Anna had been rehearsed in this argument too. 'Mum doesn't need your permission.' Karina, their social worker, had told Mum it was fine to go, time for Mum to see her parents after so many years, time for the grandparents to meet Anna and Mikey.

'Who told you? That fat social worker who can't speak English properly?'

'She's very professional.' Words came more easily. 'She says grandparents have rights, they can see their grandchildren. You said Mum couldn't manage without you, you said your job was too important for you to take time off and it wasn't true –.'

Dad rolled his shoulders. Even from the other side of the wall she could smell his after-shave, the spicy juniper cologne he must still use. She gritted her teeth and made herself stand still.

'You have no idea what you're saying. You're still a child, legally speaking.'

'I'm not, I can discharge myself from hospital if I want.' Anna had a dim memory of something else Karina had told her about her rights, but now she wished she hadn't said it. Dad was clever. He'd know how to twist her words. She rushed on. 'You could have taken Mum to Symi with Mikey and me when we were little, but you didn't want her to see her mum and dad. Mum says you stopped her talking to them on the phone. You said they weren't interested in us.'

Dad's whole body tensed, although he still kept the half-smile. She would not glance away. He'd think she was scared. The shops were not far. If she ran into a shop he wouldn't follow her inside, not if she made a fuss.

'Scraping the barrel for social workers, I'd have said. That woman couldn't string two words together. I could barely understand her. As for leaving the country – your mother won't have understood anything the judge said. You know perfectly well her English isn't up to scratch. I've told you so often enough.' He took a step forward into the fallen leaves lying underfoot – orange and gold and deep brown. Once, Anna would have crunched them, but she knew better now. Leaves were part of the tree, part of its life.

Dad kicked out, reducing the leaves to dust. Anna winced. On the magical island she and Mikey had found, LeafFall was special.

'Why are you pulling faces? It does you no favours.'

Anna's feet would not move. She suspected running away would give him the excuse to chase after her, grab her. He'd put on his best academic voice and tell anyone watching she was his 'delinquent daughter'.

At least Mikey was safe. The old lady across the road collected him from school every day Mum was at work. Taking a deep breath, Anna braced herself, hands against the wall. 'I don't care.' Her voice was louder than she meant. 'Lots of people from school come this way home. There's a football match in the park.' She cleared her throat. 'It's a grudge match,' fingering the fringe of hair swinging across her eyes. 'It could be nasty, that's what everyone says. My friends think teachers will come, try to break it up.'

Dad sniffed. 'Why did your mother let you get that ridiculous haircut?' His smile had gone. 'It makes you squint. Your mother won't have taken you to get your eyes tested. I wouldn't let you develop a squint.'

He was losing his temper. Her new short haircut was feathery, and girls at school really liked it. They said it made her jawline look like a model's. Anna tilted her head and looked down her nose, an expression of Dad's she practised in front of the mirror. He would hate it. 'I'm going to dye it this year. Mum says I can. Pink and green streaks. Pretty,'

Dad's nostrils flared and her chest tightened. Making him riled was very satisfying but scary.

'You can't — I don't permit it.'

Anna saw the lines under his eyes, around his mouth, a deeper crease between his eyebrows. 'You can't stop me ... Daddy.'

Clenching his fists, he moved, stumbled and toppled sideways. Anna glimpsed tree roots hidden under the heap of leaves. Maybe a root had deliberately caught his foot. On Pelm, trees were more alive than here, more alert.

Pelm. The very thought made her sad. They had lost the way back.

On Pelm, the trees would have used their roots to trip up Dad. They were sentient. It was a good word. Anna had just discovered it. Leaf and Stone together made the island of Pelm, and a great Sea Snake created it. Sentient trees, magical rock, birds and animals so nearly like those at home, and an amazing, wonderful Queen — they all lived on Pelm, and she and Mikey would never be able to return.

While Dad was scrambling to his feet, she walked away. She would not let him see the tears on her face. How had he discovered her favourite route home? Had he stood outside school, followed her? The air grew colder. Taking the long way home, she had to fasten her jacket.

She hesitated, peered over her shoulder. No, he wasn't there. What if he had hung around Mikey's school? Did he know Mrs Dodd would collect Mikey? He knew their street, obviously, and he could never deceive Mrs Dodd with his, "I'm a serious academic, university lecturer" act. Mrs Dodd had once heard him hammering on their door, yelling at Mum. She had come out of her house and called across the road to ask if everything was all right. Perhaps Anna should tell Mrs Dodd about Dad turning up. She was probably giving Mikey chocolate biscuits right now. Mrs Dodd was little and old but she could be fiery. She used to be headteacher of a small secondary school, somewhere in Yorkshire.

Anna had reached the main road and peered through the glass door of the corner shop. It was full of students from the college. They seemed to go in most days to buy bottles of water and crisps and chocolate, or cartons of milk and packets of cheesy snacks. A girl pushed the door, trying to leave, her arms full of packets. Anna held the door open.

'Thanks kid. You coming, Aaron?' The girl smiled, passing Anna in the doorway, her hair piled high on her head and smelling of something flowery and sweet. Her eyes were outlined in black and pink. Anna thought, *I'm going to be like her one day.* Aaron had a boy's name but long brown hair, shiny blue lipstick, and several ear and nose-rings. His – her? clothes were confusing – blue dungarees, decorated with lots of badges, a white shirt with sleeves rolled up and a red and yellow striped tie loosely knotted. There was a boy in her class who'd started out as a girl. Anything could happen.

Karina said all the time she could choose not to see Dad. It was her right.

Shame Dad didn't seem to know this.

She swung her backpack off her shoulders and rummaged for her purse. She would buy a present for Mum, something for Mrs Dodd too. She went into the shop.

Racks of newspapers and magazines lined one wall, and handmade cards were stacked in holders near the till. They were designed by students studying art at the college, and showed the old buildings in the town, especially the crooked chimneys and steeply sloping rooftops, and the huge parish church. Anna had enough in her purse to buy three of them – two for Mum and one for Mrs Dodd. Maybe one of the students who had just left had designed them.

'Here you are, love,' said the shopkeeper, handing her back a fifty pence piece. 'They're on sale now. You got a bargain.'

'Thank you.'

She ran the rest of the way home. Dad wasn't around, but she wasn't taking chances. Anyway, she had presents. It felt wonderful to be taking presents, especially for Mum. And she would never again have to hide things from Dad.

At the gate she stopped, leaned on the wall and gazed at the flowers. Their garden was still bright with orange chrysanthemums – much more luxuriant than other people's. Mum couldn't explain it, though she loved planting flowers and Mrs Dodd said maybe Mum had green fingers. Anna wondered what Mrs Dodd would say if she explained how Mikey and she had found an island, where some of the people had green skin and were bonded with the trees. The Green people had green fingers, green arms and legs but their sclera – the whites of their eyes – were white, even though the pupils were a beautiful rich green. There were Stone people too, with beautiful pearly skin, grey eyes and pale hair. The Queen was one of Stone people, and so was the King, but he was vile. They'd beaten him, though, she and Mikey.

Tears prickled at the back of her eyes. She sniffed, turned and crossed the road to Mrs Dodd's house, where Mikey would be waiting for her.

Chapter Two

Toy Horses

'Mikey has a strange view of farm animals,' said Mrs Dodd. 'Did you know? He thinks these horses can fight. He says they ought to have silver horns on their heads. I said, unicorns? He got in a bit of a temper.'

Mrs Dodd had rummaged in her attic and found the toy farm she had bought for her sons. They were grown-up now but did not have children of their own. Mikey was on his hands and knees, shoving the toy horses around. Anna suspected a tantrum was not far off. If he couldn't say what he meant he still often lost his temper.

'Mikey, shall we go home now?'

Mikey shook his head, not looking at Anna but searching through a wooden box until he found a couple of model trees. The foliage was beginning to shed bits of green felt on the grey carpet and Anna made to pick them up, but Mrs Dodd said, 'Don't worry. I like seeing it all in use again. I've made shortbread biscuits for us, if you'd like one. Mikey has eaten too many chocolate biscuits, I'm afraid. You'll have to apologise to your mother if he won't eat his supper – no, I'll apologise when she comes.'

Without glancing in their direction, Mikey said,'

Fish fingers Friday.'

Mrs Dodd laughed. 'I guess that's my answer.'

They sat together at the table, while Anna drank orange juice and Mrs Dodd poured a cup of Earl Grey tea. 'I can't tempt you to try it again?'

'No thank you. It smells like flowers.'

'That's the bergamot, the herb.' Mrs Dodd inhaled the steam and smiled. 'I must say, I do like the mountain tea your mother gave me. She says it's made from herbs picked fresh from the mountains on the island and dried.'

'Mum says mountain tea helps her relax.' They had brought several packets back from Symi at the end of their long summer holiday this year, and sometimes Mum's eyes grew damp when she was drinking it. She said it was the steam, but Anna suspected Mum was homesick.

'I looked it up. The other name for it is shepherd's tea, did you know? It reminds me of a mix of chamomile and mint.'

'You look up lots of things,' said Anna.

'I got used to it, when I was a headteacher. I had to know things, find things out.'

'You must know an awful lot.'

Mikey banged two horses together. 'These chets don't work.'

'I'm so sorry,' said Anna. The shortbread biscuit snapped in her hand and she began to sweep the crumbs into a pile.

Mrs Dodd put out a hand to stop her. 'It's all right, Anna. I'm glad to see Mikey playing, being a proper little boy. It's perfectly all right for him to lose his temper.' She watched Mikey for a moment. 'Better than being an elective mute, or whatever the term is these days.'

Mrs Dodd had seen Mikey with the awful black eye Dad had given him when he'd got in the way when Dad was aiming at Mum. She'd seen Mum bringing Anna and Mikey to the house with no furniture in it, and the van full of stuff which the two kind men from the charity had brought, so they'd have beds to sleep on and chairs and a table and even a washing machine. Nobody had told Mrs Dodd about Dad kicking Mum. She must have guessed because there was a short column in the newspaper about the court order, and she'd knocked on the door to ask if she could help. When Mum was offered her new job, Mrs Dodd said straight away she'd like to look after Mikey. She didn't want to be paid. She said it was lovely to have a child in the house. She knew Mikey would not talk to Dad.

'There's no soldiers in this box.' Mikey was still grumpy.

'There aren't soldiers on a farm,' said Anna, leaning down to collect a stray sheep. Mikey was manoeuvring cart horses into battle formation. The cows as well as the sheep were pushed to one side.

'Yes but –,' he began

Anna shot a warning glance at him but he was focussed on his battle. She had to stop him talking about Pelm. 'We started playing a game when — before — I wanted to take his mind off things, so I made up a magic island and we went to it, and all the animals were all a bit different from real animals.' She bit her lip. Should she say more? 'I made up horses with two silver horns, and they were called chets, and there were birds, huge birds, with, like, frills along their backs, like dinosaurs. Stuff like that.'

'I thought he was the one with a highly inventive imagination but it's you,' said Mrs Dodd, nodding at Anna. 'Of course, birds are descended from dinosaurs, aren't they? I can see why Mikey would be drawn into the game.'

Anna flicked the biscuits crumbs. 'Mrs Dodd —.'

'Anna?'

The heat ran to Anna's cheeks. 'Nothing.'

'Something's troubling you. I won't be offended if you don't want to say. You're thirteen. Tell me what's worrying you, or don't tell me. It doesn't matter.' Mrs Dodd's face lost its smile. 'You're very sensible.'

'Do you really think so?'

The old woman reached out to finger Anna's fringe. 'It suits you, this haircut. It makes you look so much more grown-up.'

'I don't want to look like a little girl.'

'You don't behave like a little girl. I like to see a girl stand up for herself.'

Anna's cheeks felt hot and she bent down, pretending to adjust her shoe. 'Our history teacher says girls still have to stand up for themselves, in some countries, anyway.' The teachers knew about the court order. They were not to let Dad into the school, they didn't ask her about it, and now she had proper friends who didn't ask either.

'She's right, your history teacher,' said Mrs Dodd. 'I'd have been very happy teaching locally. There's a wide catchment, isn't there? Your friends don't live near, you said.'

'There's so much to do in town, I suppose,' said Anna, trying not to give away her feelings. She would have loved being picked up from the end of a farm track or a long gravel drive, or in a village square. 'Actually, our history teacher's a man.'

'That's my wrist slapped then,' said Mrs Dodd, running her fingers through her short grey hair. 'You'd think I'd know not to make assumptions. Have another biscuit – no, don't bother trying to eat those bits.'

Mrs Dodd's biscuits were full of butter, not like bought biscuits. Anna sucked her fingers, unwilling to lose a crumb. 'Have you ever done the Morecambe Bay Walk?'

'Now that's a question I didn't expect to be asked.'

'It's our geography homework this weekend, Morecambe Bay. Our teacher says it's time we got to grips with local geography.'

'What's the topic?'

'Tourism and the local economy.'

'Important to know, I imagine.' Mrs Dodd bit into her biscuit without shedding a crumb. 'Morecambe Bay is astonishing. I expect you've been told about the signs warning people to stay off the shore. People are forever ignoring them and having to be rescued. The tide races in faster than people can run and the quicksands change every day.'

Anna said, 'You know lots about it.'

'I remember the deaths.'

'She didn't say about deaths. She said there are seven islands.'

'You're thinking about Symi.' Mrs Dodd's thin face creased into a smile again. 'I sometimes think about booking myself a holiday on your mother's island.'

'It is beautiful.' Anna wished she could describe how it felt when they were floating in the Greek sea. She had no idea the sea could be so blue, so warm, so full of fish. 'My grandparents' relations are all fishermen. You can see tiny little boats going round the island, early in the morning. They mend their nets by hand. It's so different from here.'

'You want to go back.'

'For holidays, yes. I loved it. But this is home. Do people live on the islands in Morecambe Bay? It would be tricky, shops and school and stuff like that.'

'Islanders everywhere have to deal with stuff like that, as you say.' Mrs Dodd poured another cup. 'More squash?"

'No thank you.'

At least Dad wouldn't be able to follow them over the sea to an island.

'There ought to be more animals in this set.' Mikey sat on his heels, pushing the hair out of his eyes and the little horses into a heap.

'Mikey, don't grumble. It isn't polite.' She glanced at Mrs Dodd, who only smiled and shook her head.

'It's all right, Anna. I can see he's tired.'

'We'd better go home.' She worried that Mikey might annoy Mrs Dodd so much she would stop fetching him from school. Then Mum wouldn't be able to work so many hours and they'd lose money. Mikey wasn't listening. He flicked at a horse, sending it tumbling. 'What's the matter? Don't do that.'

Mrs Dodd leaned down, picked up the models and turned them over in her hands. 'I know these are rather old but I thought they'd be fine to play with. I'll put them away.'

Mikey glared at Anna. 'I had a horrible dream. You don't care.'

Anna tried to put her arms around him but he pushed her away. He hadn't pushed her away for a long time. 'Mikey, did something happen at school today?' He shook his head but the twist of his mouth worried her. 'Did Dad – something about Dad?' She clapped a hand across her mouth but it was too late. The words had escaped.

'Anna? What do you mean?'

Anna thought her brother had stopped breathing. She took one of his hands, pressing it between her own. It was hot. 'Mikey, if Dad came to your school today it's not your fault, truly.'

His fingers twitched and he stared at her with round, dark eyes.

'Anna, why would your father have turned up at Mikey's school?' Mrs Dodd's voice was sharp. 'That would be very serious.'

Mikey wriggled his shoulders, grimacing as if he did not want to cry. 'If he comes I can shout at him. I shouted at him before.'

'You did. You were very brave.' Anna began to pick up the farm animals, her own fingers trembling.

Mrs Dodd put a hand on her arm. 'Anna, what makes you mention your father? 'She frowned, pinching her chin and appearing, for a moment, as she must have done when she was a headteacher. 'Have you seen him? Is that the issue?' She breathed out in a long, heavy sigh, rose to her feet, and pushed back her chair. 'Surely your father would not ignore a court order

'Please don't tell.'

Mikey jumped up, his fists clenching. 'I will give

him a punch if he comes.'

'No – no, that wouldn't be right.' Mrs Dodd seemed taller than usual. 'Anna, if your father approached you that is very serious.'

'I got rid of him.' Anna stood up carefully, one hand on the table. Her knees seemed not to work properly.

'You got rid of him.'

'Please don't say anything to Mum. I'll tell her.' She glanced at Mikey and was surprised when he nodded.

'What happened exactly?' Mrs Dodd raised her eyebrows.

'He just – he sort of turned up. He only talked. I walked off. You don't have to worry about me.'

Mrs Dodd rubbed her mouth. 'An injunction can't be brushed aside. I can't ignore what you've told me.'

'It's okay, I'll tell Karina, you know, our social worker.' Karina had drilled into them that she was their first helper. 'I've got her phone number. She says I must let her know if something happens.'

Mrs Dodd gave her an unblinking gaze. 'Not your mother?'

Anna noticed how blue her eyes were, despite the lines around them. Something inside her was not as old as her face. Anna's eyes blurred and she blinked rapidly. 'Mum's good at her job. She sings when she's making breakfast.' She felt sick, remembering Mum being too afraid to sing. 'I'd rather tell Karina first. She'll know what to do.'

The doorbell sounded, the front door opened and Mum came into the room. She held a bunch of flowers. 'Hello my darlings. Have you been good? Miranda, these are for you.' The flowers were huge, long orange petals spreading around a deep red centre.

'Sofia, how lovely. Chrysanths are always wonderful at this time of year. Thank you.' Mrs Dodd took the bunch from Mum's hand and kissed her cheek. 'From your garden?'

Anna's hands were twisting together. 'Mum's a great gardener,' she said, hoping to stop Mrs Dodd from saying anything about Dad.

'I don't really know how to account for it but everything in our garden grows perfectly. I don't do anything special.' Mum unpinned her coppery-black hair from its tight bun and ran her fingers through it. 'Ready to come home?' The curls rippled to her shoulders, catching the light. 'Oh – a farm. You did not buy this specially? Mikey, what have you done with the sheep? These are beautiful models, Miranda.'

'I've been keeping them for when Joe and James have children of their own.'

'How kind of you to bring them out for Mikey.' Mum knelt and began to gather the animals together. 'Let's put them away. What elegant horses. Mikey, there's one behind you. Have you been racing the horses?'

Anna dropped to her knees. 'Come on Mikey, help.'

'I don't want –.'

'Mum, can I join another after-school club?'

'As well as the reading club? It rather depends on Miranda.'

'I don't mind if you want to stay late on another day,' said Mrs Dodd, but Anna sensed Mrs Dodd's gaze drilling between her shoulder blades.

Mum began to scoop the animals into the wooden box where they were stored. 'Which club do you wish to join?'

'There's a sort of eco-club,' said Anna. 'Mum, I'll do these. Come on, Mikey, you can do this too.'

He crawled towards her, mouthing something. She shook her head, scowled, said under her breath, 'Tell me later'

Mum told Mrs Dodd about the clients she'd met today, the time spent commissioning a printer for the new leaflets she'd designed, while Anna slid the lid across the box and nudged Mikey to lift it back into the corner cupboard where it was kept.

As they said goodbye, Mrs Dodd gazed at Anna, nodded slightly, and Anna knew she would have to do something about Dad – ring Karina, but tomorrow, maybe – nerve herself – people would get upset. When she crossed the road, her breathing eased. Tanda, her stripey cat, was waiting. She leapt off their garden wall, long tail swishing, ears pricked as she wound around Anna's legs. Mum unlocked the front door, and Tanda leapt neatly on to Anna's shoulder, nuzzling her ear. Anna read an article on a school computer about cat's behaviour and if a cat rubbed against you, it meant you were okay and the cat was in charge.

Mikey tugged at her backpack. 'We got to go back, find Kazan.'

Anna dropped her voice. 'There's no way back to Pelm. The prints were all painted over, you know that.'

'But he says I've got to come.'

For a second it was as though the old, black bruise reappeared around his eye. He rubbed at it, and the shadow vanished. Anna said, 'Was that – is it sore? Don't rub it.'

'What's the trouble, darlings?'

'Mikey's got a speck in his eye but it's out now.'

He said in a whisper, 'We got to find a way. I'm not being silly. Kazan's frightened, Anna. I don't like it.' He shivered.

Anna thought about Dad turning up. It was all too much of a coincidence. She heard Mum in the hallway and said under her breath, 'I'll think. We can talk later.'

'Promise?'

'Promise.

Chapter Three: Friday

Secrets

*A*nna couldn't settle. All through Fish Fingers Friday, with Mikey shovelling peas off the edge of his plate, Dad's words chased through her mind. She had promised Mrs Dodd to tell Karina about Dad.

An injunction can't be brushed aside.

Law changes. Your mother took you out of the country without my permission. She took you to that Greek island without letting me know.

Mum had changed out of the smart black trousers and red and white blouse she wore for work. Now she wore jeans and a long-sleeved white tee-shirt with a rainbow across the front. Anna wore the same tee-shirt in a smaller size. She loved being like Mum.

She had rushed in and out of her bedroom to take off her uniform. The bright, white walls brought light into the room, even on this early November evening. Only Mikey knew how frantic she had been when a man from the charity, Roger – being helpful – had painted over the dusty, flowery wallpaper left by the previous occupants of the house. Only Mikey knew about the green streaks, remarkably like handprints, stretching from floor to ceiling on one wall. Mum hadn't wanted them to use the bedroom. Its windows had been dirty, the paintwork flaked and wallpaper hung off in strips. Flies had been trapped in large, dusty cobwebs, and spiders ran into corners.

It had seemed such a generous offer, painting the room, Mum said. Anna could have a private space of her own. She was eleven, she would soon need it. Mum was right. Now that she was thirteen, Anna loved having her own space, where she could sit with her little cat and let her mind wander.

'Anna, you are very quiet tonight. Did something go wrong at school?'

'No, Mum, of course not.' Anna dropped her fork to the floor and dived under the table. Fumbling around to find it might explain her hot cheeks.

'Well, I have a surprise for you. Dave rang me earlier today.'

'Charity Dave?' Mikey picked up stray peas with his fingers. 'Charity Dave's nice.' A squashed pea shot across the table and Anna caught it as she stood up, relieved at the change of subject. Dave, the other man from the charity, was a big, round man with a soft voice, red cheeks, and wispy white hair.

'I know peas can be tricky. Yes, Charity Dave. I thought they'd finished helping us but a kind donor gave them two reconditioned laptops and he is offering them to us.'

Dave and Roger managed to be helpful without making anyone feel as if they ought to have been able to fix problems themselves. Anna cheered up. 'We haven't seen him for ages – not since he and Roger brought that filing cabinet for you. Is he coming soon?'

'Perhaps at the weekend. He asked me to think if there is anything else we need.' Mum paused. 'It would be greedy to ask for more.'

Anna wanted to ask for a winter duvet, and maybe thicker curtains in her room, but Mum was right. It was time they fixed things for themselves. They began discussing the laptops, and whether or not Mikey would be allowed to use one.

'Why can't I use one? We have computers at school.'

'Do you mean to finish your fish fingers or are you going to chop them into bits and leave them?'

'They went cold.'

Mum leaned over to smooth the black hair from his face. 'You're tired. It's the end of the week. Maybe you'd just prefer a cheese sandwich.' His face almost crumpled, as if he were about to cry. 'It's okay, little one – all right, Year Three boy. Give me your plate.' Mum flashed a smile over her shoulder as she went into the kitchen.

Anna banged her fork on the table. 'Do you really have to make a fuss?'

Mikey's eyes filled with tears. 'We got to –,' waving his hands. 'I got to see Kazan, he's – I dreamed he was in a cave and he couldn't get out. It was horrible.'

'It was just a dream, Mikey.' A cold dread sat at the bottom of her stomach. 'I'm sorry you had a bad dream.'

'It wasn't just dreaming.' He swept the tears from his face with the back of his hands. 'The handprints all went. How do we get back to Pelm? I got to help Kazan.'

Mum reappeared, carrying a sandwich and Anna sighed with relief.

'Cheese, Mikey. Eat it all. I'll chop up an apple.

No arguments.'

Mikey pulled a face and Mum said, 'Do you two have secrets again?'

'Everybody has secrets.' She had to distract her mother. 'Harry Potter had secrets.'

'Harry Potter had very unpleasant relatives.'

'Have you read Harry Potter books?'

'Why should I not? You were reading one and I borrowed it whilst you were at school. I wanted to see what so interested you.'

'Oh. What interested me?'

Mum leaned across and ruffled Anna's short hair. 'This cropped hair suits you very well, but your face shows every thought.' Anna resisted the urge to push Mum's hand away.

Then Mum said, 'I thought you would like stories about young people facing great danger and overcoming it,' and Anna's heart fluttered in her chest. Had Mrs Dodd already mentioned something about Dad? She chewed the inside of her cheek.

'I finished.' Mikey slid from his chair and stood up. His cheeks were rounded, still full of cheese sandwich, and he bounced from one foot to the other, leaving the room.

Tanda brushed past Anna's legs, making the hairs on her body quiver. The cat's tail was more fluffed than usual, curling like a question mark as she sidled out of the room. 'I'll – I'll just give her a brush, Mum, she needs a good brush.'

'Your homework, moro mou?'

'I'm not your baby.' Anna tried to sound cross but Mum was in a cheerful mood.

'Well, my love, homework? What is your homework tonight?'

'I've got all weekend, Mum, it's only Friday.'

'Of course, but you will want to be busy tomorrow. Make a start tonight?'

Anna swallowed the sigh. 'We've got stuff to do about local geography. Rivers.'

'You are learning about our river?' Mum nodded as if she were interested.

Anna was more intrigued than she wanted Mum to know. 'The river flows so fast across Morecambe Bay it makes its own channel, and huge sandbanks keep changing. People drown when the tide comes in. I'd like to see that.'

'You want to see people drowning?'

'Now you're making fun of me,' Anna said. 'I'm going to check on Mikey.'

Mum rested her chin on her hands. 'When I'm earning more money, would you like to live by the sea, or near a river?'

In the past, Anna would have been horrified at the idea. The night they'd run away from Dad, they'd met a woman in the hostel who had spent two nights under one of the bridges over the river. She couldn't find anywhere else to go. She had a tiny baby. The river Kent was so black and noisy at night, dashing through the town, it had scared her. Anna liked water now, as long as it wasn't full of other people's poo and plastic. 'I suppose I might.' She hesitated. 'Is it because of Symi, Mum?'

Mum's eyes were very bright. 'I would love to be close to the sea again.'

'Our geography teacher said the Kent can be dangerous. It floods into houses and factories and warehouses. That's why they've built all the flood barriers. They aren't very pretty, are they?'

Mum laughed. 'I imagine there is not enough money to make flood defences attractive. Is Mikey all right? It isn't so easy to work out what he wants.'

'I might get his dinosaurs out for him to play with.'

'You are my lovely helpful girl,' said Mum. Her long black hair, lemony from her favourite shampoo, swung over Anna's face and Anna inhaled the warm perfume, her heart jumping with guilt. She had not told Mum about being stalked.

Mikey was in his bedroom, lying on the floor and kicking the small wooden bed.

Anna folded her arms and said, 'Mikey, what's this dream about Kazan?'

Mikey rolled over and sat cross-legged. He held his T-Rex toy, snapping its jaw open and shut. 'We got to go back to Pelm.'

Anna's nostrils flared. 'Well, we can't. You know that.'

He said, 'You got Tanda,' and he gave her a look from under his eyelashes.

'Tanda's just my big kitten.'

'You didn't have to call her Tanda. Why did you call her Tanda?'

On Pelm they had met a squillkit — a beautiful cat-like creature with two tails, whose touch enabled Anna to link her mind with other people's. Her name was Tanda. After the way back to Pelm disappeared under a layer of white paint, a kitten appeared in their garden, stalking out from under a bush and leaving no trail of pawprints. It was too much like magic to ignore and Anna knew she had to be called Tanda.

At first she thought it was coincidence but when the kitten nuzzled into her neck Anna was transported to Pelm and its tangled trees full of strange fruit. She saw again the orzels — great white birds with crests along their backs, and bright blue eyes. The Green people knew how to see through the eyes of the orzels as they flew, and the King had captured two or three, using them as spies. Then there were the chets. Anna and Mikey had met these sleek horses, ready for battle, the two silvery horns on their heads catching the light. Best of all were the chiriku, tiny birds all the colours of the rainbow, flocking together as if they read each other's minds.

Anna sensed the link between Tanda the squillkit and Tanda the kitten in her garden was strangely magical. It ought to be impossible. How could she see through the eyes of her kitten? And yet she did.

She did not want Mikey to know how badly she longed to see the creatures from Pelm again, and she did not want to explain the link in case talking about it made it disappear. 'It's a nice name. I like it.'

Mikey scrambled to his feet. 'We could take Tanda into your bedroom, she might make us see the prints.'

'She comes in all the time and we don't see anything.'

'Please, Anna, please. We got to try. Please?' He came up to her and wiggled his T-Rex under her nose. His curly black hair tickled her chin.

'Why was your dream so bad?'

'He was crying. Kazan doesn't cry. I never saw Green people crying.'

'I suppose we didn't.' She looked at her brother more closely. 'What's wrong really?'

He rubbed his eye. 'Mum's being funny.'

'What do you mean?'

He was right, though she could not say why. She would not accept what Dad had said, that time they had been eating lunch in a café on the high street with their friends, Diego, Tara and baby Andrea. Dad came in with a solicitor. He said he was sorry for Mum because she had mental health problems. He thought she might be 'bipolar'. Anna had looked it up afterwards. Dad had no right to pretend Mum was ill. People who were bipolar suffered dreadfully in their minds and sometimes didn't know what was real and what was a kind of dream. Some of them had hallucinations.

In the café, Dad pretended they had made up about him hitting Mum. He said Mum was a bad influence. Mum – Anna still went cold when she remembered – Mum had stood up in the middle of the café and taken off her blouse. People had gasped. Women didn't take off their tops in public, well, not in a café, not women like Mum. They gasped even more when she turned round and they saw all the scars and bruises and burn marks on her back and front. Mum usually wore a scarf around her neck to hide the red finger-marks. Customers got out their phones and took photos and the solicitor made Dad go away.

Mum didn't have mental health problems. She wore the prettiest clothes now, and if she wore a scarf it was silk, from Rhodes.

Mikey looked so like Mum it seemed obvious he was half-Greek and everyone on Symi said so. Anna thought she was the one with the problem. People used to say she was the image of Dad and even her short hair was not enough of a disguise.

'Kazan was crying.' Mikey's eyes were damp.

'Let me think what to do. Not tonight. I need to think. Tomorrow. Maybe.'

Tomorrow she would ring Karina. Mrs Dodd would be sure to ask.

When she could not sleep, she sat up in bed, arms folded over her knees, Tanda purring at her feet, and worried about Mikey's dream. Kazan was the green boy who waited for them the first time they crossed the magic bridge to Pelm. He said he'd been waiting, expecting them. They were going to set the Snake Queen free from the King's horrible spell and stop the King attacking the Green people.

They had three Tasks to complete and they had completed all three.

She shook her head. Mikey must just have had a bad dream.

Chapter Four

You bear my marks

*A*nna was in a cave, deep underground, but it wasn't dark. Her skin prickled as she twisted round, squinting. Everything sparkled. Above her swung oval lanterns, glass-sided, candlelight flashing off the crystals in the rocks and giving them the radiance of diamonds. She backed against the nearest wall, fighting against a passionate desire to reach out - touch - the crystals. Her heart began to race and sweat broke out on the palms of her hands.

It was a warning but she could not name the danger - not at first - not until her forefinger throbbed. A fine line of dark moisture appeared on the finger. She licked it, tasted the salty, metallic tang of blood. Even as she stared, the line of blood vanished. Her finger retained the memory of a scar.

In the distance was the sound of running water. Maybe there was a way out. Instinctively her feet moved and she walked forward, until the walls of the cave receded and she was in a huge cavern. Lanterns shed enough light for her to see the rocky path glimmering ahead and she moved towards it. Water skimmed over the path, deepened, becoming a stream because she could not step aside. Soon, her feet were wet - ankles - calves - she had to wade - she must get out of the water or she might have to swim for now there was the tug of a current, pulling her on, on, faster, faster –.

A voice spoke from the darkness. 'Reach for the bank. You will find a rope to guide you.'

Breathing hard, she groped with her left hand and found a rope attached to a rock. The rope ran above the stream, threaded at regular intervals through holes in the rock. Her feet were bare as she made her way over tiny stones on the path, afraid of bruising a toe or stumbling. Her whole concentration was on each step. Somewhere ahead was a man whose voice sounded familiar.

'Anna.' He spoke again, softly, and her heart beat so fast it was hard to breathe. He was moving towards her. 'Come to me, Anna.'

'I can't see you.' She did not mean to speak but her body was making its own decisions.

'I will bring you the light.' Seconds later, he stood on the opposite bank, dressed in silvery armour and a silver cloak. His hair, so nearly white it glittered, hung softly to his shoulders, and he leaned on a great, curved sword. Behind him, the crystals on the cave walls pulsed like stars. 'I knew you would come when I called. You bear my marks. One day you will be entirely mine.'

Anna wanted to speak but her throat had closed tight. Inside her head a voice screamed, but she could not find the words of the spell – the spell? And then it seemed that not speaking was better than answering this person, this King. Yes, he was the King. The small silvery circlet sitting around his forehead could have been for a knight, only he wasn't a knight.

She had escaped from him before. She must wait for

the moment. He wanted to boast, had thrown back his head, was looking down his elegant nose.

'The Queen thinks she has won. You were foolish, helping her break out of the snake body I gave her. Now she is marked as a snake. She is no better than the Leaf people. LeafFall has begun and she will have nowhere to hide. I will use the Shrivelling Spell. She will be no larger than a worm. And those children, that child who assisted you –,' swinging the sword in a lazy arc to point it at her, 'he will be easy to control. He cares too much for the small ones. Their fears overwhelm them.'

Tanda. The word swam into Anna's head. She did not know what it meant, but it felt strong and warm. *Tanda. Queen.*

A rush of wind gusted through the cave, lifting the man's cloak and bringing with it the roaring, salty scent of the open sea. The walls of the cave began to shake, and the King swung round to face the change. He swallowed hard. Anna sensed a mighty presence rising from the ocean deeps, a creature swimming to the surface, a creature she did not need to fear, whose mind she had joined before.

And she said aloud, 'Tanda.'

Chapter Five: Saturday

Looking for the Starstone

*A*nna lay sprawled on the bedroom floor, in front of her mirror. It had swung sideways, as if somebody had kicked it. It was a long and heavy, had needed special fixings to stop the plaster cracking under its weight. She had Roger to thank for drilling the holes.

Slowly she got to her feet. Goosebumps freckled her bare arms. She must have been lying on the floor for a while. She straightened the mirror and winced. The forefinger on her right hand was sore. She couldn't remember trapping it or dropping something on her hand.

There had been a dream ...

It would be hopeless trying to get back to Pelm through the green handprints. Roger had painted them so carefully she had burst into tears. To distract her, he had pulled Liquorice Lips and Fizzy Fangs from his pockets and it was impossible not to laugh. She found herself telling him a bit about the jealous King, the Queen he had turned into a snake, and how Anna had helped her to become her true self again ... and the green streaks he'd painted over were the way she and Mikey got into that other world. He had listened and said she would find another way.

It was hard to keep her face calm during breakfast. Mikey kept kicking her under the table but she didn't want Mum to notice and tell him off. She knew what he wanted. She ought to be like Roger and Dave. They didn't try to be nice, they just were, especially Roger.

Roger hadn't made fun of her when she asked him about things being real or just fantasies. He said sometimes what people believed in was as real as what they could see and touch. Maybe those weren't his actual words but Anna had brooded over them. Roger's twin brother was a teacher in prisons and Roger was training to be a social worker like Karina. He believed in people's feelings. He didn't think Anna was making things up.

Dad did, like when he made fun of Mum's beliefs.

Mum was Greek Orthodox but the nearest Orthodox church was so far away she had started taking them to the local Roman Catholic Church. Anna supposed they'd be going tomorrow. She didn't really understand what Mum believed except, maybe, when she stood in the great church at Panormitis, on Symi, asking the Archangel Mikhael to help them out, something had worked. When they got back Mum had been offered the job at the agency. That was two years ago.

Mum said if St Mikhael answered prayers a gift had to be left and the church was stuffed full of them. Anna thought, though, if you were giving something to an angel a 'thing' couldn't be right. It would have to be something better than that – a promise, perhaps?

After breakfast, she tried being helpful, carrying the plates and cutlery into the kitchen and putting them away in the cupboard. Mum said she was going to the shops. She knew she could trust Anna to be sensible with Mikey, waved, and went out of the house.

Mikey had not left the table. She said, 'Come on, let's try now. Let's see if we can find the handprints.'

'Are we going to Pelm? Right now?' He jumped up, raced towards the stairs and fell into her room before she had time to invite him. He stood in front of the wall where the handprints had been, legs astride. She could almost hear him holding his breath.

'Mikey, what do you think will happen?'

'I'm thinking. You got to imagine me thinking.'

Anna folded her arms. She knew the handprints would not appear. How often had she stared at the wall as soon as the room was ready for her to move in, staring and staring, wishing and wishing? Mikey ran at the wall, kicked it, burst into tears and threw himself on her bed.

She was surprised by a pang of sympathy. 'Mikey, we'll find a way. Don't mess up my bedspread.' She tugged at the end, trying to smooth it. 'Look, I know it worked before. The handprints were real, but they've gone. Roger thought he was making the room nice for me.'

He sobbed out loud in great gulps.

'Now you're pretending. What's really the matter?' The little shred of sympathy would disappear any time now.

'I lost my Starstone.'

'Oh.' Anna's heart sank. 'That's bad.' The Starstone he had brought back from Pelm wasn't like an ordinary pebble. It held powerful magic. 'No wonder you're making a fuss.' Anna sighed, grasped his shoulders and heaved him forward until he sat on the edge of the bed. "Didn't I say don't put it in your school trousers? Did it fall out?'

He used the hem of his yellow tee shirt to scrub the tears from his face. 'A boy threw it away.'

Gradually the story came out. Some of the bigger boys had picked on him. A group had pinned him down and emptied his pockets. The more frantic he became, the louder they laughed and one of them threw the Stone over the wall.

Anna plumped down on the bed beside him, closed her eyes and thought if she ever saw one of those boys she would punch them. She ground her teeth and then broke out in a sweat. Punching had been Dad's special way with Mum when he was cross ...

'Did you tell a teacher about your Starstone?'

'No.' He sounded more miserable than ever. 'A teacher came and told them off for pushing me. She sent them to Mr Carey and she took me in the office and gave me a drink of squash. She said bullying wasn't allowed.'

'Was that Miss Morgan, the one who used to be your teacher?'

'She's nice.' Mikey slid off the bed, wandered over to her chest of drawers, picking up a bottle.

'Don't mess about, that's my bottle of perfume. Mum said I could have it.'

Mikey pressed the top. 'It smells like in our garden.'

'Not now,' said Anna, rescuing the perfume. 'It's rose. Our roses are dying.'

'There's still roses.'

'A few.' She watched Mikey wander around the

room, picking up books, her hairbrush, a framed photo of Yaya and Papou on one of the beaches with Mum between them- an old photo, before she met Dad.

'Will we go and see them next year? Do they miss us?'

'Of course they do. They're our grandparents. They always want to see us.'

Mikey picked up the photo of Panormitis monastery. Her grandfather had bought it for her, because she had loved the monastery. 'Papou said you got to remember him when you look at this. Can I have it in my room?'

'You can borrow it if you like.'

'I wish we could see them now.' He rubbed the photo against his chest.

Anna's stomach churned. Yaya was thousands of miles away. When she had told Roger about going to Symi for their first visit he scratched his head and said he thought there was a very famous monastery on the island, with a patron saint called St Mikhail. She had stood beside Papou in the middle of the great church, and thought, *St Mikhail, I know the Snake Queen was real. Are you real? Other people could say I was just dreaming but Mikey had the same dream.*

The church at Panormitis had been enormous, with a high roof painted all blue and gold, and saints with golden haloes, and angels with wide wings spread against orange backgrounds. On upper levels, like balconies, people wandered over great white arches, looking down at Anna as she stared up. Light poured in through the huge windows and Anna had felt so full of light herself it was almost like being back on Pelm, when the Queen rose out of the lake, transformed into her proper self again – more than herself. Her skin was covered with the same markings as the Sea Snake. It had been a mystery.

A shiver ran up her spine.

Tanda arched her back against Anna's legs and feeling of lightness spread through her body.

Tanda is giving me pictures in my head, making me believe I can see Pelm. Are my dreams real? St Mikhail, dreams are in my brain but my brain is real and my thoughts are real. When I do Maths in my head it's real. What's truly real?

'She never purred so loud before,' said Mikey, clutching her hand.

Anna's vision wavered. She saw a tall boy, his skin the colour of sycamore leaves in summer, and a small child beside him, equally green. The tall boy was frightened. How did she know? The boy was Kazan, yes, it was Kazan. Her legs felt cold and the picture disappeared. Tanda stalked away towards the door, twitched her tail, and slipped out on to the landing.

A burning sensation flared across Anna's cheek, so strong she ran to the mirror to stare at her reflection. A bright red scar blazed, vanished, flamed again. Shaking, she touched the reflection, and the scar disappeared. This shouldn't be possible – the King's touch had scarred her cheek but that was when they were on Pelm. How could the old magic be coming to life at home?

She drew a deep breath. 'When Mum comes back we're going for a walk to your school and we're going to find your Starstone.' She held up a hand. 'Don't shout, Mikey. We'll take Tanda and she'll help.'

Mikey's eyes grew huge and dark. 'Like magic,

you mean?'

Anna rubbed her nose. 'We can't go back the way we did before. There must be another pathway, and maybe your Starstone can show us. We'll find it.'

'How we gonna do that?'

'Not sure.'

He picked at a loose thread on his tee-shirt. 'I couldn't tell a teacher.'

'Well, the Starstone looks like an ordinary pebble, doesn't it? Teachers wouldn't have understood.' She touched Mikey's hand. 'Don't pull – the hem will get undone and Mum will have to sew it up. Don't make faces, Mikey. You discovered the Starstone. It's the most powerful Stone on Pelm and the King would do anything to get it, but we know he can't. It doesn't belong to him.'

'Is magic real, Anna?'

She hesitated. 'Well, it is on Pelm. I suppose, on Pelm everyone believes in it and it works, so they call it magic. For us magic isn't real. I don't know.'

She wasn't telling the truth. Something *was* happening in their garden – something connected with Tanda sleeping under the bush by the fence, her disappearing pawprints, flowers the same as in other people's gardens but bigger, richer, stronger.

Lunch was simple – chunks of bread, cheese, crisps and slices of apple. Mum said she had work for the agency and could they occupy themselves for a bit. Mikey made great dark eyes at Anna and Anna said, 'I'll take Mikey to the park.'

Mum gave a sigh and lifted her dark hair away from her face. 'Thank you.' She opened the laptop case, lifted out the computer and set it on the table.

'I won't be long, I promise. Take care crossing the roads, won't you?'

'Mum! It's practically my way to school and I go on my own."

Mikey said, 'We use the crossing lights. We learned at school. It's simple.'

Anna smothered a laugh at the startled expression on Mum's face. Mum would be even more surprised if she knew they were taking Tanda on their walk.

The bigger surprise was Tanda knowing how to cross roads at traffic lights, how to sneak past people on the pavements. One girl pointed and laughed, and a man said he took his cat for a walk every night, though probably it was true to say the cat took him.

When the park came into view, Anna said, 'Maybe I ought to let Tanda take me for walks every day. What do you think?'

Mikey shook the hair out of his eyes. 'She's got to find my Starstone.'

Anna wondered what was going through his mind. 'I thought you could stand by the wall where that boy threw your stone.'

'He's a horrible boy. He's a big bully.'

'Is he much bigger than you?'

Mikey frowned, flexing his fingers. 'He's a Year Sixer.'

'He'll find it much harder to be a bully in big school,' said Anna, although she wasn't sure this was true. Bullies had their ways. She sighed. Mikey wouldn't be happy till he had his talisman, his Starstone.

A car horn blared and Anna started, jumped back, her heart hammering.

'Look out, stupid kid, you want to get yourself killed?'

She had stepped off the kerb without noticing. The motorist was right. Mikey and Tanda were safely on the other side of the pedestrian crossing. The lights had changed from green to red while she had stopped concentrating. She bunched her fists. The smell of exhaust fumes filled her nose.

There were no cars on Pelm.

They were soon at the school. Along one side of the playground ran a lane lined with trees and bushes. Leaves were falling fast and Mikey's stone would be hard to find. If it was there. They walked along the lane, staring hard at the ground, until Mikey stopped dead and stamped his foot.

'We can't never find it.' His face contorted, and then Tanda leapt past him, chased her tail, and sprang into the bushes. 'Where's she going?' He pulled back the branches and scrambled into the shrubbery. Anna pretended to look at leaves and weeds, hoping no passerby would ask what they were doing.

Mikey reappeared, grinning so hard she wanted to hug him. 'I got it,' he said, disentangling himself from a thorny branch.

'How do you know it's the Starstone?'

Mikey held up his fist. It glowed, showing the small bones of his hand as if on an X-ray – not that Anna had seen an X-ray, only photos. 'It's all warm.'

'You won't lose it again, will you?'

'I got to look after it. Pelm gave it to me.' His eyes glittered and she saw that he was proud. He had a right to be — not just for carrying out Tasks on the island, but standing up to Dad, like the time on Windermere, on a steamer, when Dad had sneaked on to the boat. Mikey had shouted about Dad punching him, and Tara overheard. After that, she became their friend.

They grinned at one another. Mikey said, 'It's real proper magic here. My Starstone is magic here.'

'I'm on my way.' The loud comment came from further along the lane — a man's voice. Anna grabbed Mikey's arm and pulled him back along the path, away from the voice.

'Is it Dad?'

'I don't expect so,' said Anna but her heart was racing. 'Where's Tanda?' What if Tanda were to be squashed by a car, her beautiful fur all bloodied and torn? She glanced back and gasped with relief, bracing herself for Tanda's leap. The little cat's claws snagged in her shoulders, but did not pierce through the fabric of her coat.

They walked quickly, trying not to run. Anna practised explanations all the way home. "There were too many big boys in the park and Mikey didn't like it", or "Tanda followed us so I had to bring her back". She wanted to skip.

At bedtime she remembered the designer cards again, and not ringing Karina.

Monday would do. She couldn't ring Karina on a Sunday. As long as she'd made the call before Monday when she went to Mrs Dodd's to fetch Mikey, it would be fine.

Chapter Six: Sunday

The Tin Man, the Scarecrow and the Cowardly Lion

*M*ikey didn't want to go to church. He dragged at Anna's arm, hissing. 'What about Kazan? Why aren't we finding the way now I got my Starstone?'

'Keep your voice down. Don't let Mum hear you..'

'But I got my Stone.' He patted the pocket of his jeans.

'Do shut up —.'

'Please don't quarrel.' Mum glanced back, zipping up her grey and green jacket. 'It's cold today.'

Anna chewed her thumb and spoke in a whisper. 'There's going to be a way but I can't work it out if you keep complaining.'

They reached the church, and Mikey ran up the steps. Mum turned, frowning, but all Anna could do was shrug and spread her hands.

Mum stroked Anna's cheek. 'What was that about? I suppose he's gone to find the boys. I hope they are here.'

Anna stared across the riverside garden opposite the church, and wished she could find a boat or a kayak, scull down the river and escape to the sea. Sighing, she followed Mum into the porch. The woman who was always there on Sunday mornings smiled at them as she handed a church newsletter to Mum. 'The weather's getting chilly, isn't it? You must miss Greece. It's so warm there.' Her puffer jacket was bright red.

'Yes,' said Mum. 'I'm glad it's warm in church.'

'Father Bernard has turned up the heating, he says.'

Mum made for the metal rack of little candles beside one of the aisles and stopped to light one. She knelt, murmuring. Anna had given up wondering what she was saying. When Mum stood up she said, 'Mum, why did she have to say you must miss the warm weather? You haven't lived in Greece for years and years.'

'She's friendly. Don't be cross.'

Dad said people who believed in God were feeble-minded but the church was quite full — old men, young men, women and girls, lots of children, black and white people mixed together. Anna thought they couldn't all be feeble-minded. Dad said people were "feeble-minded" when they disagreed with him.

The priest, Father Bernard, watched films on TV, made jokes that were actually quite funny, and said it was everyone's duty to look after refugees and prisoners and poor people. He didn't know Mum and Anna and Mikey had relied on the charity to get them furniture.

Mikey was already sitting with a couple of boys in the front pew. Mark and Nathan were the big brothers of Sam, who was getting the hang of talking and kept on, whatever was happening in the service. Their dad, Jake, stood in the aisle, talking to Father Bernard, holding Sam in his arms. From halfway back

Anna could hear, 'Book, book, book.' Jake ruffled the baby's fine red hair and carried on talking.

Had Dad ever ruffled her hair and hugged her as if she were precious?

'Come and sit with us,' said Abigail, shuffling along the pew. She was their mum.

It was the day for the music group – two guitarists, a violinist, a child with a tambourine, her mother playing little drums, a woman playing the flute and a man striking chords on a keyboard. Everybody sang. It was still a surprise to Anna.

When it was Father Bernard's turn to talk he started by telling everyone about a film he'd just watched on catch-up television. It was called *The Wizard of Oz*. 'Hands up if you've seen it.' Practically everyone had, and Anna leaned down, pretending to adjust her shoes. She did not want to be noticed. Mikey put his hand up even though she was sure he hadn't seen the film. She had heard of it, of course, but Dad wouldn't let her and Mikey watch much television.

'You remember the main characters of course,' said Father Bernard. His hair was almost white, cut very short, but his eyes were bright and his voice carried clearly to the back of the church. Anna had not expected to like him and was surprised to look forward to whatever he was going to say, even if the rest of the service sent her into a doze. 'Apart from Dorothy, who's trying to find her way home, there's the Tin Man, who hasn't a heart, the cowardly Lion, and the scarecrow with straw instead of a brain.' A woman in the row behind Anna began to sing under her breath. The song was so famous even Anna had heard it and in seconds the singers had joined in and even the man playing the keyboard struck the right chords. "We're off to see the Wizard, the wonderful Wizard of Oz." Around Anna everyone joined in the song and people started to clap. Father Bernard laughed and waited until they had finished.

'Dorothy wanted to find the way home, Tin Man longed for a heart, the Scarecrow was in search of a brain and the Cowardly Lion pined to be brave. The Wizard handed out tokens which he said would give each of them what they wanted but it turned out he was a bit of a cheat. He was just an ordinary man, not a Wizard. The tokens weren't magical at all – the truth was much more interesting. The Tin Man had always had a heart, the Scarecrow always had a brain, the Lion wasn't a coward at all and Dorothy's red shoes knew the way home. Each of them realised that the truth was inside them all the time.' He paused for a moment.

Anna gazed up at the big stained-glass windows. Perhaps she and Mikey were like the children in the Wizard of Oz because Mikey had discovered on Pelm how to be brave and she had realised how to use her wits – but she'd always had her brain and Mikey must always have been brave. He just had to find his courage. Her mind drifted. Perhaps Mum had always been brave too.

Someone patted Anna's hand. 'Are you awake?' Mum gave a little tug. It was time to stand up for more prayers.

Mum said it wasn't the same as her church back in Greece. She supposed the Greek Orthodox Churches in Lancaster and Preston might be similar but she couldn't be sure. She didn't mind, though. Father

Bernard was very easy to talk to, and after the service they went into the parish hall and had coffee or orange squash and biscuits. Mikey went with Mark and Nathan to the gang of boys at one end of the hall. They practised standing on their heads and kicking. It was very noisy.

Today, Mum was quieter than usual on the walk home. Anna slid her hand into the crook of Mum's arm and tried to keep in step but Mum was taller so it didn't work – in fact, she began to think it was Mum who didn't want it to work. 'Thank you, dear girl, but – do you mind?' She let Anna's hand slip away from her arm.

Anna wanted to ask what she was thinking but Mum got in first. 'Did you enjoy the homily today?'

'What?'

'The Tin Man and the Lion?'

'It was okay.' Her mind had wandered. Was Dad ever really nice to Mum? Had she fallen in love with him?

'Anna?'

'What?'

Mum sighed. Mikey was playing a counting game, jumping off the kerb into the gutter and back again. There were no cars driving past.

Mum said, 'I wish I could make the right decisions about us.'

She sounded sad and Anna gripped Mum's elbow. 'Mum, you do. You got us away from Dad and you found a job and we're doing fine at school and we've got friends now.'

Mum slung an arm around her shoulders. 'You're going to be as tall as I am soon.'

After lunch, Anna couldn't settle, though she had homework to finish. What made Mum worry about making decisions? She found Mum in the kitchen, her long black curls tied high on her head and her neck bare. Anna loved that Mum was singing under her breath. She did not want to spoil it, talking about Dad lurking in the park.

'What are you making, Mum?'

'Where is Mikey?'

'Playing with his dinosaurs. What are you making?'

'Sokolapita.' Mum dusted her hands on her stripey apron.

'I can smell chocolate,' said Anna, ducking under Mum's arm to read the recipe. The book was propped on a stand and the writing was Greek. Dad would never let Mum talk or sing in Greek.

'It's a special Greek chocolate cake. Yaya gave me the recipe book.' Mum smiled at Anna, her deep brown eyes looking slightly damp. 'She was afraid I would forget the language I grew up with.'

Anna tugged at a flapping apron tape. 'You chat all the time in Greek when we're on Symi. Why is it a special cake?' Dad used to tell Mum she ought to forget her past, ignore her parents and concentrate on becoming English, *"for the sake of the children."* It was all wrong, making someone forget the past in favour of a horrible present.

Mum went on weighing out ingredients for her special chocolate cake and Anna gave up. Mum was in another world.

She went into the garden. Leaves had fallen here, as everywhere else in the town, but they lay in neat heaps as if someone had swept them up. Some of the

47

shrubs had produced red berries. The grass was still green. Anna had never really paid attention to plants, or trees and flowers and shrubs, until she and Mikey had discovered Pelm. She picked the seedhead off a grass and gazed at the seeds in the palm of her hand. How delicate the seeds were, fluffy and light, ready to float away on the breeze.

On Pelm, LeafFall was the signal for the Green people to tuck themselves under tree roots and dream the Great Dream of Root and Branch. She and Mikey had never seen this happen but they'd been told it was vital for the island. There was some kind of magical link between the Green people, the trees, and Pelm itself, so when the King started chopping down trees and burning them, it was terribly dangerous.

Anna blew on the seeds, sending them into the air and wondered what happened in the Great Dream of Root and Branch. A light wind lifted the edge of her tee-shirt, making her shiver. She remembered dreaming about the King and the scar he made on her face, felt the burn again, saw the flare of the red mark across her cheek in her reflection.

'He's so dangerous.'

She had not meant to speak out loud, and glanced from side to side, hoping nobody had heard. An idea had sneaked into her mind.

It she took seeds from pine cones to Pelm, those leaves would not fall – well, some of the needles might drift down but mostly the trees would stay green and the Green people would not sleep through LeafFall. They'd be awake to fight the King. They would not have to rely on their Great Dream of Leaf and Branch.

She found Mikey in his bedroom, setting up a battle between a T-Rex and a diplodocus. He caught her eye and tilted his head. 'Do you think there were dinosaurs on Pelm?'

Anna dropped to her knees and gently lifted a model. 'I love these. I really like the brontosaurus.' He chewed the tail of the diplodocus, watching her. 'I do wonder about the big birds with crests on their backs – you know birds come from dinosaurs.'

'Course I do. Everyone knows that.'

'Well, it's like the animals and birds on Pelm, they're like our animals but not quite – like, evolution was different for them.'

'I don't know about evolution.' He pronounced the word very carefully, giving weight to each syllable. 'What's that?'

'Tell you later. Let's try if your Starstone works. Do you want to put it on the wall where the handprints used to be?'

Afterwards, Anna realised she should have planned what to do when nothing happened. At least Mikey did not have a tantrum. Instead, he became very quiet, picked up his small grey Starstone, and walked into his bedroom, closing the door. She knocked, asked to come in, but he did not answer. She caught up with homework. It was Geography, Maths and English. She enjoyed it, rather to her surprise. Everything in her secondary school was a surprise – the oldest boys (some of them with beards), the chemistry laboratory, the huge school hall, the studio theatre, the humming computer rooms, the quiet library, the oldest girls with their long, swinging hair, turning their backs on the oldest boys, the music centre, the Hub where students went who needed to calm down, or to talk to someone who probably wouldn't tell – it was all still intriguing, even though she was now in Year Nine.

Downstairs, Mum sat at her new, second-hand laptop, working on leaflets for the travel agency.

When she called them for supper Mikey did not appear. 'What's wrong with Mikey today?' Mum rattled plates on the table. 'I met his teacher on Wednesday. He does well in his lessons. He is a good boy.'

'He was in a big dinosaur game earlier.'

Mum shook her head. 'He must come downstairs to eat with us.'

'I'll make beans on toast, if you like.'

Mum kissed her, and fetched Mikey downstairs without any shouting.

Anna burnt the toast and the smell stuck to her fingers, even after she had thrown the crisped dark bread into the bin and washed her hands. The chocolate cake wasn't quite ready. It had to cool down before the rich chocolate sauce could be poured over it.

The evening seemed very long. Mum said she had backache from carrying a big box of leaflets from the delivery van into the storeroom at work. 'My shoulder aches too. I think I pulled a muscle.'

Mikey drifted back upstairs to play, and Anna stuck it out until she had yawned so often, so hugely, Mum told her to have an early night. Quietly she knocked on Mikey's door and crooked her finger. 'Come on. Let's try something different. Mum won't hear. She's doing work stuff.'

Chapter Seven

Return to Pelm

*T*he sun had set ages ago but light from the houses made it easy to see Tanda. She sat beside the hydrangea bush from which she had pranced out as a kitten. Now she was a very graceful cat, the brown, orange and creamy white stripes of her coat often becoming the colour of sunshine, or of autumn on a bright, windy day.

The long, low branches of the hydrangea still brushed the grass. A few of the shining pinky-purple flowers had fallen off but most remained, still firmly attached to their stems. Anna dropped to her knees and clicked her tongue. The cat yawned, stretched, turned with a flick of her tail, and stalked under the branches. Despite herself Anna held her breath and crossed her fingers. She watched Tanda's pawprints fill up. Her trail vanished with each step.

Mikey's voice in her ear made her jump. 'I got an idea.' He stretched forward to drop his Starstone into the last print.

The trail sprang back, showing exactly where Tanda had walked. Mikey sat on his heels and nodded. 'My Stone did it.' His teeth gleamed white.

'That's amazing – wait, don't rush, don't smudge the pawprints,' but Anna knew she was wasting her breath. She scrambled after Mikey, trying to keep the tip of Tanda's tail in sight. Their garden was separated from the neighbours' by high wooden fencing. Anna found Mikey in the space between the bush and the fence, alongside Tanda. The cat's back was arched, her fur bristled and her tail was rigid. Anna's nostrils stung from the tarry varnish the neighbour had used on the wood. She could hear Mikey's heavy breathing and tried to control her own. He had collected the Stone, once it had done its work, and held it so Anna could see how fiercely-white it glowed in the night. His bones stood out, black as shadows.

Tanda raised a paw, stepped delicately forward and leaned her head against Anna's.

Anna grabbed Mikey's hand. Together they toppled towards the fence –.

Thick tree roots surrounded them. They lay half-buried among red, brown and gold leaves, and watching them was a squillkit, no more than an arm's length away, her two tails winding around one another and her eyes gleaming in the light of a setting sun. The long low rays of golden light slid between tree trunks and set fire to the tips of ferns.

Anna could scarcely breathe. Mikey pressed his face against Anna's arm, and she shifted him off, adjusting herself until she was on her knees and could look around. They seemed to be in the middle of a forest.

Mikey wriggled forward, wiping his nose on the back of his hand. 'Is it Pelm?'

'It must be.' They both whispered. The forest was so quiet it didn't seem safe to talk out loud. 'Are you okay now?'

'What's that?' He pointed.

A chet trotted into the clearing, a catlike creature on its back gazing at Anna. Its many-coloured coat rippled gold and yellow, orange and red. Anna sensed a command. The chet came to a halt, lowered its head, and laid its long, silvery horns on the ground. The squillkit sprang down and stretched, its two tails coiling over its back – *her back.*

Anna felt the touch of the squillkit's mind on hers, as light as her own Tanda's paw patting her nose. Tears sprang to eyes and she dropped to her knees, holding out her arms. 'It's you.' Memories rushed back – finding the enormous Sea Snake trapped under the island and reaching into her mind through the squillkit's touch to let her know she could swim out into the ocean. The barrier of rocks had collapsed when Mikey pulled out the Starstone, and the boulders rolled down into the sea.

The squillkit stood in front of her, just beyond reach, her glittering eyes fixed on Anna's face and Anna caught her breath. Something had changed – a flicker at the back of her mind –.

'Mikey,' she said in a low voice. 'When Tanda found your Starstone in the bushes, you know, outside school, what happened?'

Mikey wasn't listening. He was stroking the chet's mane, patting its shoulders. 'What's its name?'

'He's called Caval,' said Anna as the name spoke itself in her head. She rubbed her nose, unnerved.

'That's a nice name.' Mikey twisted his fingers in the silky mane, and the chet knelt.

'I think you're meant to climb on.'

'I know,' said Mikey, tossing his head. He pulled himself on to Caval's back and grabbed the mane. 'We got to hurry to find Kazan.' His legs stuck out on either side.

Anna clambered on behind him. 'Well, if Kazan has Tasks for us to do, he'd better turn up and tell us.' Mikey wasn't listening. He leaned forward to whisper into the chet's ear. Anna willed herself to gaze up at the flaming sunset sky, framed between the bare twigs.

They set off, the chet keeping a steady pace, adjusting the rise and fall of his great shoulders to keep Anna and Mikey safe. She wished Kazan would step out on to the path and say hello. Perhaps he was already asleep, deep in the Great Dream. The logical voice in her brain said healthy trees depended on sunshine and rain and clean air. If the air was polluted by exhaust fumes and the soil was full of heavy metals the trees couldn't develop. The lessons they learned in geography and biology were straightforward. They had watched videos, followed programmes on the BBC.

Was the Dream only a story the Green people told themselves for comfort?

A soft paw patted her arm, and she glanced down at Tanda. Her eyes were fiery, staring up at Anna. Suddenly the paw became a claw, and Anna winced, knowing at once that the squillkit knew what she was thinking. In her dream the King said would put another spell on the Queen, a shrivelling spell. He would turn her into a worm. It might have been a Dream but the threat was real. The King had already felled trees and set fire to them – he hated the Green people, meant to drive them away – the Stone people were superior – of course they were – and dared that child to take *his* Starstone, his Starstone – it was his right to use its power –

Anna took a deep breath and shook her head, scattering the feelings. Her fists were clenched.

Somehow, the squillkit had sent the King's feelings into hers. Perhaps it was a warning of what to look out for?

She needed to concentrate. The trees were thinning out. They were coming to the edge of the forest.

Pine cones ...

If she brought pine seeds to Pelm, it might break the King's ability to ruin Kazan's people. Anna gripped Caval's mane too tightly and he tossed his head. She tried to relax.

The King's magic wasn't reliable. He had turned the Queen into a snake but she was able to keep her human head, could tell Anna and Mikey what had happened. He was furious when Anna showed the Queen how to become herself again. He was out for revenge. He said he had found a Shrivelling spell ...

If Dad could turn Mum into a worm, he would. Stalking Anna was the first step to getting hold of Mum again.

Glancing around, Anna saw the white-grey pebbles and small boulders which marked the edge of the forest. In front of them were the grey stone cliffs, their outlines jagged against a washed-out blue sky. The sun had dropped behind the horizon, and a pale, pale moon heaved itself into view.

Sun. Moon. Stars – just like at home.

The Stone people behaved as if the stones of Pelm were alive. People at home thought mountains were special. They named them – Scafell Pike, Blencathra, Coniston Old Man – as if they were alive and special

Kazan stepped on to the track, arms raised to stop Caval.

'Were you stuck in the cave? You were crying.' Mikey kicked, trying to dismount, but he was tucked tightly against Tanda and Anna. 'Let me go.'

Kazan stroked Caval's nose and he knelt. Mikey struggled down, lost his balance but Kazan took his wrist to steady him and scowled at Anna. 'Where have you been? We need your help.'

Mikey flung his arms around Kazan. 'The man painted the wall but I did it, I got my Starstone and we found it.'

Kazan's glare relaxed. He patted Mikey's head. 'I am very glad to see you.' He looked much as he had the last time Anna had seen him, but taller and his shoulders were broader. He still wore the leaf-shirt and trousers, but they were neat, not ragged, and his greeny-brown hair was bound into a long, glossy plait.

Anna shook her head at Mikey, mouthing at him to stay quiet. 'We found another path so we're here now.'

Mikey could not be stopped. 'I dreamed you were in a cave, and you were frightened. You cried."

Kazan heaved a great sigh and pushed Mikey aside.

Anna whispered, hoping Kazan would not hear. 'Mikey, you didn't have to say that.' She wanted to shake him.

'I told you he was frightened, I was frightened, we got to come back.'

Kazan gestured at the trees. 'Your dream spoke truly.' His eyes glittered. 'The King's power is growing again. We do not know how to stop him.'

Anna slid off the chet's back and leaned again the strong flank. 'I thought, when the Queen became herself again, she had the power of the snake. She said she was Leaf and Stone together.' She stroked the sleek coat, feeling the chet's longing to gallop. 'I thought she was much more powerful than the King now.'

Kazan rubbed his face, sighing again. 'The King has turned it against her. He says she is a witch.'

'That's not true.' Even as she spoke, Anna began to understand why they were back on the island. The King was clever.

'He says she is dangerous, she cannot control the Snake in her spirit, that she will squeeze all the water out of the island like the Sea Snake did before – before you came and set the Sea Snake free.' He rustled the fallen leaves with the toe of his shoe.

'That's ridiculous.' Anna struggled to talk quietly. The Sea Snake was frightened – she was trapped and all on her own in the dark – she didn't mean – oh, surely nobody believes him. He's just – he's horrible, he's sneaky.' She felt the scar sear across her cheek and ground her teeth.

Kazan stepped closer. 'He has enchanted you again? He placed the mark upon you before.'

Anna shook her head. 'No.'

'You are sure? He cannot be trusted.'

Anna needed to change the subject. 'How did you get stuck in a cave?' Mikey's dream was real – although she had always known it.

The leafy green of Kazan's skin took on a yellowish tinge. 'We went underground to talk where his people would not overhear. He tells everyone not to trust the Queen. Even our own people – I do not know how to explain it. They look at me in pity.' He imitated a grown-up's condescending voice. "You are young, Kazan, you cannot understand. The Queen makes use of you."

'Oh.' Anna sat down heavily on a tree root 'They treat you like a child.'

Kazan sat beside her and the root swayed. 'This happens to you?'

'Grown-ups mean to be kind but they don't listen. Well, my mother doesn't. Anyway.' She brushed a hair

57

from her eye. 'Everyone loves the Queen. Don't they? Wasn't that why the King changed her into a snake, he was so jealous?'

'Many still love her, but the change in her skin troubles them. No longer does she resemble the Stone people, or the Green.'

'Well, that makes her special,' said Anna, frustrated on the Queen's behalf. 'Anyway, sometimes in our world ...' She broke off. She had been going to say something about her school friend, Reima. Reima's dad was Indian and her mum was from Wales. She had beautiful creamy-brown skin and long, shining black hair but a few people sent horrible texts. No-one would say anything to her face when Anna was around. Anna had discovered how to be angry when it felt right.

'Sometimes in your world?'

'Your face has gone all red, Anna.' Mikey picked up a broken branch and waved it in the air. 'What's my Task?'

'Wait a minute. Let Kazan explain what he wants us to do, then we can work out what your Task is.'

Kazan's eyebrows shot up. 'You were going to tell me about your world.'

Anna sniffed. 'I think it's about how people say things. I mean, the King is using words to make people not trust – is that it? – not trust the Queen just because she looks a bit different.' An idea offered itself. 'In my school we get to practise how to persuade people to change their minds.'

'School?'

Mikey swung his branch. 'I go to school. We do maths and literacy and science and computers.'

'Maths? Literacy?'

Anna said, 'How do you learn things? You must do it

somehow.'

'Of course.' Kazan gestured at the trees. 'We learn in the Great Dream of Root and Branch. We grow with the roots, we hear the sap rise, we talk to the leaves before they bud.' He looked hard at her face. 'You do not dream as we do, I think. We are the earth, the song, rebirth. We send our spirit deep into the ground, we are the soil, the growing –.' He spread out his hands.

Anna said, 'We can't learn like that. We're not connected to trees,' and thought it did sound rather wonderful.

'What use are you?' Kazan sounded almost angry. 'What help can you be? Why did you stay away so long?'

'We didn't mean to, that's not fair.' Anna felt a prickle of annoyance. 'We love Pelm. We wouldn't dream about you unless it mattered. I told you, we lost the way back, we didn't know how to get back to Pelm, we didn't mean to let you down.'

Mikey said, 'There's bullies in my school,' prodding at the soil with his branch.

'What has this to do with us?' Kazan was on his feet.

'Mikey, don't get distracted. Kazan, we wanted to come.' The words seemed to stick to Anna's tongue. "Getting here was difficult. We're not magical. Something – something in Pelm,' waving her arms, 'wants us to be here.' She groped for the right words. 'Maybe your Great Dream calls us.' She struggled again. 'On my world, there's a sort of Tanda like this Tanda.' She gestured at the tree behind which the squillkit had vanished. 'Maybe my Tanda talks to your Tanda. Something holds them together – like a story being told in both places?'

Mikey said, 'We dream. I dreamed and it was important.'

'You're right, your dream is important.' Anna did not want to remember her own dream, and the King's threat of a Shrivelling.

Kazan said, 'This is a mystery.' He turned to Mikey, who was pacing around, waving his branch. 'You dream truly.'

Anna could not bear the idea of people not trusting the Queen who loved them. 'Even if they don't like the marks on the Queen's skin – I mean, they're beautiful. Everybody said so. Surely people remember how kind she is, how she listens and makes things better.'

Kazan rested his head against the nearest tree. He closed his eyes. Little twigs seemed to shiver and a couple of leaves drifted down to lie on his head. Was the tree speaking to him?

She wanted to poke him. 'Where's the Queen now? Is she safe?'

Without warning, a warm, muscled body leapt into her arms, soft tails twined around her neck, and she was in the dark. In a panic she squeezed the squillkit too tightly and a claw scratched her hand. She held on, but more gently. The dark was less intense, sparkles of light made her blink and she was in the great cavern under the island. A blue-green sea surged in and out, in and out, whispering of the Sea Snake and the Snake Queen and –

The squillkit wriggled out of her arms and now she felt cold. 'I saw the Queen. The Queen is in the cave.'

Her voice wobbled. Silently she counted backwards to calm herself – *four, three, two, one.*

Kazan's eyes narrowed and the tree behind him shivered, sending more dead leaves showering to the ground. 'How is this to be believed?'

Anna rubbed her face. She did not know how to

convince him. 'Tanda does something in my mind. We've to go into the caves to find the Queen. I don't know if she's hiding or what she's doing but we need to get to her as fast as we can.'

'Why does the squillkit give more to you than to us? You are a stranger – well, you are neither Leaf nor Stone and yet you dream in ways we do not.' His resentment was as clear as if he had spelt it out.

Mikey clenched his fists. 'Kazan, I saw Kazan in a cave, I dreamed and he was, you were frightened in the cave. You mustn't go in a cave.'

"Kazan, please don't be cross. I didn't choose this. We've got to find the Queen.'

'I will return to the caves if the squillkit leads us. She would not take us into a lie.' Kazan stood straight and stiff. He might be cross with Anna but he was brave.

'You might get killed.' Mikey's voice cracked.

'No, no he won't.' Anna grasped her brother's shoulders. 'We won't let anything bad happen. We came to stop bad things, didn't we? Your dream and my dream?'

'Okay,' said Mikey. He sounded resigned. Anna thought it had to be enough.

Kazan whispered into the chet's ear, stroked his mane and stood back as Caval lowered his head. The bright, deadly horns tossed dead leaves into the air. 'I am sending him back to his family. He cannot come underground with us.'

Caval trotted away as quietly as he had come.

Chapter Eight

The Search

*A*nna let Kazan take charge and Mikey trotted after him, waving his branch over his head. He had forgotten his panic. Anna had to smile, even though she felt exposed, coming last. Only a few leaves drooping from branches offered any kind of cover. At home, it wouldn't have mattered but here, where was everyone?

The squillkit padded at Anna's heels until a dark, jagged opening appeared in the grey cliff face and she sprang in front of Kazan, tails quivering like double question marks.

Mikey stopped dead. 'We went in dark places before.' He was chewing his thumb. 'We can do this. We can, can't we, Anna?'

Kazan clasped his arms across his chest. Anna was struck again by his green-tinted nails, green skin, white eyeballs, dark green pupils, black irises – a body like hers and Mikey's and yet so different.

And she felt his fear, his confusion. She badly wanted to make him feel better. 'Mikey, where's the Starstone?'

Mikey's eyes brightened. 'I never thought …' He pulled the Stone from his pocket. It glittered. 'What does my Starstone say?' He balanced it on the palm of his hand.

Kazan stared. 'You have one of the magic Stones?' To Anna, he seemed more focussed on Mikey than on the Stone. 'With the Starstone we could – you could change, change everything.'

Mikey said, 'Can I? Can I work out the big Tasks?' His pupils were almost as large as Kazan's.

'I don't know,' said Anna. 'Tell us if you find out.'

Anna hoped her face did not show how afraid she was of meeting the King again. Mikey was so full of confidence she did not want to make him nervous.

Kazan walked through the dark opening and turned back to wave them inside. They found themselves in a tunnel lit by hanging lanterns. He unhooked three from the wall inside the entrance, giving one to Anna and the other to Mikey. 'Do not light them yet. I will give you the signal. We need to save the candleflames for when we reach the biggest cavern.' He seemed more relaxed now, so Anna felt easier too.

Kazan knew the way – of course he did – and Mikey was listening intently to Kazan's explanations. 'This is one of the big entrances. I did not bring you this way before. The cave will get bigger, and we must walk through water.'

After a while, Anna discovered he was right. The path was becoming slippery and wet, running water soaking their shoes. She hoped it would be the same as before, wet shoes on Pelm being dry at home, except the trickle was turning into a stream.

Kazan said something she could not hear, and Mikey slithered, stumbling sideways. Anna caught him but she found it hard to concentrate on keeping her balance. This was the same as her dream. It was exactly her dream. *I have been here in my dream and the King was* – Anna staggered, kicked out to save herself and sprayed water over both of them. 'Sorry, sorry.'

'I could've fallen over.' Mikey's cold, wet fingers clutched at her arm.

'Please be quiet. I cannot tell who is in the cave.' Kazan's voice sounded hollow. He was some distance further along the path.

'You think the Queen is in this cave?' Anna hoped Kazan did not notice the quiver in her voice. If the squillkit had been on her shoulder, sharing pictures of what lay ahead of them, she would have been happier – well, less anxious.

Kazan swung his lantern. The lit cavern reminded Anna of the great church at Panormitis, except it was underground. The crystals formed into patterns as soon as she looked at them, then dissolved into a mass of brilliance when her glance flitted to another section of wall or ceiling. 'We should light the extra candles now.' Kazan produced a flintstone, struck sparks from the nearest dry boulder, and lit a candle. 'We will take the upper path,' he said, pointing upwards.

Anna saw a long rope strung between upright boulders, stretching into the distance – exactly as in her dream.

'Give me your hand.' Kazan had already climbed up. He leaned over, hand outstretched. 'Do not be afraid.'

'I'm not scared.'

'Your voice says otherwise,' said Kazan, pulling Mikey on to the upper path. 'Mikey, please go ahead,' before turning to Anna. 'What do you fear?'

'I'm in charge, I'm the leader.' Mikey sang out the words, beginning to march.

Anna saw no point in pretending. On Pelm, strange happenings were ordinary. 'I had a dream of being here – I mean, it was just like this, the path, the stream, these rope-holds. In my dream the King was waiting for me. He made all sorts of threats about the Queen.' She had to stop. Talking about it made her throat go dry.

'The Queen is here, not the King.' Kazan sounded sure of himself but when she glanced at him she saw the twist of his mouth.

'You said you could not tell who was here.'

He avoided her gaze. 'You told me she was near.' Kazan sprinted after Mikey.

Chapter Nine

The Snakeskin Queen

*W*here the mouth of the cave opened to the sky, the Queen stood, a dark figure outlined against a view of sunlight sparkling on a quiet ocean.

Anna could not move. A memory of terror returned – her mind merging with the Sea Snake's, the thrashing of the great body pulling her into the ocean and Mikey jumping in after her in a panic. They had been returned to their own world because they had both screamed. If they lost their tempers, or became afraid at the same moment, some magical force would carry them back to the abandoned room with its green handprints.

With a jolt, Anna realised she had no idea how they would return this time.

She began scrambling forward over the boulders. The Queen turned at the sound of falling pebbles and came towards them, holding out her arms.

'You came. I knew you would. I called for you.'

Anna was swept into the Queen's embrace. Her body was warm and strong and it was almost as good as hugging Mum. 'You sent me a kitten. She's not a squillkit, she looks like our cats but she's special and I call her Tanda too and she has magic pawprints, in my world, that is, she showed us how to get here and she found Mikey's Starstone.'

'So much to say – slow down.' The Queen brushed a hand across Anna's forehead, Anna felt her cheeks grow hot. She must have sounded like a little girl. Why couldn't she speak like her real self? The Queen smiled down at her. 'You have shorn your hair.' Her voice was just the same as before, low, chiming like a bell, and her face – Anna gazed into the bright eyes and gasped.

'Your eyes are green. You had blue eyes, I know you did.'

The Queen raised a hand to her cheek and Anna was close enough to see the detail of the beautiful snake markings which were now her transformed self. Anna had asked her to shed her snake skin, the way ordinary snakes did. When the Queen surfaced in the water of the lake, she was a woman again, not a snake with a woman's head – except her skin bore the snake's markings.

Anna was astounded. At home, there were tattoo parlours where people got patterns inked into their skin, some so complicated you couldn't tell from a distance if a shirt had patterned sleeves or the shirt was sleeveless. The Queen's skin was different, as if her own smooth, pearl-white skin had been soaked in a tie-dye, and the green, yellow, orange pattern of an autumn-coloured snake had sunk into the weave – or into the cells? – so you saw both the pearl-colour of the Stone people and the green of the forest, swirling together every time the Queen breathed or moved.

'You're like – it's like looking at the sea, looking at you,' said Anna, delicately touching the Queen's finger. 'You can't tell the exact colour of the sea, can you? It reflects the sky, and sometimes it depends what colour the sand is too. How have your eyes turned green?'

Kazan's words made her jump. 'The King says these

are a sign of sorcery.' His face was a deeper green, and the whites of his eyes stood out. Anna realised he was angry even though his voice was quiet. 'First, people said how beautiful she was – you are, I'm sorry, Lady – and then the King began telling everyone the snake is still inside you and you are a witch.'

Breaking the silence that followed Kazan's words, Mikey said, 'Snakes are good.' He nodded at Anna. 'Our Mum told us about snakes.'

The Queen glanced at Anna. '*Mum* your word for mother?' Anna nodded. The Queen turned to Mikey. 'What did your Mum say?'

Mikey's shorts were wet from falling into the stream and he had torn a button off his polo shirt, but his eyes were bright and his shoulders braced. He was excited.

'She says snakes are amazing like birds and butterflies and in the story it was Adam and Eve didn't want to own up they did the wrong thing.'

'Adam and Eve?' Kazan and the Queen spoke together.

'It's one of our stories,' said Anna. 'Like you have stories. In our story the people are told not to eat an apple but they do because a snake tells them they can if they want to.'

'Why did the snake tell them if it was forbidden?' Kazan had stopped being angry. He was curious.

'In the story, it wasn't really a snake but a devil – I mean, a bad spirit,' said Anna.

The Queen stirred and snake markings flared more brightly across her skin. 'You have spirits in your world?'

'Sort of – I'm not sure – some people believe in sort of spirits.' Anna could not help thinking of Papou in the great monastery. She sensed the Queen's gaze and shifted from foot to foot. 'I don't know what I believe.'

'We know the Sea Snake made our world,' said the Queen, 'and I know now, what I did not understand before, that when the Green people enter the Great Dream of Root and Branch, their minds grow one with the mighty force keeping the Sea Snake alive and the trees growing. This is what happens, Kazan?'

Kazan bowed to the Queen. 'Lady, you are right. We have no choice but to enter the Dream.' He tilted his head at Anna. 'If the people in your story did what that snake told them, and they knew it was forbidden, I do not understand why did they eat the apple? What is an apple? Are they afraid of snakes in your world?'

'Apples are fruit, they're nice to eat.' Mikey's voice was higher than usual.

Anna took over. 'Some people are frightened of snakes though we learned in school snakes can be afraid of people, it's only if you get in their way they might bite you or something.'

'There's poison snakes in our world,' said Mikey. His face was flushed. He wanted to be part of the discussion.

'Well, yes, they bite their prey – I mean, what they're going to eat. Some snakes. I think they bite if they're afraid, too.'

The Queen looked from Anna to Mikey and back again to Anna. 'I did not feel any of this when our minds were as one. Did you hide it from me?' Anna tensed, until the Queen took her hand, nodded, and Anna felt able to breathe again. 'Of course you did not.' She set her hand on Anna's forehead. 'Inside you is a great desire to do well. Do you sense this in me?'

Anna could not speak, but a great calm spread through her body, until the Queen took her hand away and the usual muddle of feelings and thoughts swarmed in her brain.

'I want to summon the Sea Snake from the deeps.' The Queen was gazing out to sea. 'I want to remind all our people that Pelm exists because she made us and protected us until we could look after ourselves. I want to remind them that trouble came after the King's father set out to hunt her, merely to prove his own strength. He was a vain and foolish man and he drowned in the attempt.'

'Kazan told us all about him.' Mikey chipped in. 'He said he made his little boy fight grown-up soldiers. He beat them all.'

'The soldiers were ordered to let him win,' said Kazan, scowling. 'It was never fair. Then he was the King and he does not like to lose. He will do anything not to lose.'

The Queen clasped her hands. 'He need not have become a bad man but he looked for the old magic and tried to bind everyone to him. This is like your Adam and Eve choosing to eat what was forbidden to them?'

'I suppose,' said Anna. It seemed as good an explanation as any.

'If people do not trust you of their own free will, what is the value of entrancing them? Now the King becomes more dangerous to us, and to the creatures we love. He tries to turn them away from their choices. Anna, I called for your help because the Sea Snake will remember you. She will trust you. You showed her how to be free and she discovered you spoke the truth.'

Anna felt very hot, although the air blowing in from the ocean was cool. She fixed her eyes on the Queen's face. 'She was unhappy. I knew how she wanted to swim among the fish and everything.' What did the Queen want her to do? Suppose she couldn't do it? She mustn't panic. 'Tanda did it really, not me.'

The squillkit crept out from under the Queen's long robe and stretched up to nuzzle the Queen's hand. She must have reached the mouth of the cave before them. In the dappled light from the outside world, the resemblance between Anna's Tanda and the Queen's was so strong, Anna said, 'I suppose – I don't suppose – is my cat her kitten?'

The Queen smiled, lifted Tanda into her arms. Her green eyes were dark. 'It is time, Anna.' Anna drew a deep breath. Her stomach turned over, but the Queen was relying on her. She opened her mind and the mystery inside her stirred, stretched, reached out, filling her with other voices.

Chapter Ten

Summoning

*T*he Queen was full of confusion.
Why did he turn against me? I came to Pelm ready to love him. How is he able to persuade so many people to fear me when I only want to serve them? He is still jealous, burning with resentment. I do not crave his power, I do not need to be King. I am Queen.

The anguish made Anna's mind curl into a little ball – she felt the soft paw, the claws not extended, the pat on her nose – she opened her mind again, and a new voice swam into it

... the deeps ... the plants I have rooted among the corals ... oh, the sway and green and rush of currents ... the saltiness, the tiny swimmers filling my mouth and throat ... and the hunt, the shoals, the biters and snappers and ... you call, my Queen ... my crunchy shells, my moist rock-suckers ... you call, my Queen ...

Anna's body rocked back and forth in the pull of the currents, swaying, extending sinuous coils to surround the island, carry it across the seas, plant it in another world –

Something bit her finger. 'Ow.'

Tanda's eyes were bright gold. *You didn't have to bite so hard,* thought Anna, glancing at the red marks. She had travelled too far into the Sea Snake's mind.

The Queen's questions wove once more through her

mind, so clearly Anna might have been hearing her speak. *When did I know you did not love me? I sat beside you in the great Hall to listen to our people, find justice, hear their sorrows and joys. You invited me to come to Pelm – why did you begin to fear the people's love? Why must you destroy the Green? Why do you fear the Dream of Root and Branch?*

So many questions – what did she want? The Sea Snake had heard the Queen but held back. And then came – *how can I stop him hurting others as he hurt me?*

The pain was different this time, not a throbbing finger or scarred cheek but piercing unhappiness and puzzlement, so powerful and familiar that Anna winched. The feelings were too much like Mum's – so much confusion – how to protect everyone – the Sea Snake's call, desire for all to be safe – and her own voice on the verge of tears, *I am the link and they will not let me go.*

No, no, no.

Choose. You are free to choose. We will let you go, send you back to your own world. We will not force you.

When Anna came to herself her face was wet. She frowned, brushed the water from her face and realised she had been crying.

Mikey said, in a voice that cracked, 'I don't like you crying. You aren't supposed to cry. You're older than me.'

Then the sea rose in a huge wave, throwing itself into the cave. The Sea Snake surfaced, and Anna and Mikey were hurled back by the force of the water.

Anna lay on her back in the garden, under the hydrangea bush. A branch scratched her face. She pushed it away crossly, rubbed her cheek and discovered blood. The plaintive voice nearby said,

'My legs are all itchy.'

She pushed herself up, staring around. 'How did we get back?' Mikey sat in the middle of the flowerbed where Mum had planted bulbs ready for the spring. He seemed to have dug up several. The sun had gone down. The lights were on in the kitchen and Anna's heart jumped into her throat. 'We've got to get indoors before Mum finds us. This is awful. We can't get in and out of Pelm from our garden.'

Mikey was not listening. 'I got dirt in my mouth.'

She crawled across to pull him on to the path and set about pushing the bulbs back into the soil. 'Come on, Mikey, help me pat the earth down so Mum won't notice.'

'She might say it's Tanda digging up.'

Anna spoke in a hurried whisper. 'She'd better not. Tanda uses the litter tray, you know she does. I wish I'd got my watch.'

'How did we get here?'

'I don't know. Maybe it was Tanda? I wish I knew where she was. Have you got the Starstone?'

He rummaged in his pocket and pulled out the Stone. It was marbled with red streaks, faintly pulsing, like lava. He stared from the Stone to Anna, mouth open.

'Isn't it hot?'

He shook his head, pointed at the kitchen door where Tanda sat with her tail curled around her legs.

'I really don't understand,' said Anna, but she reached out for the cat, and the mystery in her mind stretched too. Lights in the kitchen flickered, went out. With luck, it wasn't late, Mum would be going back into the sitting room to watch television. She wouldn't be going upstairs to check on them, not yet.

Tanda brushed against her legs and for a moment Anna sensed two tails, curling. She ran her hand along Tanda's spine, arching in pleasure, and found just a single tail. If only she could discover what was locked in Mum's mind, get her to accept the magic on Pelm ... They could never get Mum to Pelm.

There was no magic here, only whatever it was that Mum believed in.

Mum hadn't locked the kitchen door. They crept in, slipped out of their shoes to tiptoe upstairs, and took turns in the bathroom to wash off garden soil. She checked her little clock and saw it was only eight o'clock.

Later, she went downstairs, deliberately noisy, going into the kitchen to fetch a glass of water. Mum came in, her face rather red. 'Thank you, my love. Sweet of you to put him to bed.'

'He was fine,' said Anna. Mum was in a state, she could tell. 'I read him a story in the end. We had a bit of a fight getting his teeth cleaned. Mum, what is it?'

A year ago, Anna would never have asked her mother such a question.

Mum said, 'Ask me tomorrow, moro mou.'

Anna wanted to argue but she saw Mum's eyes fill with tears. Her fingers twitched as if to pull her arms up and around Mum, whether to comfort her, keep her close or make Anna feel better she did not know — but a shiver ran through her whole body, a fear so deep her lungs refuse to swell.

Mum rubbed a hand across her mouth. 'When you come home from school.'

'I'll go to bed then,' said Anna. Her voice sounded in her own ears like a stranger's.

She could not sleep. It had occurred to her that no soil from Pelm stuck to their clothes even though they arrived in the roots of a tree and crawled through the forest, but she was seriously thinking of taking pine cones to Pelm to plant them. Maybe it wouldn't be possible. Maybe some sort of barrier would kill off the pine cones before she could get into Pelm.

What happened to Kazan when he went into his Great Dream? Was it anything like her own feelings when she was in the mind of the Queen or the Sea Snake? She didn't expect to change anything, only to be the link. Kazan said in the Great Dream the people of the Leaf sent their own spirits deep into the roots and soil and helped everything green to grow. Was his mind changed when he woke up?

Was her mind changing?

Kazan said they had no choice but to enter the Great Dream.

She said to the dark, 'I could give them a choice, if my pine seeds grew into evergreen trees,' and pulled the duvet close.

Chapter Eleven: Monday

Only a Dad

*A*nna's day at school started out the same as every other school day. She met Polly and Reima by the lockers and they leaned against the corridor wall to compare notes about science homework. Polly said she'd spent Saturday morning with her grown-up lamb, Suki. Suki was poorly and she wanted advice when the vet came to check out the whole flock.

'What's wrong with her?' Reima had been at Polly's village primary school and knew Polly's mum and dad. They were farmers in the hills and kept sheep, goats, a few cows.

'She's got foot scald.'

'Is that bad?' Anna's jaw still wanted to drop when Polly talked about learning to lamb when she was very small because she had little hands and could get inside a ewe without hurting her. Lots of people in her class lived in the town and didn't know anything about farming or weren't interested. Ever since Anna had discovered amazing creatures on Pelm she wanted to know more about the animals in the fields around them, and Polly was keen to tell her.

Polly and Reima came to school on the same minibus. They'd been put in the same class as Anna when they'd started secondary school, it hadn't taken long for the three of them to suss each other out and become friends. Reima had a cat, too, though Anna guessed he could never be as *interesting* as her Tanda.

'It's okay if we treat it straight away. It's like getting a sore place between your toes. If it's left and turns into foot rot it can be horrible.'

'Infectious,' said Reima, who rarely said much but nodded a lot.

Anna said, trying to sound as if she understood, 'Your mum and dad must be worried about foot rot?'

Polly laughed. 'You know you haven't a clue. You ought to come out for a day. Would your mum let you? You can get the 555 bus. You'd love the farm. You could be a farmer. I'm going to college when I'm sixteen. I want to be a partner with my mum and dad.'

Reima said, 'My father says I should be a vet or a dentist or a doctor. I want to be a dancer.'

'Well, be a dancer,' said Polly. 'I'm not letting my dad tell me what to do.'

'Your dad won't let you leave at sixteen.' Reima laughed and prodded Polly's arm. 'You know he says you've got to get a degree or something.'

'He thinks.' Polly rolled her shoulders and adjusted her backpack. 'He can tell me all he wants but he'll let me do what I want in the end. He's only a dad.'

Anna at once knew she would have to get to the bus station, find the 555 bus, buy a ticket and go to Polly's farm. She had to meet someone who was "only a dad".

When she arrived at Mrs Dodd's to fetch Mikey, Mrs Dodd said, 'Your mother's going to be a bit late. Have a glass of orange?'

Although she smiled, her mouth was tight at the corners, and Anna's heartbeat quickened. 'Is Mikey okay?' Her voice came out as a squawk.

Mrs Dodd put an arm around her shoulders and led her towards the kitchen. 'Come on. You are a very good sister. He's fine.' She pointed at Mikey, sitting on a stool at the kitchen table. His nose glistened from the honey dripping off his slice of bread – at least, that's what Anna hoped. 'I made bread today,' said Mrs Dodd. 'I haven't made it for months, so Mikey is testing it. How did I do, Mikey?'

His mouth was full so he gave her both thumbs up.

If Mikey was fine, why was Mrs Dodd so uptight? Anna allowed herself to be seated on the opposite stool with a plate, a hunk of warm brown bread, the butter dish and the jar of honey. 'Help yourself.'

Anna pulled the butter towards her. 'When's Mum coming?'

Mrs Dodd turned her back and fiddled with dishes in the sink. 'I believe she's gone to visit your social worker. I don't think she'll be long. She rang me a couple of hours ago so I expect the meeting will soon be over. She suggested you should both stay here and I'm happy for that.'

'I can take him home,' Anna began.

'Of course you can but your mother would prefer it if you stayed with me, just for today.'

Anna drew a deep breath. Mrs Dodd was a very wise old lady. She wouldn't tell Anna something that wasn't true. 'If you don't mind — I mean — do you know why Mum's gone to see Karina? Is it about Dad hanging around?' This time, her voice was too loud

79

and Mikey dropped his bread. His mouth fell open. Half-chewed bread and honey dribbled on to the table. He tried to scoop it up.

'I know she has gone to Karina for advice.' There was a pause. 'You didn't ring Karina, did you?'

'I was going to, really I was, only not at the weekend, I thought, today. Only I forgot.'

Mrs Dodd rubbed her eyes and sighed. She helped Mikey spread another piece of bread with butter. 'Well, Anna, at least your mother is taking advice now. You must realise you put me in a very difficult position.' She glanced up at Anna and Anna felt as if someone had opened the door and pushed her out. 'If your mother knew I had information I hadn't passed on she might not let Mikey come home with me.'

'I couldn't - it's not your fault - she's been so funny lately - she says the agency wants her to do more hours, to work longer hours only she can't without —.' Anna broke off, afraid she was going to cry. This was Mum's business. Mum was going to ask Mrs Dodd if she'd mind them both staying on with her after school. Now Anna might have ruined it all if Mrs Dodd thought Anna couldn't keep her word.

It was nearly six o'clock when Mum came to say she was home. Her eyes were large and dark, and her eyelids were red. Mrs Dodd said, 'Oh my dear,' and put her arms around Mum. Mum seemed to relax against her, even though Mrs Dodd was shorter than she was, and then she stood back.

'Thank you. I did not mean to take advantage of you. Would you mind hanging on a little longer to Mikey? I want to talk to Anna.'

Anna could not bear to look at Mum or Mrs Dodd.

She glanced at Mikey but he was setting out a flock of sheep with two sheepdogs to guard them, so she followed Mum across the road and into their own house.

They sat opposite one another, Anna on the sofa and Mum on one of the dining chairs. 'I've been talking to Father Bernard.'

'Mrs Dodd said you went to see Karina.'

'I did, yes. I had to, because of what I am thinking of doing.'

The look on Mum's face made her feel slightly sick.

Mum stared at her feet. Her work shoes were thin, black slip-ons and Anna knew she wanted sturdier ones for the winter but she had bought new school shoes for Mikey instead. 'I am troubled in my conscience. Do you understand what that means?'

Anna said, 'You don't have anything to be troubled about, Mum. You're a wonderful mum, the agency likes you lots. Why are you saying this? What's Father Bernard been saying?'

Mum crossed the room, knelt in front of her and put her arms around Anna's waist. 'Don't complain about Father Bernard. He has just been listening. Talking to a good listener is so very helpful. I've been thinking for a while — ever since we started going to Mass and I have remembered all that I was brought up to believe, that I *do* believe —.'

'What do you mean?' A small fire lit in Anna's brain. 'Is this what you were saying about whatever, about choosing wisdom, stuff like that? If Father Bernard's been saying stuff, I'm never going to church again.'

'Father Bernard does not give advice – except to

81

follow my own conscience. Don't, please don't, little one.' After a pause, she said, 'I – your father has been to see me.'

There was no air to breathe.

'He wants to come back, try again. He promises not to hurt me, or you or Mikey. In my conscience I believe I must let this happen. We made promises to one another when we married. I made a promise.'

'He broke his promises.' Anna felt very tired. The story of Adam and Eve floated through her mind. Adam blamed Eve.

Mum got up, smoothing her trousers. 'We have to forgive one another.'

Anna thought if Mum knew he'd been stalking her, saying dreadful things about Mum, she might think again about forgiveness. 'I'm not forgiving him,' she said, but Mum seemed not to hear.

'I will carry on my work at the agency, and Mrs Dodd will collect Mikey from school. I said I would not change the arrangements we have made.'

'Yes but – I bet Karina didn't like it.'

Mum rubbed her face and stared into her hands. 'She is worried. I can ask for the court order to be lifted but she believes it will be a mistake.'

Dad had tricked Mum. He must have done. 'When are you telling Mikey?'

'I will tell him on Friday evening, when we have the weekend to think it over. This is my burden, not yours. Now, you can change out of your uniform while I collect your brother and then we can have a late supper.'

Anna trudged up the stairs, feeling sick. On Pelm, the King was spreading stories about the Queen and some people believed him. It was the opposite with

Mum. She must have decided to believe Dad. Anna's eyes filled with tears. Mikey would stop talking again. She was sure of it. Mum was crazy.

They had to get back to Pelm. The Queen had asked for her help. At least the Queen listened to her. At least the Queen knew the King was bad.

Mum said Father Bernard just listened and didn't give her advice. Anna couldn't believe it. Of course he told Mum stuff about what her conscience ought to be telling her. What about Anna's conscience? Didn't she have a right to tell Mum it was totally wrong to let Dad anywhere near them?

Chapter Twelve: Saturday

Second chances

*A*nna was woken by Mikey's shouts. He was cross there were no sausages for breakfast.

Anna said, 'We never have sausages for breakfast.'

'Why can't we have sausages? I want sausages. Everyone in my class has sausages on Saturdays.'

'How do you know?'

Mum said to leave it, not to get into an argument.

Mum had told him last night about seeing Dad again.

Mum carefully buttered his toast but Mikey pushed it away, and Mum turned her toast into crumbs. 'Tara and Diego are coming to see us later.'

Mikey straightened. 'With Andy?'

'With Andy. They've got a surprise.'

'Bet it's nicer than ours,' said Mikey, but the tight, angry twist to his mouth relaxed.

Anna realised she was hunching her shoulders and tried to relax. At least they would be with a lovely family they'd known for ages. Vaguely she wondered why Tara let the baby be named Andrea. She supposed it was because Diego was Italian but when Andy was old enough to go to school he'd have an awful time when other kids found out.

'Please eat something,' Mum said. 'We're going

for a picnic but I don't want you eating everything fast because you haven't had breakfast.'

'Is that the surprise?' Mikey pulled the plate towards him.

'No,' said Mum. 'They'll be here soon.'

To Anna's relief, Mikey ate his toast though she noticed Mum didn't.

When the doorbell rang it was Tara. 'Got your text, Sofia. You want to try out our new car with us?'

'You got a new car?' Mikey ran to the front door. 'It's huge, Mum they got a huge car.'

'It's a people carrier,' said Diego, swinging out of the driver's seat. 'Big enough for our family and all our friends.'

'We're driving up to Scout Scar. Walk? Picnic?' Tara stood in the hall. 'Morning Anna. Are you okay? Sofia, you're looking worn out already.'

'Where's Andy?' Mikey rushed back into the hall, bouncing. 'Mum, I got to go in their new car.'

Tara put an arm around Mum's shoulders. 'You need a bit of time to get ready? We can wait. Mikey can sit in the car if you like.'

Anna avoided looking at Mum as they cleared the table, brushed up the crumbs, stacked the plates and mugs in the sink. Then Mum said, 'I texted Tara last night. I told her about your father. We thought going out together might clear the air.'

'Mikey doesn't like it.'

'No.' Mum avoided looking at Anna. Anna felt her heart almost hiccupping with worry.

Diego parked the big new red car outside an old church where other cars were lined up side by side.

Below them the land was criss-crossed with waterways and the view across the valley made Anna hold her breath. She turned from side to side, as if looking hard could pull the horizon closer. Tara said this was the Lune valley, with newly-planted reed-beds to help the water birds. Beyond, on the skyline, outlined between the hills, was Morecambe Bay, the sea glistening in the soft autumn sunshine. The hills were turning gold and red from heather and fading bracken.

'Helsington Church,' said Mum, reading from the church noticeboard. 'And what is Scout Scar?'

Anna knew about Scout Scar from geography, but she didn't want to make things any easier for Mum by answering a question. She had no intention of "clearing the air". She knew what it meant. At school they had talks about how to resolve quarrels between friends. Friends quarrelling was nothing like letting back into the house a father who had beaten up your mother for years and years. Had Mum forgotten all her bruises and burns?

Diego lifted Andy out of his car seat and put him into a backpack. He shouted and kicked like Sam in church. Now he was nearly three he was certain he could walk everywhere. 'I can do it I can do it.'

Tara said, 'Oh, let him walk for a bit. He'll soon get cross and ask for a carry.'

Diego laughed and set down the backpack. Andy kicked against the frame, making it difficult to lift him out. Mikey took his fingers. 'I can hold his hand,' and the child immediately smiled, raising his arms to let Diego release him.

Anna wanted to say "Be careful" but Mikey surprised her. Andy gripped Mikey's hand and pulled him forward, but Mikey tugged him back. 'You got to walk carefully,' he said. 'There's roots and things under the earth and you might fall over.' He glanced at Anna and she wanted to hug him. He was still remembering how things happened on Pelm. She drew a deep breath. Her little brother was pretty special, even if sometimes he had pretty special tantrums.

Mum made to take her arm but Anna stepped sideways. She was not going to let Mum think everything was fine when it was going to be horrible.

They crossed the narrow road, carefully looking in both directions because of the bend, but no cars came. On the other side a path zigzagged up the fellside between dying ferns. The branches overhead were bare. Keen walkers were out already, silhouetted on the skyline. Diego caught her glance. 'It's very popular. We often come here. It blows all the worries out of my head.' He smiled and gestured lightly towards Mikey, who almost lost his balance as Andy crouched to pick up an important feather.

'Keep an eye on them, do,' said Tara, pushing her arm through Mum's. 'We've stuff to talk about it.'

Diego sniffed and pretended to be offended before growling like a bear and heading for the boys. Andy gave a scream and Mikey got between him and his dad. They were going to have fun. Why did the boys always get the fun? Anna fell behind Mum and Tara, kicking at little stones. After a while, she found she had to tune in.

'Are you sure? Is this wise? After all that's happened?'

Mum said, 'I think it's right. I am not at all sure about what is wise.'

'How can it be right? You've had years of worrying and getting hurt and trying to protect the kids.' Tara quickly glanced around at Anna, but Anna had pulled out her phone and was pretending to take photos of the view. The camera wasn't very good and Mum knew it, but she wasn't attending to Anna.

'I know it must seem strange to you.' Mum spoke quietly and Anna strained to hear every word. 'When we fell in love, he was sweet and generous. He was my lover. Everything changed when we came to England. He said he wanted to protect me. I know now it was a means of control. I do understand that, Tara.'

'Well then?'

'Well then, all the time I could not help feeling sorry for him.'

'You don't mean that.' Tara sounded shocked. She tugged Mum's arm. Behind them, Anna had fumbled with her phone, nearly dropping it.

Mum gave a small laugh and threw back her head, red glints in her dark hair catching the light. 'I don't quite understand it myself but I've been talking it over with our priest.'

'He thinks it's going to be ok letting – letting Anthony come back?'

A shiver ran through Anna's body. She folded her arms across her body, pulling the fleece closer. *Anthony.* How long had it been since she heard her father's name? She had once looked up the meaning of his name on a school computer. It meant *ruler.* She tried imagining him as a stiff bit of wood, evenly marked in inches and centimetres, but the website said it was a name meaning power and control. Like Dad.

Mum was talking again. 'Father Bernard never tells me what to think.'

Anna tugged at the zip. She didn't think any priest could be trusted. 'I don't mean to let Anthony come and live with us, well, not straight away. We've got the house through the charity Karina found. I've talked it over with her. I thought he could come and visit, see the children, have meals with us. But I might try to get the injunction overturned or he could be prosecuted and I wouldn't like that. It wouldn't be good for the children to have their father in court.'

Tara stopped dead and swung Mum round to stand in front of her, face to face. They seemed not to notice Anna standing nearby, or shouts from Diego, who had lifted Andy on to his shoulders and was running a race with Mikey. 'It wouldn't be good for the children if their father returned to his old habits. What do you think will happen? You told me Mikey stopped talking for years, all because of his father.'

Mum loosened Tara's hands. 'But that's the point. He is their father. They have his inheritance, his genes. I must believe he has changed. People can change. I believe people can change. I believe in forgiveness, in second chances. We all get second chances, Tara.'

'And this is what you talked to your bloody priest about, is it? Sorry. That got away from me.' Tara took Mum's shoulders again and gave her a little shake. Anna wished she would shake Mum so hard her teeth would clatter and hurt. She knew what that felt like, of course, from *Anthony.* Dad had been great at shaking till her bones hurt. 'Does your priest think it's a good idea then?'

Mum said, 'I think he does not like it but it's my

conscience not his. Don't be afraid for me, Tara. I know I must put the children first. Father Bernard says that. I just want to give Anthony a second chance. I've had a second chance. I don't know what made Anthony so controlling and cruel. Maybe I turned myself into a victim when I came to live here, because I was out of my place, out of my home.'

Tara said, very quietly, 'You're crying.' She fingered a tear on Mum's face and Anna's heart creaked.

'Of course I'm crying. It's a risk.'

Tara put her arms around Mum and Anna heard, 'You don't have to aim for sainthood, sweetheart.'

'No,' said Mum. 'I must be sure in my conscience. Anna, you've been listening. Come here, my little one.' Anna found herself pulled into a three-way hug with Tara. She felt hot and uncomfortable.

Apparently it was called the Mushroom – it did look like one, a circular building at the top of the Scar, with a mushroom-shaped roof. Scout Scar was made of limestone, Anna had learned. It was an escarpment, a great cliff rising like a wave made of rock and freezing into place above the valley below. At the top was the Mushroom, where people could stand and look, or sit and look, and see all the distant hills. As she followed the others up the side of the fell, Anna stopped beside a circle of stones someone had laid out. It wasn't like a cairn, marking the path. In the middle of the circle was a low-spreading green shrub Tara said was juniper and the berries were used to flavour gin. Anna stepped inside to pull off several berries. They smelt spicy and woody as she rolled them between her fingers, and the rough texture gave off their perfume, making her skin smell spicy too.

She wondered about taking these little berries to Pelm, along with pine cones. They might grow into green bushes and stay green all through winter. Green people could stay awake and fight.

Somebody had to fight Dad.

Somebody had to stay awake and not think everyone deserved a second chance. The King said he would turn the Queen into a worm. If Dad got inside their house, what would he do to Mum?

Okay, Mum was being saintly, but she hadn't asked Anna or Mikey to be saintly.

She stood up, stuffing the berries into the pocket of her blue fleece. 'Why do people make stone circles?'

Tara laughed. 'Well, the Park authorities don't approve but I guess some people can't be stopped. They think stone circles are special, like corn circles.'

Mum said, 'At the agency one of the staff told me about corn circles, and ley lines? Is that the correct word? It seems very superstitious to me.'

'Some people have strange convictions,' said Tara.

Anna wished she'd told Mum before about Dad stalking her. Now, Mum would have a story in her head about Dad trying to get in touch. What could she and Mikey do to make Dad go away, except find Pelm again? Maybe the Queen, or Kazan, or someone, would let her discover what to do about Dad.

Would Mikey be all right with that? He seemed to think getting back to Pelm was mostly to help Kazan.

The edge of the escarpment was steeper than she

had expected. It would be too easy to put a foot wrong and fall over the edge. Diego said there used to be a viewfinder pointing out all the hills so he would be the viewfinder instead. 'Look north, no, Sofia, look where I'm pointing. Can you see those faint outlines? That's Scotland.'

Mikey poked Anna in the ribs. 'We got to talk.'

Chapter Thirteen

Shrivelling practice

*A*nna found herself under a tree. She reached behind to touch the trunk, but the bark flaked off into her hand. Branches brushing her face felt brittle. She knew she was dreaming and yet she was here. Across the clearing the King leaned against another tree, the silvery-grey of his cloak merging with the grey of the trunk. Her heart sank.

He gestured at the tree beneath which she stood. 'Well, I might not have shrivelled this tree but I have made a dent in its life force, wouldn't you say?'

Anna dug her nails into the palms of her hands. 'Why are you attacking a tree? What's a tree done to you?'

He smiled, pushed himself upright and crunched towards her across the brown, dead leaves. Her forefinger throbbed and the scar on her cheek burned. His footsteps slowed and he reached overhead to a branch, snapping it off with a sickening click. 'The roots are growing weak, you see?' He waved the branch in front of her and she saw the interior was a dull, brownish grey instead of a sappy green. The air smelt of dead tree, of dust.

She straightened her shoulders and stared down her nose. 'It's petty, trying to kill a tree.'

He stroked her cheek, and she had to grit her teeth.

The pain was so acute, it was as if he had found the nerve connected to her most secret, sensitive feelings. 'I am practising, my dear child. I haven't found yet how to shrink my enemies but I will. This is a first stage.'

Anna's fingers twitched. How she longed to punch him in the stomach – no – that was Dad – she was not like Dad – never – not even when people still told her she looked just like him, thinking they were making a compliment. Cutting her hair short had not been enough to make her totally different but people must have worked out by now her character wasn't a bit like his.

'Killing things off is your plan, is it?'

The King's face produced a smile. 'Not at all. How naive you are. I have decided to eliminate the Green people from Pelm. They contribute nothing, and when the weather grows cold they hide.'

'You can't get rid of them,' said Anna, sick at the idea of Kazan and the others being forced to escape. Of course it might be worse. He might mean to practise his new spell on them. There was a lump in her throat. 'Pelm is made of Leaf and Stone. You don't decide on your own.'

'Stories, my dear, stories.'

Anna's breath came in short bursts. 'You *know* the Sea Snake made Pelm – your father got in a ship – he tried to kill the Great Snake and he drowned. Or is that a story too?'

The slap across her face made her head spin and for a moment she could not see clearly. A gasp of pain escaped but she drew a deep breath, determined not to give in. 'You're telling lies about the Queen.'

The squillkit dropped on to her shoulders, dug in her

claws and hissed. It was a wonderful sound and seemed to affect the King. He stumbled back, almost losing his footing. 'I'm getting rid of those creatures too.' He half-drew the sword from its sheath and it caught the light of the sinking sun, long, yellow rays penetrating through the bare branches. His eyes glittered and he seemed to be seeing something inside his head, not Anna or the forest or Tanda. He had gone inside himself, into some other world. His eyes narrowed, his lips grew thin and his pale skin whitened.

Tanda curled her fluffed tails across Anna's face and rubbed her head against Anna's right ear. The pressure from the small skull was soothing. Her fur was warm and voices spilled into her head. Tanda must have brought them.

Please come. I am afraid. He wishes to kidnap my little brother. We have hidden Nazan with the other little ones in the caves but the magic is growing too strong for us.

Anna shuddered. How did she know these were Kazan's words when he wasn't nearby?

Her racing heart slowed when the Queen spoke.

The King is afraid his troops will desert him. They cannot forget how he twisted their minds, making them lose their own will and follow him. He boasts. He does not have true power.

Anna exhaled in a long, slow breath. The Queen was right. Brave soldiers had stepped forward the last time the King had tried to work his worst magic. Leaf and Stone people swam out into the lake where the Queen had taken refuge. They meant to protect her when she shed the snakeskin and became herself again. The people who'd been there would know she wasn't a witch, whatever rumours the King spread – unless they doubted their own memories.

People did misremember. Dad did. Did Mum? She was telling herself a story about how Dad really loved her when they met so perhaps he still did. Only he didn't behave as if he loved her.

Tanda jumped lightly to the earth and dug into the soil with her claws, hissing at the King. With an exclamation, he pulled the sword fully from its sheath and raised it over his head. 'I'll slice off your head, you disgusting little creature,' but when he tried to slash downwards the tip caught in a branch and he could not dislodge it. He roared, tugged and kicked at the tree trunk, as if the tree itself were responsible. Anna recalled the very first time she and Mikey had reached the island, when Mikey had run up a hill, stood under a tree and found its branches dropping down around him. He had screamed, thinking he was in a cage but the tree was trying to be helpful.

Perhaps the trees had not lost their power, even if their leaves had fallen.

Tanda bounded off between the trees, turning to stare at Anna with her huge amber eyes. Anna followed as fast as she could although the squillkit was so quick Anna kept losing sight of her. She was so scared she wasn't certain her eyes were warning her what was ahead. The ground was thick with dying shrubbery, fallen branches, heaps of leaves, tree roots twisting above ground, until it was harder and harder to see the path. She kept sliding, tripping, with the twinge of a stitch in her side, but she ran on regardless, terrified the

King was chasing after her so silently she could not hear him.

At last she had to stop. She stared around. Tanda was nowhere to be seen. The sun must have dropped below the horizon for the forest was much darker now.

Anna began to shiver. *How did I get here? I don't remember –*

Chapter Fourteen: Sunday morning

Crossed Loyalties

*A*nna sat bolt upright, her heart banging against her ribs. A silver moon appeared through the gap in her curtains and she sank back against the pillow, gasping. It had been a dreadful dream, had followed the dreadful bedtime. Mum had tried to get Mikey to talk but he'd put his hands over his ears and ducked under the duvet. Mum had said, 'Darling, it's all about second chances. Everyone deserves a second chance, don't you think?' Mikey had said nothing. Mum had beckoned Anna to follow her out of his bedroom. 'What am I to do?'

'He gave Mikey that awful black eye and all because he was trying to stop Dad from hitting you. He'll be thinking the same thing will happen again.'

Mum shrank as if Anna had hit her but Anna was not sorry. 'It will not happen again,' Mum said, but her eyes were damp.

Anna would not be sympathetic. Going out with Tara and Diego had been lovely, and Mikey had been great with Andy, but nothing would make better what Mum had decided. Dad was coming to tea.

Anna said, 'Dad's not allowed here. What about the court order.'

For the first time, she and Mum quarrelled. Mum got very stiff and said, 'If I decide to see him and do not complain, he will not be prosecuted.'

This made Anna lose her temper. 'He stalked me, he was hanging around in the park, he got me after school, he said horrible things about you —.'

Mum became very stiff, and her mouth tightened. 'And you decide to tell me now? I am sure he was trying to rebuild trust with you. If what you say is true, he should have come first to me, of course, but he always came to you because you — he feels close to you. You look so much alike - even the way you move.'

'How can you say I'm like him? He just wants to get at you, he doesn't love me, he's horrible.' Anna went to bed in a fury.

Trying to convince herself she'd been right, she began to replay Dad's words to her outside the park, and a wave of heat made her throw off the duvet. Dad had been very rude about Karina, and about Mum's English — and Mum's English was good, the agency said so — but he hadn't actually said anything bad about Mum. She'd lied to Mum. No, she hadn't. He hadn't changed one bit. He was cunning, that was all.

She tried to apologise to Mum before breakfast, before Mikey came downstairs, but Mum had brushed it aside. 'You are emotional, I am emotional, moro mou. Don't let it stand between us.'

At Mass, Anna decided to go out with the children to the children's service. She didn't want to hear Father Bernard being funny and reasonable and talking about loving your enemies. He hadn't the faintest idea about being kicked and burned and made to look and feel stupid by someone with a blond ponytail and lots of university degrees and a profile that made stupid women who didn't know anything about him say he was *drop dead gorgeous.*

Most of the children sat on mats, and somebody told a story but Anna managed to close her ears. It was almost like wearing invisible earplugs. Abigail brought Sam and Anna sat with them, showing Sam how to colour in with a crayon. He wasn't very good at it but she guessed every baby had to learn. Then the woman in charge got out her guitar and they all sang and clapped and Anna had to swallow hard. Were some of the others from homes like hers, where a dad made everyone scared? Maybe there were awful mums somewhere too though Anna found it hard to believe. Once you'd been through all the trouble of having a baby, why would you want to hurt it? They'd done stuff at school about sex, birth control, getting pregnant, having the baby. It all sounded grisly. Periods were bad enough. Boys had it easy.

She stopped herself in mid-thought. What had turned Dad into the truly nasty man he'd become? Mum didn't think he was evil but Anna thought Mum wasn't watching – she wasn't paying attention to the glitter in his eye.

The Queen was beautiful and the King wanted to turn her into a worm. Why? If Mum was going to be stupid about Dad, Anna would get back to Pelm and make sure the King's plan fell apart. She'd make him understand human girls could be strong. It couldn't be right to forgive someone who was evil.

Mikey rushed off into the parish hall as soon as the service had finished, determined to carry on playing with his friends. Anna picked up Sam and went with Abigail to the counter where people on a rota were pouring out coffee and juice. Sam made a grab at a plain biscuit, Abigail laughed and said that was okay, and then his dad arrived and Sam reached for him, wriggling out of Anna's arms, and wiping his nose in Jake's neck.

For a moment Anna stood still, blinking hard. The baby had been heavy and warm and had put his arms around her neck and now he was burbling at his father. She turned away and made for the ladies' loo. Mum was waiting in the corridor outside and caught Anna by the arm. 'Someone has made you cry? Who has done this?'

'I'm just going to the loo.'

'You have your period?'

Anna shook her off. 'No. It's ages yet. You always know. You keep count.'

'Things change. Little one, let's not argue.'

'I am not a little one, hadn't you noticed? I'm thirteen.'

Father Bernard appeared, fresh from saying goodbye to people in the church porch. Mum and Anna went in different directions, and Father Bernard waited as Anna tried to pass him. He said in a low voice, 'If it all gets a bit much, I'm a good listener.'

'Yeah,' said Anna. It came out as a growl. 'You listen when Mum says it's okay for our dad to come back but it isn't. He's cruel and horrible and you say it's okay.'

Father Bernard raised his eyebrows and Anna clenched her fists. He said, 'Loyalties can sometimes be so hard to work out, the lines get crossed.' She turned her back, and moved past into the hall, to join everyone drinking coffee and tea.

He must have followed. One of the women behind

101

the counter handed him a cup. Her voice was high and loud. 'Kept your black coffee for you. It's all go in here today.'

Anna almost ran out of the hall, dodged across the road to the common and leaned against the wall. Below, the River Kent churned and murmured. A few ducks dabbled along, swimming against the current, and she wondered what they would find for food, where they were heading. Did ducks get bullied and beaten up by drakes?

What did he mean, *crossed loyalties*? Did he mean Mum being loyal to Dad, taking marriage vows, stuff like that? Well, Dad had broken all his promises. He might have been lovely in Greece. Perhaps that was being in another country.

Anna rooted in her pocket for the plain biscuit she'd surreptitiously scooped up and tossed it to the ducks. The biscuit circled in an eddy, disappeared under the surface, reappeared a bit further downstream and vanished altogether. She didn't want her life to be like that, turning in circles and going under because of the current.

The river rushed towards Morecambe Bay, and seven islands, and a lot of sandbanks, and people drowned where the river lost itself in the sea. She bit a nail. *If we could get the King to another country would he be nice? Nicer?*

Mum nudged her elbow and held out her anorak. 'You left this hanging up, my darling. Aren't you cold?'

Anna stuffed her arms into the padded blue jacket. 'Not really.' She thought about it. 'Thanks.'

Mum took her hand. 'Please do not shrink away from me. I wanted to tell you earlier, I cannot invite

Anthony to tea yet. It would be too soon. I've made different arrangements. We'll meet him on a bus and go to Bowness, to the lake.'

'Oh.'

'Is that acceptable?'

Well, it was better than having to open the door of their house and letting him inside.

Mikey appeared from behind Mum. 'We went on a train before and we went on the boat in Windermere and Tara heard me telling Dad he wasn't meant to talk to me.'

Mum sighed. 'It isn't helpful to bring this up today, Mikey.'

'Diego's much better than Dad.'

Anna said, 'Is Dad coming on the bus too?'

'We will meet him at the bus stop.'

'He's not paying for our tickets.'

'No, Anna, I have money enough to pay for us. Does that satisfy you?'

'You really think he will let you pay for us?'

'I will not allow anything else. And we will not be indoors with him.'

'The bus is kind of indoors,' said Anna. Her heartbeat would not settle to a steady rhythm.

'There will be other people. Mikey — is that all right with you?'

Mikey kicked at a stray leaf and shrugged. Anna had a bad feeling but now Mum had fixed it they would have to go through whatever happened. At least it would all be in public.

Dad was waiting at the bus station. 'I could have driven us, Sofia. It's rather cold and it's almost midday.' He wore a waxy green jacket, blue jeans and trainers with fat white soles. His hair was tied back in its usual ponytail and a girl and her mother, also waiting at the stop, nudged each other. The girl fished her mobile phone out of a bag and took a photo. From the corner of her eye, Anna glimpsed Dad lift his chin. He always posed when there were girls around.

She'd heard of media celebs losing their jobs because they were abusers. Maybe Dad could lose his job at the university ... Did they know, the people in charge, did they know he'd got a court order against him? She imagined herself in front of a row of men in suits — no, there'd be women too, wouldn't there? — while she explained how Dad had half-throttled Mum, punched and kicked her. Surely they wouldn't let him teach students, a man like that? She'd say if she was one of those students she wouldn't want anything to do with Anthony Daniels, no matter how many degrees he had.

Mum said, 'Are you warm enough, Mikey?'

'I put on my school sweatshirt. It's all fleecy inside,' and he pulled back his anorak to show her.

Dad said, 'Does it have your school logo on it?'

Mikey zipped up his anorak and turned his back.

'Your manners have not improved, young man.'

Mum said, 'We will be there soon enough. Look, the bus is coming.' There was a glint in her eye Anna had not noticed before, and it was almost comforting. Maybe Mum would not turn out to be too soft.

Mum was first on the bus and paid for herself, Anna and Mikey. Anna heard Dad say something but Mum said, 'Thank you, Anthony, I prefer to pay. Anna, find a seat with Mikey, please.'

She turned to let Dad pass. He paid for his ticket

and gestured to Mum to follow him. The woman and girl crowded behind them so Anna quickly grabbed Mikey's wrist and dragged him up to the top deck. 'We're not sitting with them, okay?' Mikey jumped into a seat beside a window. 'Mikey, are you going to stop talking again?'

He breathed on the window and traced, "No" with a forefinger.' Then he said, 'I'll talk to you and Mum and Andy and Tara and Diego and Mr Carey. Not talking to *him*.'

Anna thought about it. 'That's cool. I'll have to talk to him, but I'm not letting him be friendly or anything.' She rummaged in her pocket. 'I brought my purse. If we want crisps or anything I'll buy them for us.'

Mikey stared out of the window as the bus drew away from the station and halted at the traffic lights. 'He's not to hurt Mum again.' Mikey sounded much older than nearly eight.

She nudged him. 'We'll stop him together.'

They passed the journey in silence. It was almost fun, seeing the road from the top deck, looking down into gardens and fields, the little villages, seeing the great hills in the distance, getting closer. At one stop, Anna craned to see the name on a signpost, in case it pointed to Polly's farm. She'd know where to get off if she came to visit. Maybe Polly would meet her at the bus stop. Polly lived where the hills were huge and purple and gold. The horizon was full of mountains, clouds and a big sky.

'We don't get off till Bowness. That's the lake at the bottom of this road.' Dad's voice came from behind. Anna looked over her shoulder and saw him standing at the top of the stairs, forcing a smile. He couldn't tell them off. He'd want to make himself look good in front of the other passengers.

'I know,' said Anna, turning her back.

She heard his sniff, the soft hiss of his trainers on the steps as he ran back down. She imagined him sitting beside Mum and telling her off for letting his children become rude, and she didn't care. It was Mum's fault, making them spend time with him.

He spoilt everything. She had just been in a daydream of riding further and further, getting off to visit Rydal and Grasmere and getting on again to reach Keswick and Derwentwater ... the names were magic, like spells. She knew there were caves here too, and mines and shafts under the mountains, just like on Pelm. Lots of people practically worshipped the Lake District.

Chapter Fifteen: Sunday afternoon

The face beneath the lake

*T*here weren't many tourists, just a few taking photographs or feeding the birds on the shore. A lot of the shops were shut. Dad said, 'What had you in mind for us to do, Sofia? It's too late in the season for a rowing boat.'

Anna walked towards the water, where swans and geese waved their long necks and nipped at fingers for bird food. Little waves broke on the pebbles, rushed back into the deeper water, crept forward again.

Mum kept her voice calm. 'My first idea was we might try one of the cruises, around the islands, or to the aquarium. I would like to see what tourists expect out of season, what is available to attract them.' Dad frowned. 'For my job at the agency, Anthony. I need a better sense of tourist interests, tourists from this country, tourists from overseas.'

Dad snorted. 'I can tell you. They require clean public lavatories, decent food, well cooked and well presented, tour guides whose English is clear and good enough to be understood. Your job hasn't taught you much if you don't know this.'

Anna scowled, turned in time to see Mum's cheeks reddening. Anna wanted to kick Dad somewhere where it would really hurt but he had touched Mum's elbow and hadn't stopped talking. 'Of course, you understand what's required in the Greek islands, Sofia. Where the sun always shines tourists are easily satisfied. They only want sun beds. Rolls of flabby flesh on show. Gross.' He plainly meant this to be an apology.

Mum said, 'I booked a motor boat. I thought you would enjoy driving us around the lake.' Anna noticed the tightening of Dad's jaw and cheered inwardly. Mum had taken the initiative and he didn't like it. 'I booked it this morning online. It has an electric motor. It will be silent and we will be able to hear the birds. Have you driven an electric vehicle, Anthony?'

Anna reckoned he was grinding his teeth but he managed to say, 'This will be an opportunity. How very enterprising of you, Sofia.'

'I hope you will enjoy it. We can buy sandwiches to take out with us. Mikey, Anna, go and choose what you would like,' and she handed Anna a ten-pound note.

They found the place on a jetty where the electric boats were moored. Mum had let Dad buy her something to eat and drink but she was the one to show the online booking on her mobile, and Anna had to stop herself from grinning. Dad didn't pull a face. He let Mum lead the way along the jetty, he didn't try to help her into the boat like she'd seen some men do, making out women were too feeble to manage their own bodies. Had he truly learned something or was he hiding his feelings, waiting to take charge?

She pictured Diego opening the car door to let Mum out, being polite. He was polite when he stood back on pavements to let a wheelchair zip past – in fact, he was just a very kind person. Anna realised she was scowling and quickly smoothed out the frown. She didn't want Dad noticing anything about her.

Diego was a lovely person so she didn't mind when he was helpful. He made her feel almost grown-up.

Was Dad really able to change, the way Mum believed he could? Anna decided he had practised being horrible for so long he could have a degree in it. Dr Anthony Daniels, PhD in Cruelty. No, it was called Coercive Control and they'd done something about it at school.

Dad was already standing in the boat, looking at the controls while the man in charge explained how to use them.

Mikey said, 'I don't like boats.'

'Mikey, you liked the one last year.' Anna said it quickly. Dad mustn't have an excuse to complain about Mikey talking to her but not to him.

'That was a big boat,' he said, but he let Mum help him step down into it. She had gone a bit pale, and her glance at Anna had a kind of warning in it. Anna pursed her lips and used Mum's arm to steady herself as she followed Mikey. Once in the boat, she grabbed his wrist and made him sit at the back, under the canopy. At the front was the seat for the driver, behind a steering wheel like a car's, and Dad had already settled himself. He was talking at top speed, obviously very pleased with himself.

Maybe it was a good idea of Mum's, except Anna didn't believe in miracles where Dad was concerned. He didn't deserve to be a nice person. When they had been on Symi during the summer holidays and visited the monastery, she had deliberately not asked St

Mikhael to turn Anthony Daniels into a nice person. Would Father Bernard say she was a bad person, not wanting her father to change? He had no idea. People like him had no idea what it was like being a family.

Mikey kicked her ankle and glared at her.

'What?'

'You're wriggling, you're making me wobble.' He whispered, glancing at Dad's back.

'Sorry.' She whispered too. There wasn't much chance of Dad hearing. He was completely enjoying himself, playing with the controls. She nudged Mikey's knee with hers and gave a thumbs-up sign. He twitched a smile.

Dad said, 'Well, let's get this boat out on the water and see what she can do.' Mum took the seat beside him, behind the windshield, unwound the blue and yellow scarf from round her neck and tied it over her hair. It seemed to Anna a very important gesture. Mum had no scars to hide.

The boat rocked a little and then surged forward, the engine so quiet that all Anna heard was the hiss of the water foaming into a wake behind them. Mikey leaned over the side, biting his lips to stop himself from grinning but the grin kept breaking through. Anna was smiling too.

For a while, nobody spoke. Dad steered the boat away from the jetty and out towards the big island in the middle of the lake and all Anna wanted to do was gaze around, until Dad called over his shoulder, 'This is Belle Isle.' Anna did not say she and Mikey had heard about Belle Isle the last time they were on Windermere when he had stalked them and totally spoiled their trip until Tara and Diego turned up.

She opened her mouth and shut it again when

Mum turned round with a smile and a wave. She looked beautiful, her dark eyes glinting and long black strands of curls escaping from the headscarf. She must be thinking this trip was going well. The lake was lovely even in November, with the trees on the fellside shedding golden and red reflections on the water.

Dad turned the boat before they reached the island and headed along the lake, parallel to the shore. There were no steamers, it must be too late for them, but sailing dinghies flitted past, white sails billowing and dipping. Mikey caught her wrist, pointing. She nodded. 'Wouldn't it be great to sail? I'd be a bit scared but I'd love to try.'

As they motored along the far side of the lake a big building came into view, and Dad said, 'Wray Castle. I would like to moor here, Sofia. It would be an excellent stopping point for a picnic and the kids could run around a bit.'

'There is a jetty, I believe. I'm not sure if we are able to stop but we can look, can't we?'

Anyone listening or watching would have assumed this was a nice Sunday afternoon outing for a family. Anna kept leaning forward, gazing at the shoreline and the other boats, or leaning back and chewing her knuckles because she was not supposed to be enjoying herself. It was impossible to settle into a calm mood. In the end, Dad switched off the engine when the boat was close to the shore of a small bay. They bobbed up and down on little waves and Mum swung round on her seat, opening her packet of sandwiches. 'Time for lunch, my darlings. We're very late but no matter.'

'We should have eaten before we embarked,' said

Dad, rummaging in his bag.

'You were so excited at the idea of driving the boat you couldn't wait to start.' Mum had spoken without thinking, treating Dad the cheerful way Tara spoke to Diego. Anna's stomach churned.

Dad did not reply but his hand tightened on the paper bag holding his sandwiches. One fell out. Mum picked it up, dusted it off and said, 'This is fine for me. Have mine, Anthony.'

'My darling, you are always too self-effacing.' Dad put his arm around Mum's shoulders and kissed her mouth, a proper man-kissing-woman romantic kiss that made Anna curl her lip.

Mikey opened a packet of crisps and began to eat very noisily with his mouth open.

'Mikey.' Mum's tone was sharp.

Mikey rolled his eyes so that only the whites showed. He hadn't done this since they first started living in the safe house. He carried on crunching.

Anna grabbed the packet and threw the crisps over the side of the boat, where they floated until tiny fish bobbed up to nibble the edges and pull them under. The ducks practically ran across the water to get the crisps. Mikey shoved Anna in the back, and she clambered to her feet, making the boat sway from side to side. She almost lost her balance.

'Children, please.' Mum's voice pleaded.

Anna didn't care. 'I am not a child.' Something dark inside wanted a fight. When she saw a tear on Mikey's cheek she sat down heavily, blowing her nose so nobody would notice he was trying not to cry too.

Dad played at peacemaker. He opened a bottle of sparkling water and gave it to Mum, before taking a bite from his sandwich. 'Ice creams when we get back to Bowness, I think. Isn't there a famous shop near the roundabout?'

'It has more than forty flavours, I believe,' said Mum.

Dad stroked the back of her hand. 'You are very well informed, sweetheart.'

Mum's face was flushed. 'We've been here before, Anthony. And I did my research. I wanted to find out if the shop would be open out of season.'

'You don't surprise me.'

Somehow the time passed. Mikey threw crumbs from his ham sandwich to the ducks, and ate the small chocolate muffin Anna had bought, together with hers. She had lost her appetite.

Dad switched on the engine and turned the boat round, ready for crossing the lake. He said he would aim for the houses, to find the jetty from which they had set off. Anna could not wait for the trip to finish. The thought of catching the bus back to Kendal and having to sit with Dad for hours yet made her skin itch. Mikey kept wriggling. He still had not said a word and she didn't blame him. She reached out to steady him, touching his knee, and realised he was hot. Without speaking she knelt by the side of the boat, trailed a hand in the cool water and gestured to him to do the same. He slipped out of his seat to kneel beside her and she felt him relax against her.

Ripples flowed past her fingers, soothing them and her mind drifted to Pelm – Kazan – his little brother – the Queen, the caves – the King knew how to get underground – *Queen, take care, take care – he's finding new spells – he killed a tree...* He said he would turn the Queen into a worm – *like earth worms, wriggly and shiny –*

Without warning, Anna began to retch.

Anna, Anna, come back. Anna, Anna, I am trapped. Anna, Anna — I am here, beneath the water, drowning in slime –

Queen –?

Something reached for Anna's fingers, she felt a cold slipperiness, another hand –

She threw up. Vomit floated on the surface.

Mikey whipped his hand out of the water, rubbed it on his jeans and pulled faces.

Dad cut the motor. 'What have you been eating?' He let go of the wheel and it spun freely, sending the boat in circles until Mum grabbed it. Dad's hand on the back of Anna's neck was hard.

Her throat burned and the taste in her mouth was vile.

Dad said, 'We should never have embarked. I should have pointed out the pollution levels in the lake. Everyone knows. It's a national scandal. Hiring this boat was a mistake.'

He trod heavily back to the wheel, pushed Mum into the other seat, switched on the engine and set the boat moving.

Anna doubled over, clutching her stomach. She would not be sick again. It wasn't anything she'd eaten. It was panic.

Dad didn't say he was sorry but insisted on buying ice creams for everyone before they caught the bus back. Anna said she wanted vanilla, he said it was a bad idea, if she was sick on the bus he would not be associated with her, but Mum touched his arm.

Vanilla ice cream slipped down coolly into her stomach, taking away some of the acid.

On the way back, she and Mikey sat downstairs, in front of Mum and Dad. At the bus station, Dad kissed Mum again, and said he'd call round later in the week.

They walked home in silence.

At bedtime, Mum said, 'I'm sorry you felt sick, Anna. Was it the motion of the boat?'

Anna shook her head. 'It's gone now. Doesn't matter. Can I go to bed now?'

'Supper for you both?'

'I don't want anything to eat.'

Mikey said, 'I want sausages,' and kicked the table leg.

Mum found burgers in the freezer and put one inside a roll for him. Anna watched her careful actions, wondering what she was feeling. Did she think Dad was changing? He hadn't shouted at Mikey for not talking to him. He'd almost shouted at Anna but not quite.

The sick churn in her stomach came back.

Anna knocked on Mikey's bedroom door after Mum settled down with a book and went in although he told her to go away.

'We've got to check out Kazan, we've got see what the King's doing.'

'Don't care. Don't care. You never stopped him.'

'How was I meant to do that? You didn't help, sulking the whole time.'

'I was not sulking. He's horrible. Mum's horrible. Not talking to Mum either.'

Anna bunched her fists. 'You don't understand how Mum feels.'

'Go away.' He pulled his pillow over his head.

Anna wanted to slam the door but she closed it softly. It wouldn't help if Mum ran upstairs to find out why there was banging and upset.

She had returned to her own room and was sitting on the end of the bed when a soft knock on her door made her leap up, hoping it might be Mikey.

Mum said, 'I brought you a cheese sandwich. You must be hungry.' Dark rings circled her eyes and her hair was pulled tightly back from her face.

Anna's heart felt heavy. Words floated like soap bubbles, glistening and hollow. When they burst, nothing would be left except a bright emptiness and stinging eyes.

'Anna?"

She took the plate. 'Thank you.' Her mother's fingers brushed hers. They were hot. 'It's kind of you.'

'Kind?' Mum turned away, not before Anna glimpsed a tear on Mum's cheek. 'I am not a friend, not a stranger. A mother is not kind.' Her voice was tight, almost angry.

Anna wanted to say, "Dad is unkind, so why can't you be kind?" but she didn't.

Mikey could be so annoying ... she wanted to slap him ... he could be brave ... without his Starstone they wouldn't get back to Pelm. She could be kinder to him ...

After putting on her pyjamas she went back to knock on his door. She would have liked to kick the table leg too.

There was no sound so she opened it a crack. He was asleep, the pillow on the floor, and his arm wrapped around a small honey-coloured teddy bear. Where did that come from? Did Mrs Dodd give it to him? Mrs Dodd was definitely kind.

Mikey would be shrieking mad if he knew she was watching him. He looked younger than nearly-eight. She tiptoed between scattered dinosaurs and lifted the hair from the eye that had been so badly bruised after Dad had hit him. The miracle had happened, of course — on Pelm, the bruise disappeared. If she could get back to the island another miracle might happen.

In the church service people said prayers to a Holy Spirit, and she made sense of it by thinking of a kindness and bravery bigger than the whole universe. She knew it made all the difference to Mum, to Yaya and Papou, and they were people she loved, but no way was she going to ask any spirit or saint to make Dad turn into a kind person.

Maybe something happened to him when he was a little boy to make him horrible – but grown-ups could decide to change, surely. Dad showed no signs at all of wanting to change or trying to be different.

Dad would never change. Great.

Chapter Sixteen: Monday

New locks

*T*he next day, Mum was late again. Anna went to collect Mikey from Mrs Dodd, who said she should stay on until Mum arrived. She was so much her usual self, Anna felt all-over hot and uncomfortable. Somebody ought to tell her about Dad, but it was a relief to talk about English homework and ignore everything else. She had to write arguments for and against people having their own cars or sharing rides with other people.

'Car pools, you mean,' said Mrs Dodd. 'They're a good idea for people living in towns, I think, but I don't know how people living in the country areas would manage.' She frowned, sitting down beside Anna at the kitchen table and fingering her pad of paper. 'I did visit Scotland, once, the west coast, where the land jutted so far out into the sea it might as well have been an island. I remember we drove as far as we could along the road before it turned into a track, and then it was a footpath so we walked along it. And you know, what was so remarkable, we kept finding bicycles lying in the bushes alongside the path.'

'What, like just left, like rubbish?' Anna bit into her oaty biscuit. Mrs Dodd was a great cook.

'We didn't know till we reached the end of the promontory and found about a dozen cottages and other buildings. The people were living in a sort of community. One man ran a computer company with contracts all over the world. It was astonishing.' She paused, shook her head. 'My husband was fascinated. Well, they'd discovered the best way of getting to the road was to leave push-bikes they all shared, dropped off more or less evenly along the track. So, you'd start with one bike, ride till you reached the next, leave a bike and get on the next, ride on, swapping bikes every time until you reached the road. It was a very simple and effective way of travelling.'

'Whose bikes were they?' Anna picked up the crumbs from the wooden table with the end of her finger.

'I expect they all bought old bikes and pooled them. The only other way of getting off was by boat.'

'What do you mean?'

'The younger children went across the loch by boat every day for school in a bigger village on the other side.'

'Children went to school in a boat?' Mikey had abandoned his animal army and stood beside Anna, his eyes bright as he reached for another biscuit. The plate was a red and orange design of oddly-shaped triangles, so bright Anna wanted to run her fingers along the shapes.

'This is such a pretty plate.'

'Yes. It was designed by a potter called Clarice Cliff. At the time it was hard for women to get noticed.' Mrs Dodd stroked the rim of the plate.

'You don't mind us using it?'

'Are you asking, is it valuable?'

Mikey said, 'Your dishes are posh. We get ours from Dave and Roger.'

Mrs Dodd smiled at him. 'Well, I bought this from a charity shop. Sometimes you can get beautiful things from charity shops.'

Anna said, 'It makes you think, women not getting noticed.'

Mrs Dodd looked at her sideways. 'You're going to be noticed, I'm sure, Anna. As for Clarice Cliff, she meant her crockery to be used. It wasn't for decoration. A bit like the community in Scotland managed. They live in a stunningly beautiful place and they had to be practical. The older ones were taught in the village for a couple of years, and then they all went off to boarding school in – now, what was it called? Ullapool?'

Anna tried to imagine the children on Pelm being taken off to school somewhere else. The island wasn't very big. She had no idea how many children lived there. When she and Mikey went before, the young children were all in the underground caves, to keep them safe from the King. She thought they must have been very frightened, very glad to come out into sunshine when the Queen became her true self ...except now they must be hiding again.

When Mum knocked on the door to take them home, Anna was still puzzling over what the Queen's true self was, now that her skin was patterned like the Snake's, and the strength of the Snake was inside her. Maybe it wasn't such a surprise that the King could spread horrid stories about her. What was he plotting? How much time had passed in Pelm since they last were there? Would they be too late? She chewed a knuckle.

She couldn't talk to Mikey about it because there

seemed to be visitors at home. Diego was staring up at the windows, and Karina was locking her car. As they crossed the road, she said, too loudly for Anna's comfort, 'Hello children — sorry, Anna.'

Mikey swung his school bag from side to side. 'Careful,' said Anna, jumping out of the way.

He scowled. 'Why didn't she say sorry to me?'

Diego stopped an argument. 'Mikey, my man — come and give me some advice about these window locks. Maybe the front door too.'

'Why are we getting new locks?' Anna shifted her bag from one shoulder to the other. The books were getting heavier. She'd ask Mum if she could take the laptop to school like other people did. 'What's wrong with these?'

Diego winked. 'Just a precaution, Anna. Tara and I got talking.'

'Where's your new car?' Mikey swung from Diego's elbow.

'I parked it in the next street. Are you going to help me?'

Mum quickly opened the front door and gestured to Karina and Anna to follow her inside. They went into the sitting room, and Mum shook off her padded coat. 'Would you like tea, Karina?'

'That would be very nice. Your friend has made a very good suggestion about new locks.'

'I did not know he meant to come now, but he sent me a text this morning. You think he is right?'

'Yes, of course.' Karina gestured at one of the armchairs. 'Is this okay, Sofia? Anna and I can have a chat?'

'I will make tea for all of us.' Mum patted Anna's cheek and left the room.

Karina shrugged out of her jacket. 'It's nice and warm in here. I'm glad we got the heating repaired after last winter.'

Anna didn't want to sit down. 'What's this about?' She realised her tone of voice was hostile. Her fingers twined together. 'I'm sorry. That was rude. I didn't mean to be rude.'

'It's perfectly understandable.' Karina sat on the sofa and patted the seat beside her. 'Better to sit together. Your Mum's trying to do something that seems very, very ambitious to me.'

'You mean about Dad?' Anna let herself go and sank down on the sofa. Karina smelt comfortably of a soft, flowery scent. 'That's a funny way of describing it.'

'How would you describe it?'

Anna shook her head and stared at her hands. 'She's crazy. I mean, I know she's not but she's got this idea in her head and it's ridiculous. Dad's never going to change.' She felt the prickle of tears and slapped her cheeks. 'Sorry. I am not crying.'

Karina folded Anna's twitching fingers into her own warm hands. 'There can be nothing wrong with your tears, Anna. You have a right to an opinion. I'm here to listen to it.'

'Do you mean ....?' She faltered, tried again. 'I mean, if I said Dad wasn't to come back, could I stop it?'

Karina drew a deep breath, shifting the long loop of turquoise glass beads around her neck. 'I don't know what the judge would say. Your mum has the right to ask for the restraining order to be removed even if I advise against it.'

'Would you? Would you say it was a terrible

idea?'

'I don't know.' Karina rubbed her forehead, letting Anna's hand go. 'Personally, I think it's a bad idea but on the other hand your mother is the sort of person I'd describe as spiritual. She has a strong desire to do what is right, what is good. I understand that. We share a set of values.'

Anna leaned back, to get a better view of Karina's expression. She was half-smiling, her round face colouring. 'You're religious like Mum?'

Karina shrugged. 'I go to Mass when I can.' She began to laugh. 'Yes, we get everywhere. People talk about the Catholic Mafia. We're not like the Italian Mafia, obviously.'

'Aren't the Mafia bad?'

Mum came into the room, mugs rattling on the little tray. 'The Mafia?'

Diego brought in a rush of cold air with Mikey behind him, carrying Diego's work-bag and clanking it to a rhythm in his head. 'We got lots of screwdrivers and hammers and tools. Diego's going to do something to our door.'

Mum handed him a mug of tea. 'Our door?'

'The lock should be changed, I believe.' Anna watched him catch Karina's eye. Karina nodded very slightly.

'I thought it was a good lock,' said Mum, twitching a strand of hair behind an ear.

'Do we really need a new lock?'

'You could do with a multi-point lock. It locks the door in three places. I've just installed them at ours. It isn't straightforward.'

'I can find a budget for that.' Karina stood up, nursing a mug in her hands. 'We're changing locks on a lot of our houses. We did upgrade some of these after you moved in, didn't we? But I'm not sure we did much with the front door. It's a very good idea.'

Mum set down the tray. 'I am grateful for all your suggestions, Diego, Karina. I know you want to keep us safe.' She stroked her neck in a gesture Anna recognised. It made her shiver, reminding her of the mornings when at breakfast Dad was very particular about cutting toast, or cracking a boiled egg, and Mum seemed unable to sit down.

Maybe it was a very good idea for Diego to check all the locks and bolts. Their safe house did not feel quite so safe now. Suppose Mum decided it was her duty to give Dad a key for the new lock?

Anna would never be able to sleep.

Mikey might refuse to sleep in the house at all. This was such a worrying idea Anna had to get up and think of something to do.

'Are you okay?' Karina's voice was soothing – kind.

'I got homework. I'd better get on with it.'

At the door to her bedroom Anna's heart-rate settled a bit. If Mikey asked Mrs Dodd if he could sleep at her house, Anna would do the same – she would tell Mum it wouldn't be safe. It might make Mum think again.

Chapter Seventeen: Tuesday afternoon

Shrivelled Stones, Shrivelled tree

'*M*um gave me some money to take Mikey to the shop and choose his pudding for tonight.'

Anna hadn't meant to lie to Mrs Dodd but she couldn't think of how to get back to Pelm as fast as possible. She had to find out what the King was doing. The Queen said she could choose, she didn't have to be a link with the Sea Snake, and she had panicked, but now she chose to return to Pelm, find the Queen, be the link, even if it meant something changed inside her too.

She didn't like lying, least of all to Mrs Dodd, who had trusted her to tell Karina about Dad. Lying again felt bad.

Mrs Dodd said letting Mikey choose his pudding was an excellent idea.

As they crossed the road to their own house, Mikey said, 'I never saw Mum giving you any money.'

'Wait and see. We'll leave our bags inside. My key still works. Diego hasn't changed the lock yet. You need your Starstone.'

'We're going back, we're going back.' He kicked sideways in a little dance and Anna hoped she wasn't taking him back into danger. At least she knew how to hide by the fence, under the bush, with Tanda and the Starstone – and Tanda was waiting on the doorstep, exactly as if she knew what Anna had planned.

Anna scrabbled out from the hollow under the tree roots and stared up. The bare branches overhead were full of squillkits, their tails swinging individually, as if each one had a mind of its own. Their deep yellow eyes stared back. Mikey crawled out to stand beside her, scuffing his toes and sending a fine dust into the air.

'Don't do that, Mikey, you'll make me sneeze.'

It was a relief to be back in Pelm. Pelm felt safer than home. She squatted, wiping dust out of her eyes with the edge of a sleeve, wondering why the combined stare of the squillkits made her uneasy.

'They look like Christmas lights.' Mikey waved at the squillkits. 'Are you coming down to play?'

'Mikey, you can't say things like that. Squillkits don't play.'

'What do they want? Is your Tanda there?'

'I don't know.' Anna frowned. 'I don't know what they want, or why they're sitting up there like that.' The squillkits sprang from their branches, disappearing among the trees. 'Well, maybe they're like, sort of, watchers,' she said, trying out the idea. 'Maybe they're being messengers. They've all gone in different directions, did you notice? I don't know if Tanda was one of them.'

Mikey was scarcely listening. 'Where's Kazan?' He brushed the dirt from his Starstone. 'We got to find him.'

'Maybe the squillkits have gone to find him.' Anna stared around at the forest, the bare branches, the fallen leaves. She loved the idea of Pelm as wonderfully green and bright, with trees not like any at home. What happened to the orange fruit shaped like cucumbers? She didn't much like LeafFall. It wasn't the same as autumn though she couldn't have said why.

And where were the chiriku? They were her absolute favourite birds, tiny wings fluttering, all the colours she could imagine, a flying rainbow in the sky. What happened to them at LeafFall when there were no shrubs for shelter. In the pocket of her jeans the pine cones pressed against her thigh. They seemed to be okay. She could pull them out and plant them. The chiriku could shelter in pine trees.

A soft, heavy weight dropped on to her shoulders, furry tails wound around her neck and a bony little head pressed against her ear – *tunnels, caves, walls shimmering with crystals – an emerald green sea – bright fish darting through an undersea forest, the strength of the curve ...*

'Anna, somebody's coming.'

She was jolted back to the outside world when Mikey dragged at her arm.

'Don't, Mikey. If it was somebody bad, Tanda would have told me.'

'She can't talk.' Mikey thrust out his lower lip, rubbing the Starstone under his chin.

'It might be Kazan coming.'

She couldn't explain to Mikey the voices in her head, the images her eyes could not see which swam in her brain. His anxiety disappeared when Kazan's head and shoulders pushed through the undergrowth. 'Kazan, it's Kazan, I said he'd be here, I said that, Anna.'

'Hush, please do not shout.' The expression on Kazan's face made Anna shiver. Mikey did not seem to notice. He danced around Kazan as the green boy shook off twigs and dry leaves, and something else — a glittering, silvery dust Anna could not identify. Kazan grabbed Mikey's wrists and forced him to stand still. If Anna had done this, there would have been an argument, but when Kazan bent to whisper in Mikey's ear, he stood still.

'What's happening?' Anna gestured at Kazan's green-brown shirt and trousers. 'It looks like you've been crawling through one of the tunnels, only why's the dust all glittery?' She spoke in a whisper but the words seemed to hang in the air.

Kazan's pupils were huge, the whites of his eyes unnaturally bright. 'The King has been practising on pebbles.'

'Practising?'

'The Shrivelling Spell.'

Anna hunched her shoulders, conscious of a cowardly longing to crawl back into the hollow under the tree roots. 'He's been practising?'

Kazan rubbed his face. 'He's turned crystals into this dust and pebbles into sand. We have to stop him.'

She realised the green boy was on the verge of tears and it made her very anxious. She had no power to stop magic. She couldn't even persuade Mum that Dad wouldn't change.

He swallowed. 'The Queen awaits your help.'

'I do want to help.' The soft tails around her neck flicked, feather-light on her cheeks and the images flooded back –

the child hides beneath the table and bites the man's ankle – the woman sheds her garment and her skin is blistered, reddened, burned – burning I understand – why does she reveal herself, my Queen? Why does this child shrink, this child who is so close to me?

'Anna? You are ill?' Kazan's voice was anxious.

Kazan had hold of her shoulders and Mikey beside her was chewing his lips.

'I don't know.' She gulped at the dusty air, coughed. 'Sorry, no, I'm not ill, just something popped into my head.' The Sea Snake must be very close. She glanced at Mikey.

He waved the Starstone. It glowed red, as if he held a hot coal in his hand and she saw he was trying to draw her attention. 'We got to go, Anna.'

Kazan reached out, snatched back his hand. 'Does it burn you?'

Mikey pushed a long strand of black hair from his eye. 'It's mine.'

Anna hunched her shoulders, the squillkit jumped down and trotted to the edge of the clearing. Her mind felt empty.

Mikey said again, 'We got to go, we got to go.'

The tunnel was narrow but Kazan was in a hurry. He lit a lantern and plunged forward, the crystals in the walls flickering into rainbow light as he passed, and then fading.

Mikey nudged Anna. 'It's not so bright, is it?' His voice was low.

Kazan had heard him anyway. 'It is what the King wills. Watch how you walk.' The dust underfoot seemed to wink with every footstep. After a while, the path angled upwards and Kazan paused, turning to see if they were still close behind.

Anna said, 'Do you think he knows what he's doing? I mean, the crystals are breaking up. Doesn't he care?'

Mikey had been walking behind her. He said in a

loud, surprised voice, 'I can make them well.' She turned and held her breath. Mikey had laid his Starstone on the nearest wall and the crystals around it seemed to glow more brightly. Dust from the tunnel floor slid silently upwards, faster and faster, gathering around individual crystals until the path was clear and the walls and ceiling of the tunnel radiated light.

Kazan dropped his lantern. The candle-flame died and still they could see one another's faces.

Anna wanted to hug her brother but stopped herself. He had just done something wonderful and she shouldn't treat him like a little boy. When she said, 'That's totally brilliant,' he seemed to grow taller.

Kazan said, 'This is good but I do not think you can – you have to see what the King is doing now.' He sounded so gloomy Anna turned back, ready to tell him off for being pessimistic, but his mouth was tight. 'Can your Starstone put a tree back together?' He pointed at the upward slope of the track. 'We must hurry.'

Anna's heart sank. She knew the King could make the sap die. Why did he want people to watch whatever he was planning to do next?

The way out was hidden by trees and shrubs. A few dead leaves hung from the branches. They wriggled forwards on their stomachs, Kazan pressing a finger to his lips. The clearing was so full of soldiers, their cloaks flung back and their armour glinting that at first Anna did not see the Green people, huddled under the trees. Most had drawn cloaks over their faces.

The King stood with his arms spread wide. Spools of grey mist spun from his hands, curling towards a large brown branch lying on the ground. Without warning, one end of it lifted into the air, and fell, crushing the blades of grass. The King's lips moved, and again the branch leapt, flipped over, and crashed back down in a hail of twigs.

The soldiers yelled, clanged their swords against their shields, stamped their feet. The racket was so loud Anna barely heard Kazan's whisper. 'Now do you see?'

A sour taste filled Anna's throat.

The King stalked towards the Green people. They rushed to form a circle around a tree but soldiers ran forward, waving their swords, forcing them back. Green people had no weapons. The King advanced, the soldiers fell back to let him into their circle and he laid his hand on the trunk. Anna saw his shoulders heave as he took a breath. She clenched her fists, willing the spell to fail but the trunk shuddered and gave out a kind of groan. Tree roots ripped out of the earth, branches quivered, and without warning, the entire tree exploded. Fragments showered down across the clearing. One soldier sank to his knees, his face bleeding, while others covered their heads with shields.

Kazan doubled up, arms clenched around his knees, a strange cry whistling through his lips. He was obviously in terrible pain. Without knowing why, Anna laid a hand on his head. His hair seemed to writhe under her fingers, pain gripped her belly, worse than period pains, and then flowed out of her. The squillkit relaxed the claws which had dug into her back. Kazan's body slackened and Anna lifted her hand away to stroke Tanda. A warm, wet tongue rasped across her knuckles.

A finger prodded her ribs. 'What's the King doing? It's bad.'

The pupils of Mikey's eyes were huge and dark and his bottom lip had started to bleed where he had been biting it so hard.

'I don't know – oh, no, no, no.'

A young chet was dragged into the clearing. His hooves thrashed, he tossed his glittering silver horns but someone had wound a rope around his neck and he was tiring. At last they wrestled him to his knees and the horns scraped uselessly in the ground.

Anna's chest heaved. He could not mean to shrivel such a beautiful creature.

The words of the spell spun through the air –

tinier than shredded air
lighter than a blinking eye
softer than an orzel's sigh
blown apart beyond repair

finer than windblown dust –

Anna's muscles were in revolt, shaking and losing strength. Soldiers had stopped cheering. One wiped his eyes, another blew his nose while others turned away. They knew, they knew, and they weren't doing anything to stop him. She tried to close her eyes –Kazan's knees kept twitching as if he were somehow under the power of the spell too but he was just useless – anger swelled and bubbled inside her until she was about to burst – and the cry went up – tiny white chets, too many to count, galloped around the King's legs, turned in circles, lifting their minute silver horns or charging wildly in all directions.

Anna could not move – the horror was too great – and then the King lifted a foot. It took a moment for her to realise he meant to stamp on a chet. She sprang out of her hiding place and ran at him, ignoring the pain from

Tanda's claws digging into her shoulders.

'Don't you dare — you great stupid bully – don't you dare –.'

Dropping her head, she butted him in the stomach. Her head swam but he stumbled backwards, dropped his sword, and Tanda sprang through the air, landing on his head.

She was too strong for his scrabbling hands to dislodge. She raked at his forehead until blood streamed down his face and he screamed and swore, screamed again. To Anna's joy, soldiers did not rush to help him. Many clutched their own heads, blood trickling from wounds which appeared as if by magic across their faces.

Tanda's eyes blazed with the colours of fire – orange, yellow, amber, gold. Her magical power of sharing feelings was much greater than Anna had realised.

Then Mikey flew past, waving the Starstone. He flung himself on the ground, rolling over and over, banging it against pebbles, rubbing it into the sand, until, wherever he touched the broken stone, boulders sprang up, restored to their true shape.

The King roared but Tanda would not be shaken off. He reached for his sword but it had skittered away. Two soldiers staggered towards him, half-blinded by blood, brandishing their weapons and Anna closed her eyes, reaching out with her mind, not expecting to find the squillkit.

– watch out – don't – swords – Tanda take care –

Seconds later the squillkit was in her arms, still quivering, hissing, pressed against Anna's chest. She wrapped her arms around the tense body and felt tight muscles sliding under the fur. Tanda was ready to leap again.

Hush hush I've got you, don't be afraid

What had made her think she could help the squillkit? Anna had no magic of her own but for a few seconds she had remembered picking up her own little cat when she tried to escape from a snarling dog. Now, Tanda seemed able to draw strength from her and in turn her senses were sharper. She saw Mikey standing close to the King, tried not to shout. 'Mikey, come on, you did great but you've got to move, get moving, we got to get away.' Her voice shook.

'Na,' said Mikey, waving his Starstone. 'I'm gonna to save all the little chets. My Starstone can make them proper.' His voice was high but he struck a pose, scowled at the King. He was determined to try out his idea.

The King stared around the clearing and began to mutter. 'Why are the boulders standing? I have cursed them' and he started to chant once more.

tinier than shredded air
lighter than a blinking eye

Anna lunged forward. 'Mikey, get out of the way, you can't make the chets better. He's going to throw his cloak over you, just run, will you?'

'Seize that child, he's next.' The King's voice was a roar.

'But I can make the stones better.' Mikey stood with fists on hips and head tipped back. The Starstone was like a ball of fire in his right hand. 'I got to finish my Task.'

A deep rumble sent a thrill through Anna's body – something more than Tanda's purring, something huge

–a mighty, flowing presence, surging through the forest – shuddering – I come, I come –

The Queen appeared in the centre of the clearing and Anna did not know where she had come from. Green robes settled with a soft flurry around her ankles. She held out her hand to show a tiny chet, tossing its horns and flicking its tail.

Anna's vision blurred. Tanda was bounding towards the Queen, tails curved like question marks over her back, a sure sign she was very happy but Anna wanted to shout a warning. Had the King really discovered how to make the Shrivelling Spell work on living creatures? What would he try next?

The King seemed not to notice the Queen. He flung out his arms as if summoning the lost sword but it had spun, hilt over point, across the ground and impaled itself between boulders. It quivered. Anna thought of dashing to grab it so the King could not use it, but the Queen spoke and she had to listen.

Her voice raised a kind of whisper from the trees. 'This is courage,' she said. Her eyes were a deep blue-green, the colour of sea on a hot day. 'This is majesty, this is kingship, torturing our creatures as if they had no heart, no love, no worth.' The snake patterns on her skin rippled and the air was full of a salty fragrance, clean and sharp. The ground beneath her feet rolled and Anna found herself shifting from foot to foot to keep her balance. 'I call upon the Sea Snake, our maker, to restore this creature to its whole self.'

Very gently the Queen stooped to lay the chet upon

the earth. Stroking its tiny back she stretched herself in a curve around it. Anna's heart hammered against her ribs. The Queen was making it too easy for the King. He could kick her, or find his sword and slash at her flesh, he could kill her – no, he would say the terrible Shrivelling Spell and she would become ... what would she become?

Small sounds raised her hopes. A few Green people were surreptitiously shepherding the tiny chets into the forest. Anna's breath was ragged in her throat. A few soldiers seemed to be herding the chets to safety and others placed themselves on guard around the Queen. Nobody stood near the King.

Once again the ground heaved, and this time the King toppled sideways. Soldiers toppled into one another but Green people steadied themselves like sailors, and then a soldier near the Queen caught Anna's eye, placed a hand on his heart and nodded at Mikey. Anna held her breath while the soldier grabbed Mikey's shoulders and pushed him towards Anna. Mikey's body stiffened, but Kazan dragged him clear.

He tried to punch Anna's arm. 'Why did you make me come? I can do stuff with my Starstone. Why is the Queen lying down?'

'She's calling the Sea Snake. Didn't you hear her?'

'The King's skin gone all grey. I could have zapped him.' His fingers tightened around the Starstone but the colours were fading.

'We must get away.' Kazan laid a hand on Anna's shoulder. 'I have to get you into hiding.'

'But the Queen might need us.' She nodded at Tanda, still sitting by the Queen's head.

'He said, "Seize that child." That's what he said. You can't risk it.'

Anna caught her breath. 'You're right. Let's go, Mikey.'

Mikey opened his mouth but Kazan pressed a hand on his back and shoved him towards the bushes. As Anna dropped to her knees, ready to crawl back into the tunnel, she heard him muttering. 'I can zap the King.'

Safe inside the cave, she tried to distract her brother from shouting. 'You did great, Mikey. You put all those boulders back, that's okay, isn't it?' Her eyes adjusted to the dim light of the lantern, freshly lit. 'I smelt the ocean. The Sea Snake was somewhere near, I know she was. Did you smell the sea, Kazan?' Kazan was staring out from the tunnel at the clearing. 'Kazan, where are you going?'

'He will take revenge on us. We must help the chet.' His voice broke. 'What did he think would happen after the spell? These creatures belong with us. The one is many. Are the many one?'

Anna did not know how to answer. The thought of stamping on little running chets made her sick and angry at the same time. She caught sight of two bright, fiery eyes and felt a wave of relief. 'Tanda – oh, you've come. Oh Tanda, what about the Queen?'

Tanda stretched, flexed her tails, and stood on her hind legs in front of Mikey. The Starstone was loose in his hand. He scarcely seemed to notice Tanda's paw on the Starstone.

They were tightly squashed under the branches of the hydrangea bush, up against the fence. Mikey had streaks of dirt on his nose. He said, 'I could have made the chet all right again, I could, my Starstone's so strong. Why did we come home?

Anna rubbed her eyes. Dirt had got stuck in them.

'I don't know. I wanted to find the Queen ...' She blinked hard. 'Tanda did it. I don't know why. Maybe she thought we were in danger.'

Mikey was trying to extricate himself from a branch stuck under his arm. 'We got to go back, we got to find all the little chets.' He stopped and Anna heard the crack in his voice.

'Yes but first let's get into the bathroom, soon as we can, scrub ourselves. There might be dirt from Pelm under your nails, and mine.' She pulled the branch away from his tee-shirt. 'We've got broken twigs on our legs.'

'So what?' Mikey sniffed, turning his face away. She would not notice he was upset. He would hate it.

'As long as they're from our bushes, not Pelm.' At least in her world the bushes grew strongly every spring. She sighed. 'I don't think the Starstone works with living things like trees and chets. It's a stone and it's really, really powerful, Mikey. I'm so proud of you.'

Mikey flexed his fingers around the stone in his hand. It was grey again, any other pebble. He held it out. 'Has all the magic gone out of it?'

'I expect you used lots of power making the dust into boulders again.' She fervently hoped this was true. If he had asked awkward questions she had no answers. Did the Queen know an Unshrivelling Spell? Breaking a tree into thousands of little twigs was such bad magic. What happened to the chet was much, much worse.

She scowled, turning away so Mikey would not see. Where did the King find the spell? Was it in his head all the while? And more peculiar, why could she hear the voices of the Sea Snake and the Queen in her head when Tanda was not in her arms, was not touching her at all?

She checked her watch. Only a few minutes had passed since they had left Mrs Dodd's house but it felt like days and days. 'Gosh, it's just ordinary time. Let's go and buy something nice for pudding. I've got some pocket money left.' As they set off, she remembered to say, 'We mustn't forget to wash our hands when we get to Mrs Dodd's. We don't want Pelm dirt under our fingernails.'

'What's wrong with it?'

Anna pursed her lips. 'Nothing at all on Pelm. I just don't know what it might do here.'

Mikey cheered up when she bought little pots of chocolate pudding in the corner shop but he said on their way home, 'Don't they need us in Pelm?'

Chapter Eighteen: Tuesday night

Words are not enough

*S*he wrapped her arms tightly around herself, bit her lips hard, hoping this might shake her out of whatever fit had gripped her but something stabbed into her finger-ends, more agonising than pins and needles. Even her nails throbbed. The cold was intense.

With a huge effort, she lifted her eyelids. The darkness was complete, but there were sounds beyond the clattering of her teeth - someone sobbing, a deep, low cry that frightened her, made her ashamed of being afraid.

She rolled on to her side and tried to stand. At first her knees wobbled but she flung out an arm and found the trunk of a tree, its rough bark reassuring against her skin. She must be in the forest. A faint glimmer lit a way between trees - small, silver-veined pebbles on a path, leading her towards an open space. She moved unsteadily. Her feet were still numb but she guided herself, grasping low-hanging branches, following the track towards what must be a clearing. A kind of silver light hung in the air, although Anna could not at first work out where it came from, until she saw the Queen, face-down on the ground. Light flowed from her long, golden hair spread out around her head.

The light did not seem to be consoling. The Queen's shoulders heaved but the sob was not hers. Green people knelt nearby, their cloaks pulled over their heads, and the sob came again, a single cry, as if from a single throat. It was so piercing a sound that Anna could have wept, but something nudged her foot.

Instinctively she glanced down, and her breath caught. She had somehow avoided kicking the miniature chet charging at her foot, its tiny horns digging into the side of her shoe. She swallowed hard. How could it survive? An orzel might swoop down and carry it off, food for its young.

When the Queen spoke, her voice was horribly like Mum's in the bad days when she was trying not to cry. 'I cannot reverse the Shrivelling Spell – I have not all of the little chets and even if I did ...'

Anna wanted to weep with frustration. 'You called the Sea Snake. The ground rolled like the Snake was moving underneath,' but the Queen was not listening. Perhaps Anna hadn't spoken out loud. Perhaps she wasn't here at all, although it felt real enough when the little chet's horns glanced off her ankle.

Slowly, the Queen rose. The pearly green folds of her robe seemed to shed more light, green and golden. 'The power of the Snake lives within me. I feel it, but I cannot grasp it. I cannot use it without a bridge between her mind and mine.'

She turned to Anna, and Anna felt as if a hand had closed around her heart, ready to tear it out. She had no defence. That first time, when she leaned against the side of the Sea Snake, glimpsing her enormous mouth and eyes, Tanda had curled between them. The squillkit helped the Snake's mind leak into Anna's and Anna's into the Snake's. The Sea Snake felt as big as a mountain range, as big as the mountains at home, much bigger than Scout Scar, more like the fells rising above Windermere – Fairfield, Pavey Ark, Bowfell, Crinkle Crags – a Snake as big as a country – but she was safe –

– and Anna was in her bed, *at home*, dreaming, and yet on the island of Pelm. *I am in two places at once.*

The Queen's voice sounded in her head. 'The soldiers change allegiance, the Green people lose faith, the King has found more of the old magic. He will not stop.'

In the dream, Anna said, 'He tries to hurt everything that's beautiful. Why don't people just stop him from being King? They want you to be Queen, don't they?'

And in the dream – how did Anna know she was dreaming? – the Queen said, 'People long for kings to be great. I have the Snake within me. The King says, do not trust her. She is a Snake. Trust me, not her. What can I say when I do not know how the Snake works within me?'

Anna tried to reach for the Queen, to grasp her wrist. The words burned in her head. 'You are beautiful. The Sea Snake is beautiful. You are both so good.'

In the dream she saw her *drop dead gorgeous* father, posing.

The Queen said, 'Words are not enough.'

'That's not true.' It really was like talking to Mum. 'The King's learned a lot of words and that Shrivelling Spell is a load of words. You can say other words. Can't you?'

'The words will not form themselves in my mind, unless you help me.'

The duvet was on the floor. A white fingernail of moon edged around a curtain. Anna was on the floor, too. She knew she had been dreaming of Pelm but she could not remember anything, except a sense of being too late and useless.

She picked up the duvet and threw it on the bed. The clock said, '03:51.'

Chapter Nineteen: Friday

Magic mountains

*T*he next few days passed in a daze. Mrs Dodd was kind and didn't ask about what was happening at home, Diego fitted the new locks, Mum said she was working on new leaflets when she sat down at her laptop every evening.

Anna was afraid to go back to Pelm. She was ashamed of herself but imagining what the King might have done to more chets, or orzels, or even – the name flashed black and white in her mind: KAZAN. He was their friend, a fighter, the boy who had waited for them the first time they found Pelm. He could look after himself. Couldn't he? Worry and shame churned in her stomach.

School work had to be important.

She told Mikey she had to concentrate on school and he should stop pestering her. His disappointed face didn't make her feel any better.

On Thursday, at lunchtime, she went into the geography room, to the contour map of the Lake District mountains. As she stood in front of it, a familiar voice said, 'What are you doing? We're all outside. It's not going to stay sunny for ever.'

'I like this map.'

'You're funny. Seen Reima?'

'She's probably trying to buy crisps.'

Polly came to stand beside her. 'What's great

about this map?'

'You live closer to Windermere than me. You're just used to it.' Anna reached up to lay her fingers between the contours at one end of the lake. 'I love doing this. Can you read the names of the fells?'

Polly squinted at the ridges standing up between Anna's fingers. 'It's good, your hand kind of fits. Um. Rydal Fell, Scandale Fell, Snarker Pike, Wansfell. We've been up Wansfell. It's steep.'

'Who made up the names for mountains?'

'Dunno. I'll ask my Dad.'

'Will he know?'

'Might do. If I can get him to concentrate.'

Polly's dad organised eco-projects, helping streams to flow naturally, and stopping floods. In a geography lesson, Polly said something about 'leaky dams' and their teacher said she had to explain because weren't dams meant to keep water back? Polly went pink. 'They get tree trunks – I mean, sometimes they cut down trees, and they kind of chuck them down all higgledy-piggledy over streams. Dad says it makes the water run downhill more slowly and then it doesn't flood the drains.'

Anna wished she could tell Polly about Pelm, about the King burning trees and chucking ash into the lake beside the castle. What did the Green people do with trees when they died or if there was a storm and they blew down?

'Stop sighing, Anna. You're buying the chocolate.' Polly nudged her elbow.

As they wandered towards the school tuck shop, Anna wondered if eco-friendly projects would work on Pelm. Maybe planting different trees would keep the island strong. There'd be more shelter for the

Green people and the birds.

She knew she was distracting herself. She didn't want to think about tiny chets running away from stamping feet, or the Queen not being able to perform an Unshrivelling Spell. She badly needed to learn something useful, so she could go back to Pelm and give the Queen the right words ... if that was what the Queen wanted.

'Are you okay, Anna? You're in another world.' Polly had stopped in the middle of the corridor. 'You're like – well, if it wasn't you I'd have said you were talking to yourself.' Her blue eyes were narrowed, anxious. 'You can tell us, can't she, Reima?'

'What?' Reima stood ahead of them, texting. ''Yeah, sure.'

'I'm fine.' Anna adjusted her backpack. 'My mum's being a bit strange, that's all.'

'Oh, mums.' Polly pulled a face. 'My mum's in a state about our farm shop. Don't get me started. Chocolate-covered raisins for me. It's your turn.' She plucked at the strap of Anna's backpack.

'No, crisps, if you're buying.' Reima thrust her phone into her pocket as a teacher appeared from a classroom.

'Let's go then.' Anna tried to sound casual and grabbed Polly's arm. 'Come on, farm girl.'

Her idea of planting pine cones on Pelm was beginning to make her nervous. It was such a good idea – but the first time they met Kazan, Mikey tried to give him broken crisps from his pocket and she had stopped him in case they were poisonous to Green people. Potatoes might not grow on Pelm.

What did they really know about Pelm? Trees

bare of leaves looked rather depressing. It was hard to imagine the Green people asleep in their Dream of Root and Branch. When she and Mikey found themselves among the roots it didn't seem at all comfortable.

Anna's head ached.

She wondered what kind of biscuits Mrs Dodd would have baked today, but the sick feeling kept coming back – Mum talking to Dad on the phone, or meeting him in her lunchbreaks – only, that couldn't happen. Dad worked in Lancaster. He wouldn't take time off. Except, he must have left work early the day he stalked her. She found herself glancing over her shoulder, squinting into shops at her reflection, just in case, just in case he was behind her or about to jump out. 'I'm not running,' she said aloud, startling the old man in the buggy trying to pass her on the pavement.

She ran.

Chapter Twenty: Saturday

Teatime with Dad

*A*t breakfast, Mum knocked over her mug of tea. It spilled across the wooden table-top and dribbled to the floor. She started eating a piece of toast but said she didn't really want it. 'Would you like this, Mikey? I could spread honey.'

Mikey sniffed. 'You bit it. It's got your spit on it.'

'Don't be silly, of course it hasn't. Well, even if it did, it wouldn't hurt you. You like me to kiss you goodnight.'

To stop the argument, Anna said she'd eat it, with honey, yes please, but the tense angle of Mum's jaw made her uncomfortable. 'Mum, what are we doing today? I'll do my homework this morning.'

Mum drew a deep breath. 'Your father is coming to tea. Don't, Mikey, whatever you want to say, don't.' She held up a hand. It was shaking.

Anna said, 'Well, if it makes you so nervous, why did you ask him?' She wished she hadn't spoken because the look on Mum's face made her feel as if she had poked her in the eye.

Dad came at half-past four. He rang the bell and Mum opened the door, with Anna leaning out of the sitting room to watch, in case Dad did something awful. It was bad enough when he kissed Mum on the cheek and handed her a huge bunch of flowers. She decided roses must be extremely expensive and he was just showing off. He *was* showing off, wearing a pale grey leather jacket, a cream roll-necked sweater, jeans to match and black Doc Martens boots. His aftershave was lemony. Anna liked the smell of fresh lemons but she didn't want it anywhere near her if it was on Dad's skin.

Mum had put a cloth on the table and baked a lemon drizzle cake. This was Mikey's favourite and he'd hung around in the kitchen for the lickings. He'd also, very carefully, spooned the sugary glaze over the top of the cake as soon as Mum took it out of the oven. Mum was doing everything she could to make Mikey comfortable about Dad coming into the house.

Anna suspected she felt worse than Mikey. She had been awake the night Dad hammered on the door, demanding to be let in. She'd been the one encouraging Mum to send him away. She'd been the one to be stalked, to hear the unkind things he'd said about Mum. Anna did not for one second trust him. She knew she'd been sick into Windermere because of seeing the Queen's face under the water but being stuck in the electric motor boat with Dad hadn't helped, either.

There were small sandwiches, cheese for Mikey and Anna, smoked salmon and cream cheese for Mum and Dad, and the kind of vegetable crisps Dad approved of.

Dad said, 'So, Anna, how is school? What's the work like this term?'

'It's okay.'

Dad rolled his eyes. 'Really, Anna, you could be more informative.'

'We're doing stuff about ecology.'

'Stuff?'

'Well, um, climate-friendly farming?'

'Really?' He laughed and took another sandwich. 'These are excellent, Sofia. Where do you buy the bread? Why aren't the children having this bread too?'

'We don't like it,' said Anna, wanting to stop him having a go at Mum. 'Well, I don't mind it but Mikey – well anyway, I made the cheese sandwiches and it's easier with the same bread.'

She could not believe she was talking to this man, this horrible dad, about making sandwiches. Other dads weren't like him. Diego. Polly's dad. Any other dad. Reima's dad was bound to be nice.

'Well, Michael, what are you doing at school at the moment?'

Mikey took a handful of crisps and crammed them into his mouth.

Mum said, 'Don't answer with your mouth full, moro mou,' and instantly went red. Anna remembered the number of times Dad told her off for using her Greek phrases. "Moro mou" was only a Greek way of saying "my baby". What was Dad's problem?

Her imagination prodded her with a memory of the King, his face paler than before, gleeful at turning a single, beautiful chet into a crowd of tiny, terrified little creatures chasing in all directions to escape from stamping feet.

Mum stood up, pulled the cake towards her and cut off two slices. 'Here you are, Anna, Mikey.'

At once Mikey reached for his slice, lifting it on to his plate. It was still slightly warm, and crumbs fell off on to the table. Flashing a grin at Mum, he licked a forefinger and began to pick them up.

'Don't do that,' said Dad, reaching across to flick the plate away so Mikey could not reach it. 'Your table manners are atrocious. You should know better at your age. You're not a baby, though an observer might question it.'

Anna watched her brother's shoulders heave. He was taking a deep breath, but was that to burst into tears or shout in fury?

Dad said, 'That's good, Michael. Take a couple of deep breaths to settle yourself.' He pushed the plate back in Mikey's direction.

Mikey picked up the cake, took a big bite and seemed to know that a large chunk would fall off and drop to the floor. Instantly he slid off his chair, taking the plate with him, and sat under the table.

'Oh dear,' said Dad, elbows on the table, chin on hands. His near-white pony-tail formed a curl across one shoulder. The hair gleamed. 'I can see you are having considerable problems in managing him, Sofia.'

Mum's face could not go white – her skin was a beautiful, smooth, olive colour – but white patches appeared around her mouth, beside her nose. She sucked in her cheeks. 'He is usually a very well-behaved boy, Anthony.'

'Not on this evidence.' Dad reached over the table and took Mum's hand. Anna thought Mum was holding her breath. 'Perhaps I should take him at weekends for a while. I can instil some decent manners into him, improve his speech, wear him out with football. He might prefer non-contact rugby. I'm sure there are classes at the rugby club. What do you think, Michael?' He leaned down, peering at Mikey.

151

Anna glanced under the table too, and saw Mikey sitting cross-legged, not eating cake.

Mum said, 'You want Mikey at weekends?' Her voice was faint.

Dad was getting cross. 'Michael, I'm talking to you. I expect an answer.'

Mikey swivelled round so his back was to Dad.

'Sofia, I'm sorry to say this child has no social graces at all. He's behaving like a five-year-old. He needs some sense knocking into him or he'll be an adult with no resources, no future. We get the odd student like this, expecting other people to do the work, complaining about their assessments.' He shrugged and then shouted so loudly Anna jumped up and Mum dropped her plate. It broke into two neat halves. 'What the – how dare you – get out, get out.'

He threw the chair aside so that it fell with a clatter, dived under the table and dragged Mikey into view. 'He bit me, Sofia, that child bit my ankle.' Mikey struggled and Dad slapped his face. 'Don't you dare – don't you defy me. I'm your father.'

Mum was on her knees beside him. Tears rolled down her cheeks but she did not sob. 'Please, Anthony, please. Thank you for the lovely flowers. Mikey, please go upstairs to your room. Anna, can you help me find a vase, or a bowl for the flowers? I must put them in water. I'll put on the kettle to make more tea. Would you like fresh tea, Anthony? I haven't tried my own cake yet. Anna, have you tried it? Anthony, do sit down again and eat some cake.'

Mikey had left the room before she asked him to go.

Dad sat back on his heels. 'Sofia, I hoped for better. Thank you, I will try the cake. Anna, you must try it too.'

Anna felt she would choke if she took a bite, but the look on Mum's face made her sit down again, draw the plate towards her, and nibble the edges of her slice so that the cake turned into mush she could swallow.

Dad stood, smoothed down the invisible creases on his sweater, rolled his shoulders and set his chair in place again. He stared down at it before saying, 'Anna, you're a very reasonable child. I'm sure you think it would be good for Michael to have some strong male influence – a good male role model.'

The doorbell rang, and footsteps sounded in the hall. 'Hi kids, hi Sofia, brought Andy round, brought some books for Mikey and some of that new shampoo for you and Anna – oh. Hello.'

Tara stood in the doorway with Andy in her arms and a bag slung from her shoulder.

'Good afternoon,' said Dad. His face was without expression. 'We have already met on two or three occasions.'

'Yes,' said Tara. Anna watched the expressions chase across her face – the widened eyes, the glance at Anna, at the room, the table set for tea. 'I didn't realise – well, you did say.'

Mum stood in the doorway leading to the kitchen, the teapot in her hand.

Dad looked at his watch. 'I must go. I will be in touch about collecting Michael for the weekend, as we have discussed.'

Anna clenched her fists to give her courage. 'No, you haven't. You just said it, Mum didn't say yes. And you shouldn't have hit him.'

'The next time we meet we will discuss your

social strategies, Anna.' Dad made for the door, Tara stepped quickly aside and Diego appeared.

'Is that a fresh pot, Sofia? I see cake.' He took Andy from Tara. 'You like cake, don't you, my boy?' He scarcely looked at Dad.

Dad went. The door did not slam, although Anna was braced for it.

Tara exhaled sharply. 'My life, Sofia, I didn't think you'd actually ask him over the threshold, and tea? Really?' She sat down hard at the table, slapping her hands on its surface. 'You take idealism to such an extent – my dear woman –.'

'Stop nagging her,' said Diego, adjusting Andy's position so he could take the teapot from Mum. 'She looks like she needs a strong drink.'

Mum said, 'Could you find Mikey, my darling? Ask him to come downstairs to see Andy?'

Mikey was already on his way. He flew into the room and flung his arms around Mum's waist. She ran her fingers through his black curls, tugging them. 'You shouldn't have bitten your father, moro mou.'

'He's not my father.' The words were muffled but clear.

'Well, he is.'

'He's not a dad like Diego.'

Mum cried then, the sound as if something inside her had torn.

Chapter Twenty-one: Sunday

Snake legends

*M*ikey didn't want to go to church on Sunday morning but Mum said they were all going, and Anna, watching the way Mum stood at the sink, washing up the cereal bowls, knew she had to help Mikey stay calm. They both would have to be super-careful so Mum didn't cry. Anna didn't ever want to hear that particular sound again.

Anna's mind wandered, as usual, until Father Bernard caught her eye and winked. Anna felt hot and stared into her hands but what he said caught her attention. It seemed Jesus told people they had to be like little children, and how important children were. Anyone who harmed a child should be thrown in the sea with a heavy weight round his neck. She pictured getting Dad into another motor boat and pushing him overboard and watching him thrash around and lose his temper.

Dad was a bully. He wasn't a decent grown-up like Diego or Mrs Dodd.

Mum didn't want to go into the hall for coffee after Mass but Sam's mum stopped nearby and said, 'Coffee? Come on. You look a bit peaky.' They followed her, and when Sam struggled to be put down, because he was getting good at walking, Mikey grabbed his hand and took him to the end of the hall where the other children were already turning cartwheels or practising handstands. Anna took them each a chocolate biscuit, leaving Mum to talk to Abigail and Jake. Mum even started to laugh at something Jake said, and then Jake came to sit on the floor with Sam between his legs. Sam wanted to learn how to do a head-over-heels. Anna watched Jake's hands supporting Sam's small, tough little body, and wondered what it was like to have a dad who loved you so gently.

On the way home, Mum waited for Mikey to run ahead, counting green cars, before saying, 'You're right. It isn't going to work. Anthony can't come back till Mikey's older. I mean, when Mikey can sit at a meal with Anthony, with your father, and talk to him without getting angry.' She bit her lip. 'Without being afraid, too.'

'What will you say to Dad?' Anna hated calling him Dad but it would be ridiculous to call him Mr Daniels, or Anthony.

'I'll ring him this evening. It's all right, Anna, this is my responsibility.'

'I could sit beside you when you ring.'

'My darling, no. I must handle it myself but I am so glad of your support. I know you won't be far away.'

After supper, Anna went into her bedroom to leave Mum alone with the phone call. She was afraid to hear what Mum would say, afraid of what Mum might have to listen to, afraid of discovering Mum's reactions.

Mikey was next door, organising his dinosaurs into two football teams, whooping and cheering according to which team had scored.

Anna lay back on her bed and thought back to their last time in Pelm. If she was going to help the Queen, it might be useful if she understood more about snakes – not biology, not what snakes ate or stuff like that, but why people thought snakes were important or evil.

Why did the King decide to turn the Queen into a snake? Was it because his father died, trying to kill the Sea Snake? Was it, like revenge? It hadn't worked. The Queen was more wonderful now than even before.

It wasn't Mum who had mental health problems. It was Dad.

The Sea Snake and the Snake Queen had travelled through Anna's mind and they had left something of themselves behind. She was not the same Anna. It was a scary thought. Perhaps she really could help the Queen if she discovered more about how people viewed snakes. She opened the laptop, mentally thanked Roger and Dave for remembering them, and started a search about the symbolism of snakes.

Chapter Twenty-two

Missing

'Mikey, that brontosaurus by your foot – why've you brought that?' Anna coughed, swallowing dust. 'Kazan won't understand dinosaurs and anyway he might not know about toys. We haven't seen children with toys on Pelm.'

Mikey wriggled forward, kicking his way out of the tangle of roots. A small greeny-brown model lay on the soil, its long neck trapped. Mikey snatched it as Anna reached out. 'Might be dinosaurs here. You don't know. Kazan likes my things.'

Anna spluttered, wiping soil from her nostrils. She hadn't meant to inhale. 'It's not being a toy, it's just whatever it's made of. We can't bring stuff from home to Pelm.' Even as she spoke, rolling free of the roots, she felt the bump in her jeans' pockets from the pine cones. She had not meant to bring them, not this time, but she was desperate to get away from Mum and her phone call and she'd learned enough, she hoped, about snakes.

Tanda stretched, arching her back, flexing her tails, digging her claws deep into the soil. Her amber eyes gleamed. Anna ran a hand along the squillkit's back, feeling the muscles contract on either side of her spine, and the arch of each tail. The sensation was uncannily like stroking her own dear Tanda, and yet not at all.

Mikey stood up, brushing soil from his knees. 'What are we doing, Anna?' He pushed his Starstone into a back pocket.

'We have to find the Queen, help her make a new spell to stop the King.'

'She couldn't magic the baby chets back together.' Mikey stroked the tail of his brontosaurus. The corners of his mouth were tight.

Anna waved her arms. 'I know she couldn't before but she didn't have them all and I don't think a spell would work without all of them together.'

'How is all of them going to get together? You said my Starstone can't make them all come.'

'I think –.' Anna struggled to explain. 'I think she can do it only she doesn't know how.'

'That's silly.' Mikey turned his dinosaur upside down and scrutinised the plastic moulding.

'You know how to jump off the wall at home but you don't.'

'My legs might do something wrong.'

'Suppose. It's not a big jump.' Anna bit her lip. 'Don't try if I'm not there. I was stupid suggesting it.'

Mikey patted her shoulder. The gesture made her feel very odd. 'My Starstone can help. I know it can.' He planted his toy in the ground between the roots of the tree. 'So we know where to come back.' He pushed his hands into the pockets of his jeans, watching Anna from under his dark lashes. 'I can be a help.'

'Brilliant idea,' said Anna, disconcerted by his grown-up attitude. 'I guess we'd better look for the Queen. I wish Kazan would come.' A little, nipping wind ran across the ground, whipping up the silvery dust they had seen before, after the King's first attempt at shrivelling. She tucked her hands under her sweater and looked about for the squillkit. 'Oh. Where's Tanda? I didn't see her go, did you? She was here just now.'

'I bet my Starstone can find her, I bet she's finding the Queen,' said Mikey, pulling the stone from his pocket. Red and gold lights pulsed in his hand.

'I'm not sure the Starstone can track the Queen. I know she's one of the Stone people only she's a bit of a snake now too. I don't think the Starstone has power over the King, either. He wants it so he can use it.'

Mikey frowned. 'You don't know. Last time, last time we were here, the Starstone kind of shook in my hand when I was standing by the King. You wouldn't let me try.'

'Well, he did order the soldiers to grab you,' said Anna, beginning to worry about why she had not noticed the squillkit slipping away. Strands of grey mist wound around bare branches, stirring as if they had life of their own instead of being just –

– what was mist made of?

Fuzz filled her mind.

'Come to me, Anna.' The King's voice vibrated inside her skull. *'You know you want to. You belong with me.'*

Wisps drifted down to encircle her head, thickening fast, until with every breath she seemed to draw the greyness into her body. *'Bring the child. He has stolen what is mine.'*

Anna doubled over, coughing and retching, unable to reach for Mikey as the Starstone rolled from his hand and disappeared among a tangle of roots.

'Anna.' Mikey's voice sounded distant and feeble.

The pain of a slicing knife ran down Anna's cheek. Her forefinger was on fire, her right foot twitched and lifted.

'Anna?' He wailed again, sounding like a small child.

She wanted to shout, 'It's the King, don't let him in your mind,' but the words would not form. Her lungs seemed to have stopped working.

The spell broke with the warm weight of a squillkit landing on her shoulders, scrabbling to stay in place. She gasped, and, when Mikey ran at her, gasped again, putting her arms around him and stroking his hair the way Mum did. He was shuddering uncontrollably. 'It's all right. Tanda's here,' but it wasn't okay at all.

Tanda's claws dug deep and her tails lashed. Anna rocked backwards under the force of an approaching panic, pounding through the forest, pounding inside her head, and Kazan burst into the clearing, his face contorted, one hand clutching his side. Broken branches scattered around him. 'Can't – can't – get my breath – Nazan – gone – little ones – cave – the King –.' He staggered towards the nearest tree and propped himself against it. 'Need your help,' came out as a hoarse groan. 'Tanda brought me.'

Mikey's body tightened. Anna squeezed him again, thinking he was about to burst into tears, but he pushed himself free, waving his arms in the air as if to beat off the mist. Threads of grey curled around his head and Anna tried to follow him but she could not move. The squillkit's claws flexed against her neck.

Mikey stood in the middle of the clearing with his eyes closed and mist spinning around him. *Mikey – Mikey –.* Could he hear her? Would he know she willed all her strength towards him? All at once he flung up a hand, catching the Starstone as it spun out of its hiding place, almost as if thrown by an unseen player.

The mist vanished, and with it the fuzz in Anna's head. 'What happened?' Tanda sprang down and she could run towards him. 'You've got it again.' The Starstone gleamed more brightly than ever.

His eyes were huge. 'I called it. I heard it.'

'You mean, like a voice in your head?' She knew he could not explain, just as she could not say how she felt when the Sea Snake and the Queen met inside her mind. 'It doesn't matter. You've got it again.' She turned to Kazan. 'What's happened to your brother?'

Kazan had straightened but his face was still as pale as a new leaf. 'He's taken them. We can't find them anywhere. He's going to shrivel them. We can't find the Queen. Where's the Queen?' His voice broke and he wiped his nose on the back of one hand. His green eyes were almost black. 'My parents have been seeking her everywhere.' His shoulders drooped. 'The soldiers are guarding entrances to caves and tunnels. Many of the King's people are with us, but some of our own people have fallen under his spell. How do we trust the people we meet?'

'We can find her. My Starstone can find her.'

'Well, maybe,' said Anna, confused by the tone of authority in her brother's voice and the way he stood with both hands clasped around his Starstone. The squillkit's tails brushed against her legs and she shivered. She could smell the sea. Were they close to the coast? A salty tang filled her mouth.

Kazan dragged back his hair, gathering the long strands into a clump. 'You are not listening to me. The King's people are everywhere. We cannot get into the caves.' He covered his face with his hands. Anna did not know how to reassure him.

Mikey said, 'My Starstone flew into the tree.'

'What do you mean? You dropped it and it rolled.' Even as she said it, Anna thought, *and it flew out into your hand as if somebody had thrown it back.*

Mikey's eyes were very bright. 'The tree wanted it. You got to go to the tree.'

Anna's body did not wait for her to decide – she had to stumble over twigs and branches until she fell against the tree, her arms wrapped themselves around its trunk and her forehead pressed against the rough, dry bark. Her trunk clasped the trunk of the tree and a thrill rippled through her body, into her spine – the call of the roots, summoning the Starstone, taking it deep into the earth before throwing it back.

Mikey nudged under her arm, his small, warm body trembling. 'What is it?' His voice was high-pitched and she gave him a squeeze.

'Hush. It's okay.' Tanda crept down the tree, pressed her head against Anna's, let her tails drift across Anna's shoulders. Anna sensed the Queen, deep underground, in the cave where they had found the Sea Snake, but this power was somehow *greener*. She did not know how to express it. 'I can feel the Queen.'

'What's she doing?'

'She's by that big pool, you know, where you found your Starstone.'

'How do you know?' Mikey's sharp elbow could not dislodge the vision in Anna's mind – a mingling of the tree, the Starstone, the Queen, the Sea Snake, the sea itself – and something bright and hard, like crystal, only pulsing green and gold – a huge strength –.

Kazan cannoned into them. 'They're coming, the soldiers are coming, the orzels are coming, the hunters – run.'

They were back in the garden, in the dark, huddled under the bushes by the fence. Tanda squirmed against Anna's stomach, trying to escape from her clutch.

Mikey spoke into Anna's ear. His nose was cold.

'I don't like it, Anna.' He was shaking violently. 'I don't want to go to sleep here.'

'I'll get us indoors.' She hoped it was true. Something hard dug into her side. 'It this your dinosaur?' She pulled out the rigid toy. 'It worked, Mikey, putting it by the tree.'

'My brontosaurus.' Mikey sat up and snatched it. He brushed off specks of soil and she felt his breathing grow easier.

'It gets dark so quickly now.' Anna glanced at the luminous face of her little watch. 'Let's try the door. If Mum sees us coming in, we can say you dropped your dinosaur out of your window. It's a good thing your room's at the back.' She gestured at the dark window above. 'Best not to say anything unless you must. She might ask why you opened the window.'

She pushed very gently at the back door, and it opened without a creak. Finger to lips, Anna led the way through the kitchen and into the hall. The door to the sitting room was open. Mum glanced up. 'I put the kettle on. Have you got Tanda there? I wondered where she was.' She went back to her book.

Upstairs, Anna and Mikey stood on the landing outside their bedrooms and stared at one another. Anna said, 'Your Starstone talked to the tree. Something like that. Tanda was there. Maybe it was Tanda, only ...' Her voice trailed off.

'The tree throwed my Starstone back.' Mikey tossed the grey stone from right to left hand and back again. An arc of bright sparks traced the curve.

'Threw it back,' said Anna automatically.

'I know that.' Mikey sighed. 'I liked it better when the Starstone just talked to me and I could make the rocks better.'

'She reached out to touch his cheek, feeling the cool softness of his skin. He would not be eight for another month. 'You're being brilliant.'

He shrugged, shifting her hand away. 'It's all changing.' A voice sounded downstairs and he twitched, scowled, bit his lip.

'It's only the TV. I think it's the news. It's late. Mum'll come up in a minute.' Anna sat on her bed, slowly peeling off her socks and found herself breathing more quickly than usual. Mikey was right. The magic was affecting them both. She wished they had not been dragged away from Pelm when the hunters were coming and Kazan was panicking. She should be there, fighting alongside him, looking for his little brother, stopping the King.

Were all the little children hiding in the caves again?

Surely the King would not be so wicked as to try out his spell on little children?

Chapter Twenty-three: Tuesday

Where's Mikey?

'Gosh, Mrs Dodd. I didn't expect to meet you here. Is Mikey playing in the park? It's a bit cold for that.' Anna stopped dead in the middle of the pavement, her heart giving a lurch. Mrs Dodd's white hair wasn't in its usual neat bob. Her smile was tight. 'What's the matter with Mikey? Is he poorly?

She knew as soon as she'd said it that of course he wasn't. Mrs Dodd would not have left him on his own.

'I don't want to worry you, Anna, but he didn't come out to meet me and I didn't want to start a panic without checking first. He has been saying he could come home, well, to my house, on his own. He must have said so to you. He's got a strong sense of his own ability to look after himself, hasn't he?' Mrs Dodd's words spilled out in such a rush Anna knew she was worried. 'Anyway, I thought I'd check the roads nearby first. And I wondered, well, not likely, but – if something was happening at school that he forgot to tell us about? Only Sofia wouldn't forget.'

Anna's lips had gone rubbery and numb. She pinched them between thumb and forefinger. 'Should we go straight to school? It's right next to mine.'

'Yes, of course. I was on my way.' Mrs Dodd's mobile phone was in her hand. She caught Anna's glance. 'I was about to ring the school. Better to go in person.'

They almost ran to St Nicks, where Anna had been in Year 6 the first time they found Pelm. It was very odd to think she was in Year 8 now, but her memories of Mr Carey, the headteacher, were more vivid than the picture in her mind of the headteacher at her present school. He was a tall, stiff man she hardly ever saw.

Mr Carey had believed her. Mr Carey had called the helpline.

Anna's heart raced. What would he think about Mikey not coming home, after he had taken such trouble to make sure home was a safe place? He was the one to ring Social Services after she'd told about Dad beating up Mum.

He was in the entrance hall when Anna rang the Reception bell, turned, saw her, smiled, frowned, and pressed the entry button to let the glass doors swing open. 'Anna, how very nice to see you. Miranda, hello.' He dropped Anna's hand after shaking it. 'You're both looking worried. You're cold, Anna. You should have a thicker coat.'

'We've arranged recently that instead of waiting in the playground for Mikey I would stand by the gates, outside but he didn't meet me.' Mrs Dodd stood very erect, her black coat tightly belted.

'Ah. He's developing an independent streak, isn't he?' said Mr Carey, rubbing his chin. To Anna, he looked exactly the same as he used to, just more tired. 'He's much tougher in the playground than he used to be – well, he isn't getting bullied now.'

'Yes, but he wouldn't not wait for Mrs Dodd.' Anna tried not to sound panicky.

Mr Carey tugged his ear. 'I'll double-check the after-school club room. Might he have arranged to go?'

Mrs Dodd said quickly, 'That's what I was hoping.' She flashed a glance at Anna. 'It's not four o'clock yet.'

Already Mr Carey was walking fast along the corridor, with Mrs Dodd and Anna chasing after him.

The room was full of small boys and Lego but Mikey wasn't there.

'You've been back to the house to check he didn't slip out and walk home on his own?'

'I've walked every street between here and my home, but it's still possible, I suppose.'

Mr Carey pulled out his mobile phone. 'I'll send you my number. Check first, will you? But I might ring up anyway.'

'Who will you ring?' Again, Anna felt she might have sounded rude but Mr Carey patted her shoulder.

'Don't worry, Anna. I know you feel like Mikey's mum half the time! How is school?' All the while he spoke, he was texting.

Mrs Dodd's phone pinged. 'Thanks, Andrew. We'll go straight back to my house.'

'To answer your question, Anna, I'll ring our police liaison officer. And I might ring social services too.'

Mikey wasn't at Mrs Dodd's, he wasn't at home, he wasn't anywhere. Mr Carey rang to say he'd spoken to Karina and she was contacting the police.

Anna and Mrs Dodd sat on either side of the kitchen table staring at a plate of biscuits and cold cups of tea. Mrs Dodd had already decided not to ring

Mum but to wait for her to arrive.

Mum's face became very still when she learned Mikey had disappeared. She strode around the kitchen several times, threw her arms around Anna, around Mrs Dodd.

'This isn't your fault, Miranda. I know in my guts Anthony's got him. I don't know how he's done it but it's revenge. I know it is.'

'Oh my dear,' said Mrs Dodd. 'That's very strong. Would he really – I mean, his own son?'

Mum was already dialling. She put her phone on speaker and held it up so they could hear the answerphone message. *"Anthony Daniels is not available at the moment. Please leave a message after the tone."*

Mum did not leave a message. 'There's no point.' Mum sat down so hard on the nearest chair it rocked sideways. Automatically she steadied it.

Anna said, 'Could you try the university perhaps? I mean, if he's there ...'

'You're right.' Mum's dark eyes flashed. 'You're right. I'll try his department now.' She thrust a long black curl behind an ear. 'Perhaps I should not assume the worst.'

Dad had not been at work all day, he had left no messages, and somebody had covered for his tutorials. The lecture he was meant to have given in the morning had been cancelled.

'We'd better go home, Anna.' Mum's voice was flat. 'People will come. I'll have to ring Karina.' She gazed around Mrs Dodd's kitchen but Anna did not think she noticed Mikey's latest drawing stuck to the fridge, or the small pottery Peter Rabbit mugs swinging from a mug tree, or the Clarice Cliff plates standing along the top of the dresser.

'That's okay, Mum, Mr Carey rang her.'

'He did? That's so kind of him.' A tear ran down Mum's cheek but her words still sounded flat.

Mrs Dodd went to the fridge, opened it and pulled out a covered saucepan. 'I made a pasta sauce this morning. We'll take it to your house and eat it together. I'm not leaving either of you till you get an answer.'

Karina arrived just before six o'clock. She came in a rush, dark hair flying, her face red. 'Sorry, I had to get out of several other cases – I mean, I had to hand over to colleagues. I've spoken to the police team. Someone will come in half an hour but they're on the case already.' She sat down heavily on one of the armchairs. It gave a squeak. 'Our problem might be the restraining order. You chose to set it aside but we haven't been through the court, so if Mr Daniels has taken Mikey it will be a case of abduction. Will you want us to proceed on that basis? After what you said to me last week?'

Mum was still wearing her work clothes, navy-blue trousers and the agency's white shirt. Embroidered on the pocket was its neat logo of a green island, perched on wavy blue lines to represent the sea. Anna closed her eyes for a moment. It was almost as hard to believe in what was happening as it would be for Mum if Anna told her about Pelm, and the Queen who'd been turned into a snake. Karina might say Anna was making things up, that she was delusional.

'I rang him yesterday. I left a message saying it was too soon, but I'd be happy to go to reconciliation

– counselling? Something like that?' Mum choked, swallowed. Anna grabbed her hand, felt the pulse beating fast in her mother's narrow wrist. 'Why would he take Mikey? How would he take Mikey?' She glanced at Anna, seized her hand. 'It's Anna he's always said was his, not Mikey.'

Blood pounded in Anna's temples. 'I'm not his, he doesn't own me. Just because I look like him, I hate looking like him, I hate him.' Her nostrils flared, the same as Dad's did, she knew it. 'I hate him. He's horrible, he's an animal, no, he's worse –.' She ran out of words, leapt to her feet with fists clenching and unclenching. Her whole body quaked.

Mrs Dodd's hand on her forehead was cool. 'Steady. It's not surprising you're furious but it won't bring Mikey back, you know.'

Anna drew breath to shout, *your brother hasn't been abducted, your family's all right,* until she remembered Mrs Dodd's husband died not so long ago.

'Hmm,' said Karina, mopping her forehead with a green woollen glove. 'This sounds manipulative. Not you, Sofia, sorry, I meant, your husband's actions. If they *are* his actions. Until he gets in touch, or there's a sighting of Mikey, we can't be sure.' She stood up, stuffed the glove into a pocket and shrugged out of her red coat, throwing it over the back of the chair.

'Go and wash your face, darling,' said Mum, touching Anna's arm. 'You are hot and bothered. This is not your responsibility.'

He's my little brother. Anna still wanted to shout, but she went upstairs anyway, into the bathroom. It wasn't such a stupid idea. Cold water splashed on her face made her nerves quiver, cleared her mind. Mrs Dodd was keeping cool. She was staying with them, too.

She stared at her reflection in the mirror and scowled at herself for getting in a panic. She was supposed to be helpful. What if Mikey hadn't been taken by Dad at all? Suppose he'd found a way of getting back to Pelm on his own? She would search his room in case he'd left the Starstone in yesterday's school trousers and her hand was on the doorknob when the doorbell rang, and it was a policewoman.

Anna sat on the top stair, reluctant to go back down for the questions and suggestions and note-taking she imagined would come next. Would Mikey's photo be shown on television? Dad's? a picture of Mikey with Mum and Anna? They had several from last summer, on Symi. She heard voices, a drawer being pulled open, a radio signal – one of those police walkie-talkies? – the sound of a mobile, not a ringtone she recognised.

The stair-carpet was faded, a pattern Anna quite liked. Green ferns twisted, rubbed bare in places from scuffing feet, it smelt clean. It *was* clean. Dave had organised a steam-cleaner hired from a supermarket earlier in the year, and Anna had enjoyed helping Mum get rid of the old stains. The paintwork still smelt fresh, too, after Roger had repainted everything white, their first summer in the house.

The house no longer felt safe, and neither did she.

Eventually everyone went away except Mrs Dodd, who was heating up the pasta sauce and cooking penne. Mum had found cheese to grate over the top and Anna knew she would insist on Anna eating her portion.

'I'm not hungry.'

Mum gave her the kind of look she kept for Mikey not washing his hands before supper. 'If Miranda has made this sauce it's delicious. Come here. Smell it.'

Mrs Dodd said, 'It doesn't matter, really, if Anna wants something else. I didn't make much.'

The sauce did smell very good.

Much later, after Mrs Dodd had gone home and Anna had washed up, to say sorry, she realised Mum had disappeared. She stopped dead in the middle of the hall, could not catch her breath.

'Don't be stupid,' she said aloud. She was sure Mum had not gone out of the house ... even though she and Mikey had sneaked out into the garden and Mum hadn't heard them go... No, Mum would not leave her without telling her.

Maybe Mum had gone early to bed. It didn't seem likely, when they were both so screwed up with worry, but she tiptoed upstairs and peeped around Mum's bedroom door. The room was empty. She remembered, then, that she'd meant to check Mikey's trousers, in case he'd not transferred the Starstone from yesterday's dirty trousers.

Mum lay on Mikey's bed, eyes closed. His small teddy was under her chin.

Anna was not going to cry. She was going to *do* something – she would find the Queen, ask her, see if things on Pelm might give her new ideas.

She crept towards the clothes basket in the corner, where Mikey stuffed his dirty washing, found

173

yesterday's trousers and delicately rummaged in one of the pockets. The Starstone was unexpectedly heavy for such a small grey pebble. She stashed it in her back pocket and froze. Where were the pine cones? Had she dropped them on Pelm when she was tree-hugging, when Kazan banged into them?

Tanda waited by the kitchen door.

Anna crept outside and stared up at the moon. The stars pulsated but perhaps that was simply her own heart beating too hard, making everything wobble. Tanda brushed around her legs and sauntered forwards along the path, before taking a leap into the shrubbery. There was light enough to see, to fumble her way on hands and knees across the cold earth, into the hydrangea bush.

'I hope this works,' she said into Tanda's neck. The cat seemed more than happy to crouch by her ear, purring loudly/ Groping for the fence, she set the Starstone against it, held her breath and hoped. If she got back to Pelm without Mikey, the change was even bigger than she'd thought.

Chapter Twenty-four: Tuesday night

Underworld

*S*mall, stiff branches irritated her face and voices sounded from somewhere nearby. Anna frowned. There was light enough to see her hand, holding Mikey's Starstone. Tanda nuzzled her neck. She lay flat on rough ground, with thick bare branches overhead, on either side, all around. Several small, jagged silvery-grey stones were piled on the soil nearby. Without thinking, Anna reached out with the Starstone to tap them. Nothing happened.

Manoeuvring herself into a kneeling position, she reminded herself of what she had discovered. The Starstone, together with Tanda, could get her back to Pelm, but it would not give her the power Mikey had when he held it. Well, fair enough. She didn't need the Starstone for anything else – unless it could help her find the Queen.

A squillkit jumped on to her shoulders and nibbled her left ear.

She sighed and smiled at the same time. 'Tanda?' The hard little head butted against hers, sending fresh pictures into her mind of a great cave, filled with amazing creatures she had never seen before – a cave which was close by.

How could she find it when she had to stay out of sight? Every movement made twigs crackle. Tanda rubbed the side of her head across Anna's ear and then she heard high-pitched voices, shouting and singing. She guessed the little ones would be hiding in caves, just as they had before, when she and Mikey first visited Pelm and the Green people were protecting their youngest children from the King's threats. Anna hoped there would be more light in this cave. Last time, it had been very upsetting to see so many little ones living in a darkness barely lit by lanterns.

She began to wriggle towards the sounds, keeping low to avoid low-growing branches, and stood up when the shrubs thinned out. As she disentangled twigs from her hair, a familiar voice called her. 'Anna, at last. Where have you been? Why do you keep running away when we need you? Where is Mikey?'

Kazan looked as desperate as before, and his eyes were just as dark and heavy. His parents stood behind him and Anna was more shocked than she could say by their matted hair and the way their clothes hung on them, loose and dirt-streaked. 'I'm sort – we don't run away – we can't help it. Mikey couldn't come this time.'

'Why not? Doesn't he care about us any more? He's got our Starstone.'

Anna flinched. She had not expected Kazan to be angry. She supposed it was understandable when she and Mikey kept vanishing and she could not explain it.

Someone said, 'Kazan, do not be so rude,' and his mother stepped around him, holding out her hand. 'Come into the cave. You were kind to our sons before. I remember.' Kazan scowled but had to move aside to let Anna pass.

She took a deep breath and tried to smile but it was difficult with Kazan glowering at her. 'I thought all the caves were blocked.'

'This one is secure. Move out of the way, Kazan.' His

mum sounded so like her own mother telling off Mikey or herself that she caught his eye, pulling a face. He could not hide a smile. As she let herself be swept into the cave by his mother's arm, she thought with relief that some things were the same, whatever world you were in. Mums could nag.

Her eyes had to adjust to the flickering light. Animals and people huddled together, making it impossible for anyone to sit down. Children perched on the shoulders of grown-ups, men in uniforms stood beside restless chets, stroking their manes, orzels clustered on rocky ledges and she heard the chiriku overhead, their chittering songs interwoven with human chatter. How could birds settle inside a cave?

Gazing around she saw creatures she had not seen before – fleecy, sheep-like animals with horns curved into circles, long tails and long necks, and two or three creatures with enormous, powerful jaws, deep chests and whip-like tails, caged off from the rest. Anna had never seen a wild boar but these animals grunted and growled, their tiny orange eyes glaring so fiercely she backed away. Maybe they were a kind of pig.

'Stay away from the warchaki,' said Kazan's mother, guiding her away. 'They eat anything. We do not eat meat but the King's soldiers do.'

'You are protecting these animals?' Anna was surprised.

Kazan said, 'We will protect any living creature against the King.' He sounded defensive and Anna saw the angry glitter in his eyes. He must hate having to hide when he longed to go outside to fight. She swallowed a sigh. If Mikey had been here he'd have distracted Kazan, asking lots of questions. Kazan would have loved telling him, like an older brother – except his little brother had been seized by the King's soldiers. Nothing would matter apart from finding Nazan.

She dug her nails into the palms of her hands, trying to picture Mikey in a safe place, as if all the power of her imagination could make a difference. Maybe he'd got trapped somewhere … she shut down the thought as a small four-legged creature ran between Kazan's legs to press its soft black muzzle into the palm of her hand. Its coat was rough, wiry, like a terrier's –it was just like a terrier but for the length of its tail, and its long snout.

Anna dropped to her knees, glad of a distraction. 'Who's this?'

'She's my lapsa,' said Kazan, bending down to stroke the creature's ears. 'I called her Anna.' He sighed. 'We gave her your name.' His face relaxed a little.

'Oh.' Anna's cheeks grew hot. 'I never had anything named after me before. She's –.' She had been about to say the lapsa was pretty but bit her lip. They'd think she was showing off. Lapsa-Anna had a reddish, bristly coat, like a fox, but not foxy. 'How many are there in this cave? It's very crowded.'

'We brought in as many as we could gather. If the King used his magic on these creatures …' His voice was hoarse. 'If these creatures become many, how are they to become one again?'

Anna gazed at the lapsa's brown eyes, her twitching black nostrils, and wished she could stroke her ears too. 'I'm sure the Queen can help.'

'You think we have not been looking? This is the only cave the guards have not found and barred – the only one where we can get in and out. We don't know where she is.'

'I think she's in that big cave, the one where the Sea Snake got trapped.'

Kazan stiffened and the lapsa curled her lips, producing a throaty growl. 'How would you know she's in the same cave?'

'To get close to the Sea Snake.'

'Why should you know more about our Queen than we do?' His fingers flexed.

'Kazan, you know – you must remember.' Lightly she touched his hand. 'You know I didn't choose it – we had the three Tasks to do, and mine was being the link with the Queen, only I didn't know that at first and you didn't either.'

Kazan snatched his hand away and the lapsa growled again. 'Why did she choose you?' His face contorted. 'Why were we not good enough?'

Anna stared. The idea had not occurred to her. 'Oh, Kazan, don't be jealous.' He started, dropped to his knees, both arms around his lapsa. 'The thing is, being here, stuff we learned here, on Pelm, when we were here before, it made all the difference to Mikey and me at home.' She took a deep breath. 'We couldn't have helped our mum at home without what we learned from you.'

He rubbed his forehead into the lapsa's back and the small creature wriggled, licking his hand. 'I did not mean to complain. I am angry with myself that we could not undo the spell the King laid on her. You did it – only, you keep going away. Where is Mikey? What is your task? Can you prevent the King from using this Shrivelling spell? Do you know where he found it, how he found it?' He stood up, scrubbing at his forehead. 'Her fur itches.'

Anna wrinkled her forehead in sympathy. 'I don't know what I'm meant to do except find the Queen, help her.'

'How do you know this is so?'

'Sometimes, I dream about her and the dreams don't feel like mine – like dreaming someone else's dream.'

Kazan drew back. 'What do you mean?'

She struggled to find am explanation. 'The tree – you remember? Oh, you weren't there when the Starstone rolled into the tree and then Mikey caught it and the tree – well, it drew me towards it. I felt the power of the tree. Everything's different.'

Slowly, deliberately, Kazan straightened. 'You entered the Great Dream of Leaf and Branch? You felt the power?' The lapsa ran behind him.

'No, no, of course no, I couldn't dream your dream, I know I could not. It's just – oh, please don't let's waste time. The Queen is calling me, telling me to come. Please, can we go to that cave? How do we get there?'

'Is something wrong with your brother?'

Anna clasped her head in her hands. She could not bear to say the words, *Mikey's disappeared.* 'He's tired. He's only young – oh, please tell me, about your little ones being taken, your brother.'

Kazan picked up his pet and hugged her. 'They were playing by the sea, on the beach. He sent soldiers.' He sighed and the lapsa wriggled, demanding to be put down. 'My father says we must give them their childhood but this King would deny them even that.'

'But the soldiers saw the Queen change back from being a snake. They cheered.'

Kazan shook his head, glanced at the grown-ups gathered behind them. They were talking quietly and fast. 'My father says people must be reminded to stand firm, not to fall for his lies.' He sighed, frowned. 'I tell my friends not to be deceived.'

Anna wished she did not feel so helpless inside. 'I hoped the soldiers would stay true to the Queen.'

'So they did, for a while.' Kazan took a lantern from the wall and began to trim the wick of the candle. 'He takes a truth and overturns it – as if the sun shone by night and the stars by day. Does this happen in your world?'

Anna watched the flame flatten, stand erect. 'It's hard sometimes, working out what's truth, what's a lie.'

'Some people are very good at telling lies and making them seem like truth.'

Anna watched the skilled movement of his hands as he lit the lamp. She would not have known how to do that. 'What happened to the children?'

'My mother heard their screams as the hunters carried them off – as if they were bundles. I ran after them but they galloped too fast for me.'

'That's awful.' Anna tried not to picture what he had seen but she kept thinking of small legs dangling over the sides of the chets.

'I was so very angry but I knew we had to save the others. We gathered them as fast as we could and brought them here – and the animals too.'

Anna wished she could have done something as useful. She had no idea where Mikey was. At least Nazan must be somewhere on Pelm. 'Your King is stupid.'

'Stupid?'

'He'll destroy everything if he isn't careful.' She eyed the lapsa, her long snout snuffling against Kazan's ankle. She wished she had her very own Tanda nuzzling into her ear. 'Doesn't he realise, Leaf and Stone have to hold together, the Sea Snake made them grow together?'

Kazan's fingers ceased stroking the lapsa's fur. 'You understand this?'

She could not explain her own Dreamtime. Anna stared beyond him at the flickering candles and the thick darkness of the inner cave. The smell of salt returned, and she sniffed. 'Can you smell that?' He pursed his lips. She tried again. 'There's a way out from the back of this cave – truly there is. We need to find it, we need to find the Queen, I know she's near, she's waiting for me, for us.'

'How can you be so sure of these things?'

She took a step back. He sounded so fierce her heart began to bump in her chest.

'Kazan?' His mother reappeared. 'Why do you allow this ill-temper? Kazan, I felt a change – a blight in the leaves.' She glanced at Anna. 'You are pale, child.'

Anna did not mean to cry. The sob escaping her throat was rough and raw and completely unexpected. The ache in her heart was for Mikey. 'It isn't his fault, I don't think – he doesn't understand, you don't understand but you can't – I don't – except the Queen speaks in me and the Sea Snake too and I cannot keep them out. They said I could choose and I chose.'

The woman moved closer. 'You have allowed yourself to be their voices?'

'I can't help it.' She rubbed her fist under her nose, swallowing repeatedly to get some control over her voice. 'It's like, their voices speak in my head.'

Kazan's mother pulled her into a hug. 'You are their soil, their growing together place. This is a hard thing you do, brave.' She was cool, strong, thin, tall, and the power that poured into Anna from the tree seemed to come from her too. Anna laid her head on the offered shoulder and sagged.

Kazan said something and his mother's voice was sharp. Anna said into the cool greenness, 'I know he's frightened. I cannot be afraid or the King will come after me. He wants to own me because I have been inside the Queen's mind, and he wants to possess the Starstone.'

A ringing chime in the pocket of her jeans jolted her upright and she pulled it from her pocket.

'You have his Starstone?' Kazan's face was expressionless.

'I had to bring it to find the way here from our world. Mikey doesn't mind.' Mentally she crossed her fingers. 'Look, it's changed. Something happened to it. I think – I think –.' She held it out, seeing new colours inside, green and yellow strands twisting through the reds and oranges and amber. 'See?' Her fingers tingled but the Stone no longer burned. 'It's like, I dunno, like your Dream of Root and Branch got into the Starstone. Somehow.'

Kazan's mother grasped Anna's shoulders. 'You mean this? You believe this is so?'

Anna held out the Starstone to Kazan. 'Take it.' She held her breath.

He stared at the Stone, at his mother, at Anna. 'You offer me the Starstone?'

'No, I can't do that, it's Mikey's but I'm its bearer just now and I think maybe you should be too. I am from another world and the Starstone has been there. You are from this world and the Starstone comes from here.'

His mother reached for Kazan's hand and unfolded the fist. 'This is a test, my son, and also a gift.' She smiled at Anna. Her eyes were the same as Kazan's and her face was lined and weary but she tilted her chin.

The Stone seemed to leap into Kazan's hand. He gasped, closed his eyes and held the Starstone tightly.

The bones of his hand glowed green, like sap running through a leaf. 'I smell salt.' His mouth dropped open and Anna wanted to laugh with relief. 'I hear the great ocean too. Mother, I hear the sea.' He turned to the green woman, his fingers tightening over the Starstone.

A deep growl sounded, Anna spun around and gulped. They were surrounded by a crowd of people, holding their lanterns high, their eyes glittering almost as brightly as the crystals embedded in the walls. Even the animals were there, apart from the fearsome pig-like warchaki, snorting in their enclosure. A distant rumble suggested thunder.

Kazan's father pushed through the crowd. 'If the Starstone carries our Dream, it will know how to find our Queen.'

His face still bearing the dazed expression of someone shaken out of a deep sleep, Kazan began to walk towards the back of the cave. The squillkit nudged the back of Anna's legs. Quickly she followed, close enough to hear Kazan's breathing and aware she was seeing his mind, feeling his feelings. His thoughts were as clear to her as if he spoke aloud. It did not seem right but she could not hold back the magic.

"I hold the Stone of Power but I am Leaf. The Starstone leads me between the roots of the trees, deeper than ever the Dream has taken me, into the stones – the Stone –."

He staggered, fell sideways against the tunnel wall. *"How can this be?"*

Anna had to shield her eyes. The fire within the Starstone blazed so fiercely it made the light from his swinging lantern a pale fuzziness.

'Will everything change?' Kazan stared up at the

roof of the cave. 'Is this what you have done? Must all things change?'

Anna could not answer.

Then he turned towards her. 'I remember. We have been here before.' She nodded. The Starstone lifted his hand. 'We found the Queen by following this way?'

She was anxious not to unsettle him any more. 'Is this what you remember?'

'You are setting me a test again.' His pupils were dilated.

'No, I don't have the right. I couldn't.' Tanda leapt into the middle of the tunnel, tails waving and eyes blazing, and she knew what she must do. 'Trust what the Starstone tells you.'

'This Stone is too heavy for me. You take it,' and she felt his heart's judder as though it were her own.

'I will lend you my strength.' The new power rippled through her body and raised her hand. She placed it on his shoulder.

'I am in Dreamtime,' he said, and his pupils expanded until there was no white.

Chapter Twenty-five

A Snake to make a World

*T*he Queen was where Anna had expected, at the mouth of the cave, by the fallen rocks which once had kept the Sea Snake from reaching the sea. She lay on her stomach by the edge of the water. Waves rippled over her head and neck and lifted her long hair into wet strands across her back. She didn't seem to care. Kazan yelped as the Starstone leapt from his hand and rolled towards the Queen, settling beside her head.

The scar on Anna's cheek began to throb, as did her forefinger – both places where the King had hurt her in the past. He was trying to hurt her again.

Kazan's voice was faint. 'What is this place?'

'It's where Mikey found the Starstone.' She wanted to shake him, but he was still confused. She picked up a pebble from the beach. 'It was like this, only, like the keystone in the middle of the rockfall, the wall of rocks. Most of the rocks were great big boulders but when Mikey pulled it out the rocks all rolled away and the Sea Snake could escape. Are you listening?' The scar on her cheek began to burn and she swallowed hard, hurrying to explain what she guessed before the scream exploded. 'The Starstone must have got some of the sea in it – well, not exactly, but water – sap from the trees, something.'

Kazan gazed at the Starstone as it nudged against the Queen's head. She stirred, rolled to her side and stood. The long robe flowed over her limbs, clinging to her legs and body, lifting in a breeze that seemed to touch only her, and fluttering into dry folds.

'You are in pain, child. Come here.' Slowly Anna approached. The Queen stroked Anna's cheek. 'I see he marked you. Poor child. Not a child. You have grown taller.'

Was the red scar actually visible? It was a horrible thought. She might be scarred for life. 'Does it show?'

'Only to my eyes. I know his marks.' The Queen pulled up the sleeve of her gown. At first Anna saw only the beautiful patterning, much finer than any tattoo, but when she stared more closely she registered a long dark line, beneath the markings of the snake. 'You see? He marked me too. I am so very glad you have come. You knew I called you.' She patted a nearby boulder and sat on another. 'You have more to explain.' She pointed Kazan to a third rock but he shifted from foot to foot and Anna knew the rapid beating of his heart, the trembling of his fingers. She breathed slowly in and out, willing her own calm to reach him.

The Starstone sizzled at the edge of the water, plumes of steam rising. Kazan glanced from the Queen to the steam and bit his lip. When his gaze fell on her, Anna nodded, once more, and he sat down.

Anna's boulder was hard and lumpy but the Queen seemed to be totally comfortable. She slid her hands through her fair hair, adjusting the long curls, and Anna registered it was now faintly streaked with green and blue.

The Queen said to Kazan, 'You carried the Starstone.'

Kazan pointed at Anna. 'She gave it to me.'

It sounded like an accusation and Anna smothered

a sigh. She had to get quickly to the point. 'Lady, you wanted me to come.'

'I know you have more to tell me.'

'You said you have the snake's power inside you but you don't know how to use it.'

The Queen's expression stiffened. 'I have said no such thing.'

The rock dug into Anna's bottom, and she tried not to wriggle, not to sound as if she were making excuses. 'Maybe I was dreaming but it was a very strong dream. You said,' taking a deep breath, 'You said, "The power of the Snake lives within me. I feel it, but I cannot understand it. I cannot use it without a bridge between her mind and mine." That's what you said. In my dream.'

Kazan broke in. 'Lady, can it be right for a – a person who is not of the Leaf to enter our Dream?'

Anna forgot her worry about Mikey, Dad's bad temper, children huddled in a dark cave. The words poured out of her. 'You know how the King says you're a witch now because you were a Snake, and he says you're still a snake inside, well, I started thinking about snakes in my world so I looked it up.' She snatched a breath. 'And some people think a snake means healing, being born again but different, and some people say a snake means eternity, you know, going on for ever and ever – a snake-god circling the earth – sorry, earth is our world. I don't know if Pelm is on earth. Anyway, this snake stops the world from flying apart. It's like when the Sea Snake made Pelm in your stories.'

The Queen held up a hand. 'Stop, stop.' Her voice was soft. 'You talk so fast I can scarcely make sense of what you say. In your world a snake is a healer?'

Anna dug her fingernails into the palms of her hands. 'Well, for some people, yes, and – and transformation. I didn't know what that meant so I looked it up. It's not like a caterpillar turning into a butterfly, at least I don't think so.'

'Caterpillar? Butterfly?' Kazan had forgotten his worries about Anna entering the Dream. 'They are creatures of your world?'

Anna gazed at the Queen's face, seeing the snake pattern on her skin and under it, green and blue and yellow, like watercolours or like a dress she'd love to wear. She turned to Kazan. 'Well, butterflies don't look one bit like caterpillars but they start out as caterpillars. Like – well, think of a very tiny snake that turns into a chiriku. It's amazing, when you think about it. Caterpillars wriggle on their tummies and then they turn into these beautiful little flying creatures, all different colours. I wonder if, when the Queen shed her skin, in the lake, I mean you, Lady, I wonder if you were transformed but you don't know it yet. You're you but you're a different you.'

The Queen sat so still that she seemed to have stopped breathing. Then she rose, touched the scar on Anna's face. Her skin was warmer than usual. 'Perhaps I did not fully understand the trans – transformation, is that your word? Becoming a new form.' She closed her eyes, opened them again. 'I have not completely understood the snake inside me. The Sea Snake is my sister, the great Spirit made her and she made Pelm. If I make the connection with her again, I will know the form I must take and the power I must use. Will you help me?'

Anna wanted to say yes. She had come to find the Queen so the Queen could stop the Shrivelling, and the Queen could only do that when she knew how to use her snake power. So why was Anna's stomach churning?

Why did her heart beat against her ribs?

'Anna? You are very pale. The mark on your cheek is deepening. Has he taught you fear?'

Anna rubbed a hand over her forehead, rubbed it again, but the action could not wipe away the stabbing cold in her limbs, worse than pins and needles. What if, when the Queen's mind and the Sea Snake's mind met inside *her* mind, it changed her? What if she had a snake's mind, what if her skin turned into a snake's? What if she were transformed into a creature that could only live on Pelm?

'You are afraid.' The Queen clicked her fingers. 'Where is that squillkit?' Tanda appeared from behind a boulder with a fish in her jaws. 'You are not ready for this, Anna. I will not compel you. You must choose with all your heart and spirit.'

Anna stared into the Queen's blue-green eyes. 'You know what's in my mind?'

'The squillkit brings me knowledge, child.' The Queen's eyes darkened. 'And you have brought me knowledge, too. Why you have brought that which might poison my world?'

Anna tried to speak but the words ran round in circles. So now the Queen knew about the pine cones she'd lost? Tanda wound her tails around Anna's legs, tethering them together and Anna's head swam. Of course the Queen knew everything that was in her mind ... dimly she heard the Queen giving a command. 'Take her back to her world,' and the Starstone burned in her hand –.

She opened her eyes. She was lying on the floor in her bedroom, with Tanda sitting on her chest, kneading her with spiky claws to wake her up. A soft paw, claws retracted, patted her nose and a dim light slid through the gap in her bedroom curtains.

Slowly she sat up. Tanda hung on to her sweatshirt, refusing to be dislodged. The Starstone rolled out of her pocket although that should have been impossible. Her jeans felt tight.

How had she got from the bush in the garden to her bedroom?

The Queen thought she was not ready to help. The Queen was right. She was frightened about Mikey. No, she was frightened that letting the Queen and the Sea Snake into her mind again as well as the Queen – Mikey too.

The idea, when it came, made the hair stand up on the back of her neck. Her mobile phone lay on the end of the bed. She reached across, picked it up, opened the contacts.

Dad's phone number and address were listed under Anthony Daniels. He still lived about two miles away, in their old house, on the long hill leading up out of the town towards the sign, 'Welcome to the Lake District National Park'. She sent a message. Maybe he had changed his phone and number so he wouldn't get it but she would try.

> Hi Dad, can we meet? I'd like to talk. Same place as before, same time? Anna x

She thought hard about 'x' and deleted it, reused it, deleted it, left it.

The Starstone on her bedside table flared red, and green, and settled into a glow strong enough to keep her awake. She could not understand how she had been returned from Pelm.

She had to get back, do something about the King, help the Green people, *do* something.

Chapter Twenty-six Wednesday

Japanese Knotweed

*A*nna didn't want to go to school. She did not want to leave Mum alone when they still had heard nothing about Mikey. There had been no answer to her text and she was desperate to get to the park for the end of the school day – in case Dad turned up – but she had to stay with Mum.

Mum had to be dragged off Mikey's bed and made to drink a cup of tea. She had to be steered into the bathroom to wash her face, pee, do whatever her body wanted. Anna didn't stay in the bathroom but lurked outside, knocking on the door from time to time. When Mum eventually emerged, her eyes were bloodshot. The idea of Mum crying so hard and so quietly was almost enough to tip Anna into sobbing, but she made herself stay calm.

Taking Mum's damp, limp hand, she led her downstairs, tightly gripping the banisters, in case Mum lost her footing, and steering her into the kitchen. It was like managing someone not quite alive, not quite dead. Anna had heard of zombies. Was this overwhelming misery what gave story-tellers the idea of the living dead? Mum had been so strong before.

Once Mum had been seated on a stool, Anna found a bread roll, split it, buttered it, opened a jar of elderberry jelly Mrs Dodd had given them, and spread it thickly. The jelly overflowed on to the plate in gleaming purple drops, smelling sweet and tangy. 'Go on, Mum, take a bite. Please.'

Mum pushed the plate away, her finger brushed across the jelly and she licked it off. 'Hm.' She pulled the plate back and lifted the roll. At that moment the doorbell rang. Anna ran out into the hallway and found Mrs Dodd standing in the porch

'You should be at school, Anna.' Mrs Dodd sounded sympathetic, not bossy.

'I can't leave Mum on her own.'

Mrs Dodd put her arms around Anna. She was only a bit taller than Anna, and thin, but her hug was strong and warm and Anna found her head had rested on Mrs Dodd's shoulder, just for a second. 'I'm here to look after her. Put on your uniform? I'll stay for however long you both need me. I expect your social worker will call, and the police. Did you see the tv appeal last night?'

Anna missed the first two lessons at school but nobody nagged her – in fact, when she registered as late at the school reception, the attendance officer appeared like magic, and she hugged Anna too. It was very odd to be hugged in school by a member of staff. 'We had an early-morning call from your social worker. She sounds very nice. Do you want to sit with me till the start of break? Then you can just slip in and join everybody else.' For a couple of seconds Anna could not breathe. She might cry.

'Come on. I keep chocolate ginger biscuits for crises. Sorry about hugging you. We're not supposed to. Hug students I mean.'

'It's okay.'

'I've made you cry. There's the bell for break. Are

you okay? Take my tissues.'

Anna found Polly and Reima by the tuck shop. She had texted them on her way to school. Polly gave her a nudge and Reima offered a lightly-salted crisp. They found a quiet corner outside, away from the queue, and leaned against the wall. A faint sun straggled through clouds but the air was chilly. Polly said, 'Don't know what to say. It's crap.'

'Yeah. It's crap.'

'What shall we talk about?'

Anna swallowed the crisp and accepted another. 'Can I ask something totally wild?' 'Go ahead.' Polly sucked loudly through her straw and apple juice bubbled. Reima giggled, bit her lip and tried to look solemn.

'It's okay to laugh. Forget the crap. Polly, you know when you said about your lamb getting foot scald, well, what happens if it's like a germ from another country making your animals get sick?'

'Like bird flu, you mean?' Reima had tucked the packet of crisps into the top of her bag, and was loosening her plait, running her fingers through the thick mass. A spicy scent floated around her, from her shampoo. 'Bird flu's sorted, isn't it?'

'You've got red streaks in your hair.' Anna sniffed. 'Smells nice. Aren't your parents pissed off?'

Reima grinned. 'Dad's cross but Mum tells him to stop worrying because school will make me wash it out.'

Anna lifted a strand of Reima's hair. 'Wish mine was this colour. Where does bird flu come from, Polly?'

'Bird flu isn't sorted at all.' Polly lifted the bottle

of apple juice, swilling it gently. 'We had to lock all our chickens up last time. I hate having them inside all the time. Any crisps left, Reima?'

'I'm bored. You can finish them.'

'Thanks. Your hair's cute, Anna. Why do you want to change it?'

'Why not? Reima's done hers.'

Polly plucked the crisp packet out of Reima's bag. 'I love lightly-salted. Why do people buy prawn cocktail flavour? It's disgusting.' She upended the bag, tipped the last few crisps into her mouth, spluttered and drank apple juice straight from the bottle. 'Bird flu's difficult. Dad says the only way to stop it is a total block on everything coming into the country, only sometimes you can't. Like, I dunno, spiders hiding inside loads of bananas. My uncle moved to Australia last year and it was more expensive getting his cat there than him. And his cat can't go outside, either. They're very strict in Australia.'

Anna pictured Tanda having to stay indoors all the time. 'That's awful.'

'Well, but he says they don't want infections like we get.'

'Like what?' Reima was now brushing her hair. It gleamed, red lights shimmering along the black kinks.

'Some of our sheep got bluetongue last year.' Polly's face was pinker than usual. 'It's horrible. Midges carry it.' She glared at the bins lined up along the wall. 'I wish they wouldn't keep taking the labels off recycling bins. You're not really interested in biology, Anna, are you? Why are you asking?'

'Yes I am, well, about eco stuff anyway, what

your dad's doing on the farm.' She tried not to think about pine cones. She had ransacked her bedroom twice and had to tell Mum she was tidying.

Reima rummaged in her school bag once more and produced a chocolate biscuit in a shiny blue and red wrapper. She unpeeled it, caught the glance Polly gave Anna, and stuffed the wrapping back into her bag. 'Polly, you're an eco-bigot. Have a bite.'

'I'm not, I'm – well, maybe I am. Thanks.' Polly seized the biscuit and Reima tried to snatch it back.

Anna felt a surge of mixed emotion. It was all so silly and predictable – not at all like Pelm – for a moment she wished she had never found the island.

Polly snapped a chunk off the biscuit and gave the rest back to Reima. 'Dad says things are all going to shit because of climate change. He's damned if he's going to be blamed for not doing his bit. He and Mum nearly had a fight when she bought the wrong sort of bleach.'

'What's the wrong sort?' Reima offered a bite of the biscuit to Anna, but Anna shook her head.

Polly aimed a light kick at the brick wall. Her black school shoes were scuffed at the toes. 'It's what gets into the water and kills off practically everything and it's our fault.'

Anna yawned. 'Why's it our fault?'

'You can't be getting much sleep.' Reima put an arm around Anna's shoulders. 'You ought to be home.'

'No thanks.' Anna rubbed her eyes. She hoped the terror did not show. Whatever she said, however hard she tried to concentrate on Polly and Reima, she could not stop imagining Mikey locked in a room, or a cupboard, or even in the boot of Dad's car. Where did that idea come from? She must have seen it in a film. People couldn't breathe in car boots. She fidgeted with the strap of her bag, undoing the buckle, redoing it.

Reima stuffed the brush back into her bag. 'People do stupid things for the best reasons my dad says. You know the garden centre where he's the manager, and he says Japanese Knotweed's awful, if it gets to the wrong places they have to burn it out and it costs thousands of pounds and we've only got it in this country because some man who thought he was clever decided to import it.'

'He can't have been very clever.' Anna's mind conjured up pine trees growing all over Pelm. Would that be so bad?

'He brought it to the big gardens, Kew, somewhere like that, and everybody liked it because it grows so fast and looks great and people planted it all over, like, on steep sloping banks to keep them from falling down.'

The bell rang for the end of break. Together, they turned back towards the big glass doors leading into the corridor. Anna's heart beat so fast it was hard to sound casual, 'In Japan do people have to burn it to get rid of it, Japanese Knotweed?'

'No, not at all,' said Reima, aiming the biscuit wrapper at the bin inside the door. 'It's okay in Japan and China. No trouble, my dad says. He says, here it's a lot wetter and warmer and knotweed stops everything else from growing properly, at least, I think that's it.'

'I'm going to be late for Spanish. See you later.' Polly skidded around the corner.

Reima was going to German with Anna. She

hooked her arm through Anna's. 'Why are so you bothered about Japanese Knotweed and stuff like that?'

Anna could not tell her about the lost pine cones. What if pine forests on Pelm had to be burned down?

She could not concentrate in class.

Would Dad turn up in the park? Would he answer her text?

She hung around on the path home, but Dad did not turn up. Karina's car was parked outside their house, and so was Diego's. He said he was ready to drive anywhere they wanted, anywhere they thought Mikey might have been taken.

'That's a generous thought but we don't know where to start.' This was Karina's comment. A pot of tea, a collection of mugs and a plate of Mrs Dodd's home-made biscuits were laid out on the kitchen table. 'The police have posted something online.'

Diego paced up and down the kitchen, his chin edged with stubble. 'Tara thinks it might help to drive up the hill, you know. And maybe we should drive to Lancaster? Might he be staying overnight on campus?'

Mum made fluttery, helpless gestures with her hands. 'I cannot imagine where he would stay on the campus. Would the night patrol not notice his car?'

Anna went early to bed. Her eyes felt sticky, heavy and sore and her head ached. She was almost drifting off to sleep when her mobile buzzed. She checked.

> Will pick you up Thursday 4:15.
> Dad.

Chapter Twenty-six: Thursday

Sea Snake, Queen Snake

A flat, desolate land stretched in all directions. The boulders had been reduced to a fine silver sand. Instead of trees, there were mounds of shredded timber. The Green people seemed to have given up hope, apart from three figures, bent double, trying to shift the jagged splinters heaped over the roots of what must have been a great tree. Their hands bled. Maybe they were searching for signs of life. Did they really think the trees could grow again?

Even the mounds of fallen leaves had crumbled.

There would be no LeafFall, the Green People would have nowhere to sleep and no-one would dream the Great Dream of Root and Branch and anyway, she might have contaminated the island herself.

The Starstone throbbed in her pocket. If the King intended to destroy the cliffs, the tunnels, the caves beneath, would he attack his own castle by the lake?

What had brought her here?

A chet whinnied, trotted towards her, with Tanda perched behind the two silver horns. She knew at once she was meant to mount but she did not know how to ride – yet, in the dream, she found herself sitting astride the chet with Tanda perched on her shoulder. A slender silver rope lay across the chet's neck, a kind of bridle. She wound it round her wrists and hoped she would not fall off. Tanda nuzzled her ear, letting her know the chet was Caval. Without Tanda she would never have known him. The dream fizzed in her brain.

The great shoulders of the chet shifted under her body as Caval began to trot downhill, finding a way across a boulder-covered hillside the King had not yet reduced to dust. The squillkit slid down, curled in front of Anna, her head bouncing gently against Anna's chest.

She was a small, warm bundle, sending a stream of sensations – Caval's hooves clattering over stones, soft nose twitching in the evening air as he scented salt in the air wafting from a beach below. *We're going to the sea?* Anna framed the question to Tanda, but it was Caval who tossed his head and shook his mane.

She wished she could understand his senses but had no words to interpret them, only a feeling of joy as he thought of wading out through cool waves.

Further down the hill a scatter of shrubs and small, sturdy-looking trees found root-space, giving Anna a flare of hope. Maybe the King had run out of energy – got bored – lost interest – lost the Shrivelling Spell –.

The Starstone burned against her thigh and she twitched, almost losing her balance. Stones slithered under Caval's hooves and her fists tightened around the silver rope. She ought to keep her emotions to herself, not let Caval pick them up – only it was so hard, so hard not to picture a shrivelled child. She had seen those hundreds of little, desperate chets, running around to escape trampling feet.

He can't do it to a child, he can't.

Why don't the King and Queen have a child of their own?

Sharp claws dug into her thighs and she flinched. Somewhere in her mind was Mum giving birth to Mikey even though by then she knew Dad was - well, why did she let it happen?

If the Queen had a child, where was it?

She'd hide it, of course. Maybe the King was so enraged because she kept his child away from him.

Was that why Dad....?

The chet shifted sideways, and she slipped again. Tanda turned, stood on her hind legs and stretched up to rest her front paws on Anna's shoulders. Her warm, cat-like breath fanned across Anna's chin and the tightness in Anna's chest eased. She wanted to stroke the squillkit's head but it didn't seem right. She was not a pet.

Caval resumed his careful downhill trot, taking them through a narrow gap and, at last, out on to a long sandy beach. The sand was white, with silver-grey rocks stretching out into the sea. He stalked towards the tideline, leaving deep imprints in the sand, halted, and dropped to his knees for Anna to dismount.

Tanda jumped back on to her shoulder, and as her feet sank into the wet sand, she became once again aware of the swirl of undersea forests, the darting movements of tiny fish and the sway of the great Snake surging towards the shore.

And even though she knew this was a dream, she was afraid. Her heart skipped beats, and if her knees had not begun to tremble, she would have run away. Small waves, one after another, rolled towards her, splashing across her legs and soaking her jeans.

... my Lady, my Queen, my child from another world, my island, my dangerous, mischief-making

people, my Green children ...

The Starstone burned through her pocket and burst out in a fiery arc, diving into the sea.

Someone rushed past her, knocking her sideways, a green figure splashing face-down into the water. Kazan surfaced, spluttering as he tried to grab the Starstone. His eyes were tightly-closed. 'It hurts – why does it burn me?'

She seized his wrist and pulled him upright. *I am dreaming – but the water is salty in my mouth and what does the Sea Snake want?*

... Child of another world, my greetings and my thanks...

A mighty presence rolled around her body. Muscles flexed, lifting her clear above the surface of the sea, pulling her away from Kazan. He floundered after her, crying out but unable to reach her.

Anna was helpless. Words seemed to vibrate through her body.

... I have been waiting for you to come...

I must help him. You must let me go, no, that's stupid, I'm dreaming.

... No, you are awake ...

I can't be. The grip on her body relaxed, she fell back into the sea and choked as salt water swirled into mouth, nose, ears. *I am awake in a dream.* She collided with Kazan and together they staggered to their feet.

There was nothing to see and yet the Sea Snake had lifted her up.

The water was not deep but waves kept tumbling towards them. Shivering, she stared out at the waves and clenched her fists. 'Where is the Queen? I know the Queen is here, I came to find her.' Her voice sounded feeble.

'Anna, why are you talking to the wind?' Kazan plucked at her soaked sleeve. 'What magic are you working?' He thrust a hand over his mouth as if he were afraid to say more.

'I'm not magic, I don't do magic.'

Behind them, the soft, clear words sounded. 'I summoned you again, dear child, and you, my dear boy.'

The Queen did not sink into the sand but Anna told herself it was an illusion, because she was dreaming. The Queen's eyes were green and the snake markings rippled across her face, soft and distinct, almost like a painting.

It was hard to breathe.

The Queen crooked a finger and Tanda cavorted in front of her, leaving pawprints in the sand. Where had she been? 'I have discovered that the markings of the snake correspond with the beating of my heart,' said the Queen, catching up the squillkit.

Anna gave herself up to the dream 'What, like this?' She rolled her left sleeve above the elbow to reveal her bare arm. The faint blue tracery of veins was clear.

The Queen peered at Anna's arm and ran a finger over the veins. Anna shivered. Her skin prickled. 'You are pink, very pale, but these,' touching a vein again, 'are blue.'

'Well, my blood's red but when it comes through my veins it isn't so red.' She faltered, wondering if the Stone people had the same circulation of blood as she did.

To her surprise, the Queen handed her Tanda. The warmth of the squillkit's fur was comforting. 'You know that the Sea Snake is my sister, my sister under the skin.' She caressed her arm. 'To release her shaping power in me, I need to see her mind. For that, I need you, just as

I needed you before.'

'I never understood why,' said Anna. 'I'm not special.' She buried her nose in the back of Tanda's head, inhaling odours she could not identify but relished. They conjured up trees in leaf, damp soil, sun-baked rock, a stream trickling over pebbles. 'I'm no good without Tanda.' She was aware of Kazan standing close by, his mind churning.

The Queen said, 'But Tanda chose you, and I will always trust my squillkits.'

Why is Kazan so upset?

'This is not without risk.' The Queen grasped her shoulder. 'I must explain. When my Sister's powers run into mine, through you, you too might be changed.'

'Oh,' said Anna. *Only it won't really happen because when I'm back home I'm just Anna like Mikey's just Mikey. I don't want to be different. I don't want to be changed. What does she mean?*

'You are afraid,' said the Queen, gently stroking Anna's arm.

Kazan burst out, his body rigid, 'Why do you need her? I am here, we are here, your people are here.' He held up the Starstone, and Anna's hand trembled from the fiery scald in his palm, struggled with the shudder of his muscles under its weight — *so small a stone, as heavy as a boulder* — and she longed to reach further into his mind to help him.

The Queen smiled, as if she knew Anna's thoughts. She laid a hand on Kazan's shoulder. 'You are my brave soldier - no, not a soldier with weapons but one who fights for the Green, and we depend on you as well as Anna. Do you see?' She took the Starstone from him and flames flickered all around her hand, but still she smiled.

When she gave it back to him, he said, his hand quivering, 'I could hold it before. Now it burns me.'

'When you held it, you poured the life of the Green into the Stone. Others might have done the same but you were the one who chose to be present, to take the risk. You have set it on fire. You are the holder of the Starstone in this world.' Her gaze shifted to Anna. 'And your brother is the holder in your world. I know you have lost him, but you will find him again.'

'You have lost Mikey?' Kazan swung round to Anna, his eyes widening.

She squeezed Tanda so tightly that the squillkit growled, scratched, leapt clear. She did not want to tell him, to make things worse by saying it aloud in this beautiful world. 'Someone's taken him. Our dad's taken him — our father.'

Kazan took a step towards her. 'A father takes and hides his son?' The Starstone's bright colours faded until he held, once more, a hard grey pebble. 'In your world, such a thing can happen?'

Anna nodded, breathing hard to keep back the tears. There was something more immediate to think about. 'Lady, will you know how to stop the Shrivelling Spell?'

'It may be so.' The Queen turned to the rolling ocean, robes swishing, settling. 'She is here. She has already known your strength, Anna.'

Anna was struck by an idea so idiotic she stammered. 'Do you think the King — I mean, could he — I mean, would he stop using the Shrivelling Spell? I mean, could he decide not to? Could he change his mind?'

The Queen said, 'I have lived for many years with the hope he might change.' Anna saw the green in her eyes become almost black. 'Hope is folly where there is no love.' On the nearby rock, Tanda hissed loudly. Anna turned to see a wave receding, drops of seawater glistening on the squillkit's striped coat.

This is a dream but it feels so real. My clothes are soaked. Caval is standing in the shallows. Kazan is by my side and he is my friend. He was afraid. I am afraid. We are together.

The Queen stands in the shallows, between Anna and Kazan with Tanda on one shoulder. Surges of sensation Anna cannot name shake her body, raise her pulse-rate. Her eyes water. The Sea Snake is returning to the shore –

... oh, the green, succulent forests, long strands rooted in the seabed – swirling currents – the little bright fish, the winking seashells, the claws and tentacles reaching out to touch – the great plumes of crimson fire – blackness lit by luminous eyes – island and continental shelf, encircled, shaped, made safe – the sinuous muscle of the world – I am here, Sister, be comforted ...

The Sea Snake's green and blue head rises above the surface of the ocean. She bends her long neck, catching the swell of a great wave – she is a mountain range, a floating island – so vast Anna has forgotten. Her mind cannot hold the memory.

The Queen grasps Anna's hand, Kazan's, leads

them into the sea, wading deeper and deeper until Tanda leaps on to Anna's head to stay above water, taking care to retract her claws.

'Show the Starstone to the Sea Snake. She made it when she made the island.' The Queen's command is clear.

The Sea Snake lowers her head, allowing Kazan to lay the Starstone on her neck and immediately it rolls off into the sea. Leaning sideways, Anna sees it take fire, and then shoot out of the sea like a rocket, in a perfect tight curve.

'Anna, be ready to catch it,' says the Queen. 'The Starstone has new powers. You will need these.'

Anna thinks she will fumble the catch but the Starstone finds her hand and lodges there, a small, grey pebble, almost unbearably heavy.

'And now, climb on. She waits for us.'

Anna finds herself on the Sea Snake's back, behind Kazan, in front of the Queen. She has no sense of how this is possible. The Snake is so huge, she sits cross-legged.

Then, without warning, the Sea Snake hurls herself out into the deeps. Kazan whoops, Tanda screeches, clawing at Anna's shirt and Anna holds her tight. She cannot hang on to the Sea Snake's skin – it is too sleek, wet and taut – but the muscular surges are hypnotic and soothing and the Sea Snake's delight floods through her mind –

... crystal bright... the depths, the caves, the soaring peaks ... crimson petals pulsing, hungry ... turquoise and amber fluorescence ... clefts in the seabed ... chasms and mountain ranges .. hanging valleys cradling lakes ... one making, one story, one

dream come to life ...

There's a movement behind, a kicking out, and Queen slides off into the waves, the arch of her body sinewy and elegant. New colours ripple over her skin, within her skin, merging with the flow of yellow hair over shoulders and back – and Anna finds herself slipping down, down, into an ocean she has only ever known through sinking into the mind of the Sea Snake – and Kazan swims alongside her, his body brilliantly green, his eyes even greener in the light streaming down through the waves, mouth – and Tanda's tails swirl in the currents, paws flexing as if she loves the medium – and this can only be a dream –

– their heads break through the surface of the sea.

The Sea Snake floats nearby. Her great mouth curves as if into a smile. She scoops them into the air before catching them, setting them neatly down once more on her back. Tanda shakes herself, almost dancing, not skidding, and it takes a moment for Anna to catch sight of the Queen. The markings on her skin have taken on the green of the deep ocean, a deep sky blue, the yellow of sunflowers, the distant pink of sunsets, the pearly essence of silver-white clouds. Her eyes flash green, golden and grey, and Anna cannot look away.

Her pupils alternate between vertical slits and human eyes. The Queen says, 'Give me the Starstone.' Anna has no idea what she has done with it but the Queen reaches with a smile to catch the little pebble. Anna must have tossed it to her. She crushes it between her hands and throws up a sparkling pearly-grey dust that takes shape – flows like a wave rising to a crest, high, higher, impossibly high, a mountain – is sky, is bluer than blue – is a surge of orzels, white-winged, wider than the island – chiriku, painting a rainbow of light – weaving, curving, twining, snaking – the great Sea Snake herself, arcing across the heavens and diving down, into the blue, the green, the deep-down forests of the sea and the leaf and branch of the Dream –

Anna found herself face down on the sand. Salty water seeped into her nostrils and eyes. She lifted her head, sneezed, dug into the sand with her fingers and found tiny shells and little wriggly-fishy worms relying on the sand for hiding-places. This was not a dream. If it wasn't a dream, then where was the squillkit? Where was Kazan?

'Tanda? Kazan, where are you?'

Her voice raised an echo from the steep hillside behind the beach.

The chet's whinny drew her attention. 'Caval?' He stood where scrub gave way to sand, shaking his mane and pawing soft soil with a forefoot. Tanda sat between his horns and Kazan stood beside him, gently stroking his mane. Anna scrambled to her feet, ran towards them and stopped short.

Kazan held out his hand. 'You brought these to our world?'

Her heart sank. He held three little pine-cones.

'I wanted to help, I wanted you to be safe. I thought if I planted more trees, trees that didn't have LeafFall –.' His eyebrows contracted into a frown. 'Sorry, on our world we get trees where the leaves don't fall off in the winter. I thought you would have a better chance against the King. We do get LeafFall too, but not all the trees ...'

He shook his head. 'These would be a greater danger. Do you see?

Already the skin of his hand was peeling off, turning brown.

'I'm sorry, I did think about invasive species ...'

Kazan shook his head. 'You say things I cannot understand.'

Anna rubbed her eyes. She did not know what else to say.

'But you meant to help. Without you we would have had no hope at all. Take these back to your world. Will you return to Pelm?'

Chapter Twenty-seven: Thursday

Mikey

*A*nna felt very strange. She found herself sitting at the kitchen table, head down on the wooden surface, and she was cold. She squinted sideways at the little black and white clock and made out the hands, pointing to six and nine. Half-past nine at night or a quarter to six in the morning? She had no memory of returning from Pelm.

Surely it must be morning. She had been dreaming. Had she dreamed? Hadn't she found Mum on Mikey's bed, searched for the Starstone?

Starstone? Where had she put it? She leapt up, sending the kitchen chair rattling across the tiles. Upstairs, a door creaked. Mum's voice sounded creaky too. 'Anna? Are you up already?'

'Thirsty, Mum. Go back to sleep. It's early. I'll bring you some tea.'

'He's not here, is he? Did I dream it all?'

'No, Mum. He's not here.' Anna's throat tightened at the Mum's words. They were dreadfully hurtful.

But Dad had answered the text. She would go to school and hang around in the park, to meet him.

Her neck was stiff. She filled the kettle with a mugful of water and switched it on. At least she was still wearing her pyjamas and not the jeans and shirt of the dream. She almost expected Tanda the squillkit to be nuzzling the food bowl, asking for a refill, or a chet to be standing in the garden, flicking his tail and nodding his long silver horns.

How would she get through a day at school? Geography, science, English, history, computing ... Homework? Had she even looked at it? Teachers would probably let her off. Everybody knew about Mikey disappearing. The time would drag, people would look at her in corridors and whisper, and nobody would say straight out, 'Where's your brother? What are the police doing?'

She sniffed her skin and detected a faint odour of salt, as if she had been swimming. She ran upstairs into the bathroom, shook off her pyjamas and reached for the shower tap. In the mirror she glimpsed a white body with soft streaks of colour – blue and green and yellow – pulsing under the skin. Horrified, she stared down at herself. The faintest markings of the snake lay across her body, down her thighs and upper arms. She gasped aloud, then closed her eyes, squeezing them tightly. She was so tired, she must be hallucinating.

When she opened her eyes, the markings had gone. With a sigh of relief, she climbed into the bath and stood under a shower as hot as she could bear. Wrapping a towel around her body she went back into her bedroom. Where had she put the Starstone? The first thing Mikey would ask about would be his little grey magical pebble. Frowning, she began to rummage through her small chest of drawers, then lay on her stomach to thrash an arm under her bed, in case the Stone had rolled out of sight. By the time she had emptied her wardrobe, she was hot and anxious. The few clothes she owned were strewn across the bed and every pocket had been tested – except the jeans she had been wearing yesterday. They lay across the foot of the bed. Almost afraid to search, she tightened the towel and patted a back pocket. The pine-cones slid out into her hand. They had a faint green sheen.

'I'll plant you in the garden,' she said, tucking them into a drawer, as a warm glow of relief swept through her body.

Then she remembered the Queen throwing the Starstone into the air and how it had turned into something .... what would she tell Mikey? Rubbing her face, she caught sight of her reflection and froze. The markings of the snake rippled down her neck, disappearing under the towel. At the same time, a voice in her head said, *The Starstone fell in the sea and Kazan was there and he took it, and you went into the sea too. The Queen of the Sea and the Queen of Pelm shared their thoughts and feelings through you. And Kazan has forgiven you.*

The words were so clear that Anna glanced from side to side, almost expecting to see the speaker. *If I have the power of the Snake in me, what will I be able to do?* She stared again at her reflection. Yes, she still resembled Dad but only on the surface. She couldn't help what she inherited.

Putting on uniform was oddly reassuring. She would blend in with most of the other girls in her year. Older girls took great care to look different, especially with their hair and makeup, and they'd sometimes change in the toilets before going home into whatever clothes *everybody* was wearing, but their photos on phones were almost identical. Would she ever bother to carry extra clothes to school, or makeup?

Shaking herself, she picked up a hairbrush and attacked her hair. Gradually the marks faded. If she kept calm and steady, perhaps the marks would always stay under the skin instead of appearing to everyone. Keeping control was even more important than worrying about how to tell Mikey his Starstone had turned into something new.

It was time to take Mum a cup of tea. She glanced at her watch. Seven o'clock, much too early to go to school – how would she keep herself sane till 4:15?

She must have made too much noise for Mum opened the door and stared. 'My dear child, what have you been doing? Why are your clothes heaped on the bed?' She hurried across the room and knelt. 'You've thrown everything out of your drawers. What are you looking for? Can I help?' Already Mum was picking things up, making little piles, ready to put them away. 'I'll do these, you hang up in the wardrobe. You need more hangers. My dear girl, your pants are old. We must buy new.'

Anna grabbed her mother's shoulders. 'Mum, don't worry. We'll find him. I know we will.' Mum's mouth quivered but she bit her lips. 'Mum, you're wonderful. I do love you so much.'

They cried together for a while and then made themselves breakfast.

All day at school, Anna practised breathing in calm, deep breaths. She hoped nobody would notice but Reima did. 'You okay?'

'Course. Why?'

'You're doing those breathing things we had to do last year in Practical Citizenship.'

'Well, I thought I would.'

To her surprise, Reima took her hand and squeezed it. 'Must be hell at your house. Tell your mum we're all thinking about you.'

The blood rushed to Anna's face and her heart gave a couple of thuds. What if the snake marks showed? 'It's really kind of you,' she said, turning away, pulling the sleeves of her sweatshirt over her hands. 'I expect it'll be okay.'

'Yes,' said Reima, her voice sounding doubtful. 'I never thought those stupid exercises would be worth it but my dad says it's good for you, it's mindfulness or something. He does meditation. He's got an app on his phone.'

Anna's face was cool again. She said, 'I might tell my mum. Only she says prayers and stuff. It's like meditation, I think.' Then, 'The only thing is, what I think is, it's okay being calm and mindful but suppose something needs to be done? Suppose you have to do something?'

'Like find your brother?'

'Yeah.'

Reima fumbled in her school bag and pulled out a small cardboard box. 'I brought you some of these. I thought – my mum thought – we thought you and your mum could do with a treat.'

Anna wanted to weep. The kindness was almost too big to cope with, but she saw the anxious look on Reima's face and took the box. Inside were delicious-looking fudgy squares. The sweet caramel smell made her mouth water. 'Oh, Reima, what are these?'

Reima's creamy-brown skin seemed to glow. 'Take a bite, quick, before anyone comes. They're Indian milk cake, well, the proper name is Alwar Ka

Mawa. My Indian granny showed my mum how to make it. My mum gave her the recipe for Welsh cakes. I think she was a bit disappointed, they aren't sweet. Move.'

The headteacher strode around the corner and they ducked into the classroom for their next lesson. It was still empty, with five minutes to go before the end of break. Reima said, 'I don't think I could stop myself getting angry if someone kidnapped my sister. I'd want to hit someone. She's a pain but, you know.'

'These are fantastic.' Anna's teeth were almost stuck together. 'I'm going to let you taste sokolapita, that's a Greek chocolate cake, sort of. My Nanou makes it, she's my Greek granny.' She thought for a moment. 'I don't know anything about my English granny.' *Maybe Dad's mother was an evil witch ... or maybe she was a nice person whose son was totally rubbish as a human being.* Had Mum met Dad's parents when she landed in England? Maybe they were nice people. It would be lovely to have a granny and grandad in England. Maybe they didn't know she and Mikey existed. When Mikey was home, she'd ask Mum.

She sucked the ends of her fingers, so noisily Reima laughed. 'Scrummy.' She must not cry.

At the end of the school day, Anna shouldered her bag and walked purposefully to the park. She meant to arrive by four o'clock – with luck, before Dad turned up. After her chat with Reima she had been thinking about anger. Anger wasn't always a bad emotion. She'd been angry about the King shredding the trees on Pelm. She was even more furious about Dad. She was sure he'd abducted Mikey though how he'd done it she could not imagine. She was going to find out soon.

She took up a position by the wall where he had spoken to her, dropped her bag, and closed her eyes, focussing on her breathing. The blood pulsed evenly through arteries and veins, surfacing at wrists and throat, in the crook of her elbows, knees, ankles. She pictured the snake's beautiful patterning spreading like ink wherever blood flowed.

When Dad arrived, she would be strong and not girly – though girly could be strong. Why not?

Dad spoke from behind her. 'You're early.'

Anna gritted her teeth and did not jump. She did not turn quickly, either. 'Oh. Hello.'

'You're a bit stand-offish, my child. You texted me. I didn't initiate the meeting.'

'I thought we should talk about Mikey.' Now she had turned and stared at her father, noting the well-brushed ponytail, the thick cream gansey. 'Have you got him?'

Dad's head jerked back. 'Are you accusing me of spending time with my own son?'

Anna folded her arms, felt the heat of the blood-surge in her temples. 'If he doesn't want to see you why should he? You do tend to hit him.'

Something in her manner – or maybe it was what she said – seemed to annoy him. He mimicked her pose, his grey eyes focussed on her face, but not her eyes.

He's avoiding eye contact. The thought gave her a thrill. 'He's far too young to make reliable decisions.'

Again, Anna tensed as the blood pounded in her head but she tightened her arms and breathed in steadily to the count of ten. 'Children are entitled to protect themselves from bullies. Mikey was old enough to stop you punching Mum. He was better than me. Of course he's old enough to decide he won't see you.'

A flush ran over Dad's cheeks and a tic started under one eye. He sniffed, and Anna wanted to say, "Blow your nose," but she didn't. How could Mum think he would change? Why did she want to give Dad a second chance? 'Well, have you got him? Did you take him? Where is he?'

'You want to see your brother, you come with me.'

Anna said, 'I'll come with you after you bring him here, to the park, so he can go home.'

'You're offering a trade, is that right?' Although Dad spoke sharply, he was startled. She knew from the way his fingers twitched.

'I'll wait, shall I?' She leaned against the wall, sensing its solid, rough surface as a strength.

'You're assuming he's nearby.'

'I'm assuming you took him back with you, whatever you said to make him come. He'd be okay for a bit in the old house, I suppose.'

'Don't fake a maturity you do not possess.'

'So the police haven't checked the house?'

Anna was amazed at the way she was able to bargain with him. The words appeared in her head as though a script unrolled in front of her and all she had to do was read aloud.

Dad's mouth opened, closed, and he exhaled loudly. 'Well, young lady, you've some nerve. If that's what living alone with your mother inspires, the sooner you have a strong role model, the better.' His hand wandered to his ponytail, stroked it, tugged it, unfastened the band so let long white hair spread over his shoulders. In the fading light, as he straightened, he looked a bit like a knight of old. All he needed was a gold circlet round his head, a cloak and a sword. Anna half-smiled and Dad mistook her expression. 'You'd be better off with me, wouldn't you, sweetheart?'

'I don't know,' said Anna, not wanting to give away that she had, suddenly, glimpsed Dad's self-image – or maybe he'd been influenced by all the *drop dead gorgeous* comments he'd heard. It was rather strange to think of Dad being influenced. 'I won't go away, Dad. You won't be long, will you? It's getting dark.'

He put out a hand in a welcoming gesture. 'Come with me now.'

'No, I'd rather wait. You bring Mikey and I'll come back with you on my own.'

After he'd gone, Anna's teeth began to chatter. What had she done? And yet the steady beat of her heart, the throb of strong pulses in her wrists, at her temples and throat, made her feel wonderful.

She picked up her backpack and began to run. She would just have time to get to Mrs Dodd's, ask her to come back, maybe phone Diego. When Dad brought Mikey, convinced she would exchange herself for her brother, he would have a shock – or she would have the shock. If nobody came, she'd send Mikey home alone and go with Dad. She could escape from him, she was sure. Probably she could escape. Probably.

Mikey would have to go along with the plan, though, not start showing off. He wouldn't have the

Starstone to make him brave. She wanted him to know he didn't need a bit of magic to be brave. He had it inside himself, like the Cowardly Lion.

Chapter Twenty-eight:
Thursday evening

A gathering

*W*hen Anna reached her street, she was horrified to see Mum standing with Mrs Dodd and Diego in the middle of the road. The van from the charity was parked outside their house, and Dave and Roger were unloading something. How could she get Mrs Dodd's attention without having to get into a big explanation, and Mum would hear, and everyone would say her plan was crazy.

She pressed back against a wall, keeping out of sight. Street lamps flickered on, casting long shadows, and people were switching on lights without drawing curtains. In one room two small children were sitting on a sofa, sucking some sort of juice from squashy packets, their faces changing colour in seconds from whatever was on the television they were watching. It had to be a cartoon of some kind, otherwise their faces wouldn't have been so very purple and orange. Their mother – was it their mum? – came into the room, bent down and changed the programme. One of the children started to kick the sofa. Anna remembered Mikey at his worst, when he was five or six, and her throat tightened. Dad never understood Mikey's tantrums, how they got worse and worse the angrier Dad was with Mum.

She hesitated. She couldn't risk going up to Mrs Dodd because there were all these people and in any case Mum would stop her and Dad would hang on to Mikey. Whatever he said, Anna was sure he wanted to hurt Mum and this was his way of getting at her. She would have to go back on her own and risk it.

Risk what? She pulled back the sleeve of her anorak and sweater. The bunched fabric was tight around her elbow but she saw on her bared arm faint swirls of colour. The sign of the snake ran through all her arteries and veins. Her stomach tightened and she straightened, dropping her backpack to the pavement.

The sign of the Snake – Sea Snake, Snake Queen, Queen – was hers now, whether she wanted it or not. She had no idea what it meant. *I've got to find out, and fast,* she thought, as she picked up the bag and walked back to the park, not running, trying to think clearly. She had to be there before Dad drove up, to look as if she'd been lounging, or playing a game on her phone. She had to take him by surprise, get Mikey free, grab him and run. It wasn't a very promising plan. Would the sign of the Snake make a difference?

'Hello Anna.' Anna jumped, gasped, and the man said quickly, 'I'm so sorry, I didn't mean to scare you. Father Bernard? You remember me?'

'Oh yes.' Her breathing came far too fast. 'You didn't scare me, only, it's getting dark.'

'And I'm all black in this outfit.' Father Bernard gestured at the long black robe he wore, under a black jacket. 'I'm sorry. I've been taking a funeral. You're on your own? It's a bit dark round here for a girl walking on her own.'

Anna said through clenched teeth, 'I'm absolutely fine walking on my own. I know all the roads round here.'

Father Bernard moved to stand under a lamppost, where the light could show his face. She had seen him, of course, but never really looked at him, and now she realised he might be younger than she'd assumed. His hair was white and fluffed-up, but thick, and his skin was smooth. He said, 'You had a rather fierce expression on your face and you were clenching and unclenching your fists.'

Anna's mouth dropped open. She wriggled inside her jacket, trying to gather her thoughts. 'I expect I was daydreaming.' She glanced aside, not wanting to meet his gaze. She couldn't tell what colour his eyes were but his gaze was too direct and bright for her to be easy about telling a lie.

'Would you mind if I walked with you till you get to wherever it is –?' He gestured. 'I'm a safe person. Safeguarding, all that.'

Several ideas flashed through Anna's mind. 'Yeah, I suppose.' The statement sounded unclear. She began to walk on, and he stepped beside her, not close, but near enough for her to be surprised at how relieved she felt. For several paces neither of them spoke, and then she said, 'She's talked to you about my dad, hasn't she?'

'Your mother has told you? Well, I'm glad.'

'You're glad she wants to let Dad off?'

'No, no.' He sounded shocked. 'I'm glad – relieved, shall I say, she took you into her confidence.'

'Oh.'

'I am sure you are old enough to be consulted. She tells me you have been a tremendous support to her for the last couple of years.'

'Do you think she's crazy?' Anna did not mean to blurt it out but now that she had started she had to continue. 'He's awful, he makes people think, because he's clever and he's sort of good-looking if you like that sort of thing, he makes you think he's a nice person and Mum's got mental health problems, making things up but she isn't. I mean, he really did kick her. He burned her arms, he burned her back. Mikey and me, we saw stuff. Why does she think he can change? Why does she think she's got to let him off? She's crazy – well, not like he said, but – I don't understand.'

Father Bernard stopped. They had reached the edge of the park, near her meeting point with Dad. He sighed. 'I believe that forgiveness is required because we are all made in the image of God, and God loves all his creation. In particular, we are told to love our enemies. You've heard me say so.'

Anna slapped the top of the wall and winced. 'What's the point of that? He won't suddenly get kind and loving. He's been to the house, and Mikey won't talk to him so he slapped him, Dad slapped Mikey across the face.' Father Bernard leaned against the wall and waited. 'Well, Mikey did bite him but he deserved it and now Dad has taken him.' She broke off, cross with herself for saying the words aloud.

Father Bernard stiffened. 'You know this for sure?'

She drew a deep breath but the words kept spilling out. 'I kind of arranged to meet him here and he came and I said if he brought Mikey I'd go with him instead.' Father Bernard's intake of breath was almost a groan. Anna sniffed. 'I can manage him better than Mikey. Anyway, I had a plan.'

'You had a plan? What happened to it?'

Ann shivered and pulled her anorak tight. It was a bit too small. She couldn't zip it up but she hadn't told Mum. Mikey was growing fast. 'Well, I went home and I meant to ask Mrs Dodd, she's our friend, she lives opposite us. I was going to ask her to come with me so Dad would be far too embarrassed to do anything.' Father Bernard raised his eyebrows. 'Mrs Dodd used to be a headteacher and Dad's a lecturer and he's a terrible snob. He'd have hated Mrs Dodd seeing him do something bad, like stealing Mikey.'

Father Bernard's laugh completely surprised her. She was about to stamp away when he said, 'You are a very astute reader of human nature. Will I do? Would I be a suitable substitute for your Mrs Dodd?'

Anna caught her breath. Could she trust this man who thought Dad could be forgiven? A wave of something like anger made her eyes burn. She swung around to stare into his face. 'Did you persuade Mum to see Dad again? Did you tell her it was her duty?'

Father Bernard took a step back.

Anna chewed her cheek. It was all a horrible mistake. Dad was going to steal Mikey whatever she did. Tears prickled the back of her eyes.

'I think you are a very brave young woman.'

A tear rolled down Anna's cheek. She looked over her shoulder, so he would not see.

'I encouraged your mother to follow her conscience, and nothing more. We have to live with our own sense of what is right. I could not possibly tell her what to do. She is a very faithful woman, a lovely, wise person. I think she must be a wonderful mother.'

Anna blinked hard. 'She is.'

'I'm more than happy to come with you, if that would help. I don't want to make things more difficult for you.'

'He'll be horrible.' Anna hesitated. 'He says religion is useless, it makes people weak.'

'You think your mother is weak?'

She did not have time to answer. A car slowed and drew up. The driver switched off the headlights, opened the door, climbed out and locked the car. It wasn't Dad's car. She couldn't see the driver because he was still in the middle of the road.

Father Bernard had not moved, but he said, very quietly, 'Is that Mikey in the car?'

Anna groaned. She could not help herself when she saw the pale, small face pressed against the window.

Dad came to the back of the car and rested his hand on the roof. The car was a deep red, a bit like a Land Rover, with huge wheels and wheel arches splashed with mud. Had Dad bought a new car? Why was it so big? 'Who is this, Anna? What are you doing with a priest? You know they're all paedophiles, don't you? Living off other people's money, not doing a decent job of work.' His voice was hoarse. He broke into a coughing fit before carrying on. 'Your mother plainly has no idea of how to protect you. You're coming with me,' and he lunged towards her, taking her by surprise.

Father Bernard was unbelievably fast, standing in front of Anna to protect her. She had not expected him to be able to move so easily. Dad made a growling sound, lifted his right hand into a fist and made to punch Father Bernard, but the priest was, again, too quick. He grasped Dad's wrist and held his arm tight. Dad punched with his left hand but Father Bernard neatly swung his body aside and caught the other wrist. Anna heard him say, 'I believe your name is Anthony. Anthony, think. You want your children to witness this?'

Dad spat in his face and Anna closed her eyes for a second. She had to do something herself, if Father Bernard was being so strong on her behalf. She ran to the car and heaved on the doors, but none of them would open – but Mikey's face split into a huge grin at the sight of her. He gave her a double thumbs up, scrambled between the front seats and began to hit the car horn. It took a few goes for him to settle into a steady rhythm of pressing and releasing, pressing and releasing.

Anna spun round to see Father Bernard pulling Dad's arms down, until his wrists were together. Dad was shaking with the kind of rage she had seen before, when he had totally lost control of himself. 'Call yourself a man of peace? Think you can hold me? I'm reporting you for assault.'

Father Bernard's shoulders were still bunched, and he trembled slightly. His whole body was tensed. 'Will you be calm, Anthony? I want to release you. I don't like doing this but you did threaten to abduct your daughter.'

'She's mine, she'll come with me, I know she will, she offered.'

'Be rational, man. Can I release you?'

'Yes. Yes.' Then, as Father Bernard let go of his wrists, he swung out again.

Anna was there. She grasped Dad's left hand, caught his fingers, and let the power of the snake ripple through her body – *dark forests – reeds rooted in the depths of the ocean – currents lifting and carrying – the sway and the joy – bright fish – claws scampering across the rocks –the surge and eddy of the ocean where I have my being – the land I raise into sunlight through the long rays slanting down –*

Dad was not moving at all. His eyes had rolled up to show only the whites.

Father Bernard said, 'You can let him go, Anna. I don't think he's going to do anything.'

A man and woman ran across the road, the door of their house banging open. 'What's the trouble? The child in that car needs a real talking-to, sounding that horn all the time.'

Father Bernard turned in their direction and said something under his breath. It seemed to satisfy them, because they stood watching, arms folded, like an audience.

Anna said, 'Dad, unlock the car, please.'

Dad seemed to come back to life. He put his hand in his pocket and clicked the car key. Mikey fell as he climbed out of the car but he did not whinge or burst into tears. He rubbed the sleeve of his blazer over the graze and ran at Anna.

On their way home, Father Bernard said, 'Well, I used to play rugby and then, when I got too old for it, I began going to the local gym. Weight training. Keeps me fit.' He shot a glance at Anna and said, 'I'm not sure what happened there when you took hold of his hand.' He laughed. 'I've come across enough situations I can't explain.'

Anna nodded. She could not have found the words to tell him what had happened. She didn't know what she would say to Mum. She thought of another question instead. 'Mum's going to have to tell our social worker, Karina, she's been round lots. And the police. Will they put Dad in prison?'

Father Bernard was holding Mikey's hand, or perhaps Mikey was holding Father Bernard's hand. 'What do you think, Mikey?'

Mikey didn't reply.

Anna said, 'What was it like with Dad? Did he take you to the old house? Did you talk to him? Actually, how did he get you to come with him? He must have done something.'

'He came to the playground. It was playtime.' Mikey's voice was quiet but he spoke clearly. 'He said Mum had a really really really bad accident and she was in hospital and she was so bad he was taking me to see her first. He said we'd get Anna later.'

Anna blew out her cheeks and glanced up at Father Bernard. He said, 'Good story. Mikey, did he tell anyone at the school he was taking you?'

Mikey seemed to perk up. 'I said that, we're not to go with anyone except the person we're meant to go with. I go with Mrs Dodd, that's what Mum fixed.' He rubbed a hand under his nose. 'I didn't think. Was it wrong?'

'No, Mikey,' said Anna, taking out her phone. 'You were frightened about Mum.' She texted Mum.

When they got to the end of the street, people were running towards them.

'You've got him, oh, Mikey my man, how are you?'

There were more questions than answers in the next two minutes.

'Did you talk to Dad?'

'We brought a new chest of drawers we thought Sofia would like we had no idea –.' That was Dave.

'Where did you learn to fight like that, Father Bernard?'

'You will have noticed I didn't fight?'

'Dad had lots of new toys but I didn't like them. Can I have them here?'

'Didn't police come to Dad's house –.'

'Will I be on television?'

'Shouldn't we ring the police straight away?' Roger's voice was steady, breaking through Mikey's explanations. 'I think we should – sorry, Sofia, I'll ring Karina.'

It was very crowded in their sitting room. Dave and Roger stayed for cups of tea and cake, and Roger said he thought Karina would give the best advice about who to tell and what to do next. Anna listened carefully. 'Are you trained now? I mean, are you qualified as a social worker?'

He grinned at her, retying the green ribbon on the end of his thin plait. In the half-light from the lamp his dark skin had a polished gleam. 'More or less. I've asked for Karina as my mentor. She's terrific.'

'I love my laptop. Thank you so much.'

'You're welcome. We knew you and your mother would make excellent use of them.'

Then Mum asked him something, and Dave started playing a dinosaur game with Mikey and Mrs Dodd went across the road to her house, to collect special biscuits she'd made for when Mikey came home.

Father Bernard had seated himself in a corner, cross-legged on the floor. He had unbuttoned the black robe and Mum had hung it up along with other people's coats. He said the clothes he wore underneath were much more comfortable and he did look easy in his green corduroy trousers, green shirt and thin blue woollen jumper. He'd said he was glad to get out of the dress and Mikey had fallen over, laughing at the idea of a man in a dress. Anna felt him looking at her and squatted beside him, more comfortable herself in jeans and jumper than school uniform.

'You took your father's hand and he came to a stop. He just stopped.' He bent forward over his shoes, retying the laces and waited, resting his hands on his knees.

Anna said, 'I can't really explain. I said I'd exchange myself with Mikey because, well, because – Mum said something funny about giving him another chance. I never wanted to give Dad another chance but I was, just a bit, well, sorry for him.'

Father Bernard tipped his head back and stared, apparently at the ceiling. 'Tell me a more about being sorry for him.'

'You won't tell anyone, will you?' Father Bernard shook his head. 'I keep thinking, he's very clever, he's got all these degrees, but he has to be so horrible to Mum and us and really, he must feel horrible inside. He's got to know he's being stupid, hasn't he? All of a sudden I was a bit sorry for him behaving like that. It's a funny sort of feeling.'

'You think he knows you're sorry for him?'

'I don't know. He'd hate it.'

Later that night, curled up in bed with the first hot-water-bottle of the nearly-winter, Anna relived the sensation of Sea Snake and Queen and Anna, three very different beings, joined together, and stopping Dad. If she got back to Pelm could she share this with the Queen? She'd have to take Mikey. If she didn't they might not find the other little kidnapped children. He'd be so upset about the Starstone.

Kazan was the Keeper of the Starstone on Pelm, only the Starstone had disappeared into the air. What had the Queen done with it, to it? Did it still exist somewhere? Could it be in two places at once?

Chapter Twenty-nine Friday

Unshrivelling

*I*t was hard to work out who was more worried – Mum about Mikey going to school, or Mikey worrying about Mum, until Mrs Dodd said she would take him, talk to his teacher and Mr Carey, go back at the end of the day, the same as always. This time she would ask Mr Carey to make sure the staff on playground duty kept watching everyone who came through the gate.

'I don't blame them for not seeing Mikey go off with his father. Well, perhaps a little, but this will have scared them into being extremely vigilant. Sofia, you are not to worry. If I know Mr Carey, he will let the playground duty staff fret and worry and that will be enough.'

Mum was paler than usual and she hadn't brushed her hair properly. The curls were wildly knotted. 'Karina will come this morning, and the police. I must decide what to do. What will be for the best?'

Anna had the same thought as she went off to school. Polly and Reima were waiting for her by the lockers. 'You got your brother back, everyone says.' Polly had already packed her bag for the morning's lessons but a boy crashed into her and she dropped it. The books spilled across the corridor floor.

The Year 9 kid kicked at them and Anna grasped his wrist. He was so surprised he stopped kicking. 'Are you worried by books? Frightened?' The boy's eyes opened wide and for a second, before the usual swank and swearing began, he was properly startled. Anna simply tightened her grip and felt, again, the power of the snake, flowing through her. She knew he could not move, except to rant. 'You'll pick up Polly's books. It was an accident, wasn't it.'

She released him. Bits of white spit flecked the corners of his mouth. 'You're sick in the head, you are,' he said, and but he picked up a couple of books, handed them to Polly before running off.

Anna knelt to collect the rest, finding Reima by her side. 'What's got into you?' said Reima, nudging her. 'I want you on my team. You can be leader.' Anna giggled and the snake feeling sank down.

'I wish you could come to tea with us. I asked Mum about sokolapita but she says it's too messy to bring to school. It's the most amazing squidgy chocolate cake you ever tasted.'

Polly said, 'Cakes make people happy. Can I come too?'

When Anna got home she found Mrs Dodd and Mum in the kitchen, talking, while Mikey played upstairs. He said he was tired. He hadn't been able to sleep, even though Dad shut him in his own old bedroom.

'It's hardly surprising,' said Mrs Dodd. 'It will have been a traumatic experience for him. You've settled with your social worker what to do.'

Mum held her mug between both hands. 'I do not want him to be questioned any more than necessary. There's no point in dragging Anthony through the courts. I spoke to my parents earlier today. They're coming over. I must find a hotel, somewhere not expensive –.'

'Nonsense,' said Mrs Dodd, leaning forward and taking Mum's hand. 'Sofia, they must stay with me. I have plenty of room. They can spend lots of time with Mikey.'

Mum hiccupped, stood up, sat down again, covered her face with her hands and began to cry.

Anna had been staring at her schoolbag and wondering if she could bear to start her English homework. She jumped up but Mum waved her off, swallowed, coughed, blew her nose. Then she pushed her hair behind her ears and smiled. 'I can't apologise, although I am embarrassed. Miranda, you are so good. How can I ever thank you?'

Mrs Dodd knotted her fingers together. The knuckles were knobbly and Anna had never noticed this before. Mrs Dodd had an old body and a young mind. 'You thank me every time you allow me the pleasure of spending time with your children. I hardly see my own. You know I have no grandchildren. My sons live so far away. Getting to know you and your children has completely changed my life.'

Anna picked up her bag and crept upstairs. She had just opened her poetry anthology when Mikey came in, banging the door. 'I can't find my Starstone. Do you know where it is?'

She had known she must tell him, but what could she say? She took it into a dream? It vanished in a dream? She rubbed her forehead. 'When you were gone I had to go back to Pelm. I did something bad, Mikey – well, I was wrong, I took some pine cones to

Pelm, I didn't mean to leave them but I did and I had to get them back.' She glanced at him and saw his fingers tighten around a model T Rex. 'You weren't here, so I borrowed the Starstone to get me there, and it worked, I did find them.'

He was interested, to her surprise. 'Why were pine cones wrong?'

'They might have stopped other trees growing, or chets or orzels or chiriku or other animals might have tried chewing the seeds and got tummy aches.'

Mikey frowned. He was thinking. 'Like when you wouldn't let me share my crisps with Kazan the first time we went?'

'That's what Kazan said. He found the pine cones. He said they might make everybody sick.' Relieved, she sank down on to her bed.

'Where's my Starstone then?'

'I haven't got it. I had to give it to the Queen.'

Eventually she led him on tiptoe, downstairs and into the garden. It was still daylight, and Tanda followed, miaowing loudly about not having had her supper. When she took Mikey towards the fence at the end of the garden, he said with a wail, 'This isn't the way. We got to have Tanda, and the Starstone too.'

Anna placed an arm around his shoulders and waited. Tanda appeared on top of the fence, balancing as a dog yapped on the other side. Her fur stood on end.

'He's a nuisance dog,' said Mikey.

'Well, don't forget, we've seen Tanda terrifying him. Come here, Tanda, settle down.'

The little cat leapt down, curled around Anna's legs, and mewed. Mikey said, 'She never cuddles me,' and leaned down to stroke her.

The King's castle rose up in front of them, the lake lapping at the shore on which they stood. Mikey grabbed Anna's hand.

'It's okay. We've been here before, remember?'

'Where's Kazan?' He squeezed her fingers. 'What's that nasty stink?'

Anna sniffed, pressing her lips together. 'I think it's the lake.' She pulled away and walked across the sand, now covered with a fine, silvery dust, and squatted so she could dip her finger into the water. Long strands of something green and sludgy hung just below the surface, moving lazily as a light wind ruffled the water. She tipped forward until her nose was close to the water and squinted. The bed of the lake was covered in shredded wood and something else. She caught her breath, sank back on her heels, and dug her fists into her stomach. She felt very sick.

'What? What is it?' Mikey thumped her back. 'Are you being sick again?' Mikey was intrigued by other people's vomit, terrified of throwing up himself.

Anna stood up, slightly unsteady, propping herself against Mikey's shoulder. She could not tell him she had glimpsed the corpses of tiny chets half-buried among pebbles and grit and what looked like sacking bags. Maybe someone had collected them up and thrown them into the lake instead of burying them, as they deserved.

How long did it take for water to become so slimy and foul?

'I don't like that lake. Where's Kazan?'

'I expect he's looking for – for the lost children.'

'Yeah, Nazan. Got to find him.' Mikey put his hands

to his mouth to make a funnel and shouted at the top of his voice. 'Ka-a-a-z-a-a-n.' The sound bounced back from the castle walls.

Previously, Anna would have tried to shut him up but she wasn't nervous now about soldiers coming, or the King. An arrow zipped past Mikey's arm and plopped into the lake. He jerked back, but Anna saw he wasn't bothered either. He grinned at her. 'We don't get hurt on Pelm do we?'

Anna pulled a face. 'I wouldn't rely on it.' The scar on her cheek had stopped throbbing but she knew it was still there, under of the new snaky markings. 'We ought to be careful. We've come to help, haven't we?'

The ground trembled and Anna spun round, staring up at the hillside. An army of soldiers on chets was trotting down, sheer numbers producing a sound like thunder. The chets were moving faster than before. Nothing barred their way. The King had ordered the trees to be shredded and all the tiny wooden splinters to be thrown into the lake. The landscape made Anna recall photos she had seen, of war zones.

'You cannot stay here. They will see you, you are not safe.' The voice was Kazan's. 'Why are you standing here? Come *on.*'

Mikey jumped up and down, shouted, clapped his hands. 'Kazan, Kazan, Kazan.'

Kazan's green shirt was torn, his hair was wild and his knees were bloodied but his face was bright. He grabbed Mikey and slapped a hand across his mouth. 'You cannot let everyone know you are here. Stop shouting. Stop.' He shook Mikey hard, making his head loll.

'It's okay, Kazan, you can let him go. Mikey, shut up.'

But Mikey was bursting to say something. 'Have you

got my Starstone?'

Anna tried to shush him. 'I told you, Mikey.'

Kazan said, 'The Queen knows. You can ask her. I did not understand.'

'She said you are the Keeper of the Starstone here and Mikey is the Keeper of the Starstone at home. I don't understand either. It's what the Queen says. Okay?'

In her head another voice called, one that made her bones feel soft and fluid. She breathed in and out, closing and opening her eyes to the rhythm of a sea breaking on a shore

... I am here, little one. You can draw on me ...

She drew a deep breath and focussed on the army thundering down the hill towards them. 'Oh my, oh, look at the soldiers – it's amazing.'

Kazan covered his face with his hands. 'We cannot escape – we are doomed.'

'Kazan, look.' Anna prised Kazan's hands away from his face. 'Look properly. The Stone people are wearing the green and the Green people are wearing silver. Do you see?'

At the head of the troop was the Queen, mounted on Caval, and the colours of the Snake flowed, spread on the ground before her, streamed down the flanks of the chet. Anna felt his snorts, the muscles bunched in his shoulders, his joy as he gathered speed and his hooves struck fire from the boulders. The squillkit sat between Caval's horns, her eyes glittering.

'Kazan, look, the dust is turning back into boulders.' Anna's heart raced at the sight of boulders leaping into shape, taking on the colours of the green, the Snake, the sea.

'Where is my brother?' Kazan's yell sounded above the rattle of sliding pebbles, chets whinnying, riders shouting as they dismounted, throwing back their cloaks and gesticulating. 'What does it mean?' Someone called his name and he staggered into Anna. She had to steady him.

'My boy, my boy.' A soldier ran forward with arms outstretched.

Kazan backed away. 'He's got the wrong armour,' but Anna grabbed his shoulder.

'You're not looking properly – Kazan, look again.'

'That's your dad.' Mikey hopped from foot to foot. His shout was almost as loud as Kazan's. 'We saw him before. It's your dad.'

The man's silvery cloak was draped over one arm. 'Yes, yes, we are Leaf and Stone, we are one.' Tears shone on his face. 'My boy? Kazan? You do know me?' and Kazan threw himself into his father's arms.

Mikey began to jump up and down, screaming at the top of his voice. 'There's Nazan, it's his brother, it's Nazan,' and Anna had to grasp the back of his tee shirt to stop him charging off. People surged forward so quickly she would have been afraid for him, except this was Pelm and people did not bump into each other or knock each other aside.

Without warning, her eyes prickled. 'How – how –?' She could not complete the question, but one of the soldiers halted nearby, unstrapping his armour. He turned in her direction and his blue eyes were bright – so bright she knew he too was not far from weeping.

He gestured vaguely. 'There was magic in the air, the caves opened, all the caves opened.' Running a hand through his tangled hair, he sighed. 'We felt it, we felt the power under our feet. The island opened and the children were free.' His voice cracked. 'Our children ran out and they were free and we are free too. He cannot hurt our children. The Stone and the Leaf are one. We do not know how it happened or when but we are glad. And you are from the old tales? You are neither Leaf nor Stone and yet you stand with us?'

Anna did not know how to answer. She remembered the Starstone crashing into the tree and hurling itself back towards Mikey, Kazan grasping the Starstone, his whole being focussed on it. She thought of the Starstone flying into the air and dissolving into rainbow colours, and it was all very wonderful – but what about the King?

Quite suddenly there was no noise, and the Queen was gazing down at her from Caval's back. 'You have a question for me.' The chet knelt and the Queen slipped off. As she set foot on the sand, it changed colour, from a flinty white to yellow, orange, green, blue, red, violet – like a rainbow pooling on the earth instead of springing across the sky.

Anna found her voice at last. 'Can you undo the Shrivelling Spell?'

The Queen gestured, and Anna slowly turned. Three strides away stood the King, holding a great silver sword over his head. Behind him more soldiers stood in long, straggly lines.

'Your time to become a worm,' said the King in a loud, clear voice. 'Many little worms, in fact.'

Tanda leapt off the chet to balance on the Queen's outstretched arm. Her claws dug deep but the Queen did not wince. She caught Anna's hand. 'You will join me? Kazan?'

'Yes, yes.'

'Although it is the Shrivelling Spell?'

'Yes.'

'You are not afraid?'

Anna said, 'Are you going to turn it back on him? Can you Shrivel him?'

The Queen's eyes flickered, changing shape into yellow slit, green orbs, and the deep, bright blue eyes of the Snake Queen. 'Oh yes, I can.'

The King began to chant.

Anna's breath came in short bursts. 'Will you be happier – if he is shrivelled – like, like the chets?'

'He deserves to suffer.'

'Yes.' She swallowed, remembering. 'But will you be happier?'

'Woman, prepare yourself –.' The chant grew louder.

softer than an orzel's sigh
blown apart beyond repair

finer than windblown dust –

Tanda leapt to the ground and wound between their legs, just like a cat. The Queen pressed her hand. 'What do you want to show me?'

Kazan said in a fierce voice, 'He deserves to be shrivelled.'

Anna said, 'Wait,' and closed her eyes. Mind shifted to mind until she did not know what separated Sea Snake, Queen, Tanda, Kazan, Anna – tree and sea and cave and cliff and mist and rain and starry sky – and all the cells of her body seemed to dance with the words of the chant.

Leaf and Stone flow together, grow together
We make the world, we do not break it
Let him be his own true self

'Oh,' said the Queen in a low voice.

Colours rippled across Anna's skin, sand shifted beneath her feet, saltiness filled her lungs, carried on the wind blowing over the sea. Leaf and Stone, root and rock, air and ocean –.

'We release him from magic. Let him be a man of Stone again.'

The world shifted. Anna found herself back in her own mind.

Tanda's tails were neatly curled. Her purr was so loud even Kazan's dad knelt beside the squillkit and pressed his forehead into her side.

Although the King continued his chant, the words of the Shrivelling seemed to unravel until he fell silent. Anna heard the world's stillness, its held breath. No pebble moved, no chet snorted, no orzel swooped across the sky.

The King dropped his sword, scratched his nose and lifted one foot to inspect the boot. 'In Pelm's name, are these the best I can find? No heft on the soles. No good for riding, far too much fancy work. Where's my bootmaker?'

Still muttering, he wandered down to the lake, and stood with hands on hips, seeming unaware of the water lapping over his feet. He gazed up at the clouds, where a couple of orzels now swung lazily, before disappearing into the clouds.

Anna remembered the first time she had seen an orzel – the great white bird with a crest down its back and intense, watchful blue eyes. 'They are so beautiful.' The Queen nodded. 'He can't hurt them now, can he?'

The Queen squeezed her hand. 'He will not.'

They watched the King bend, dip his hand into the water and shake off the drops as if they were poisonous.

His yell brought servants running from the castle. 'How have you neglected your duties? How has the water become so degraded? I expect a plan tomorrow for clearing and cleaning. I cannot imagine fish will survive in filth like this.'

Someone said, 'Sir, you commanded us to throw in all the –.'

The King threw up his hands. 'I will hear no excuses. Do your duty or expect to be chastised.' He picked up the sword, swung it loosely to and fro and dropped it in the sand before stalking off towards the castle.

'What happened?' Mikey prodded Anna's arm. 'Why didn't he get shrivelled?'

The Queen said, 'It would not have been right.'

Mikey frowned. 'Why did he drop his sword?' He folded his arms and tilted his head.

The Queen caught Anna's eye and cleared her throat. 'He does not need it any longer.'

'Isn't he King?'

'Yes, he is King, but he will be an ordinary king, a king without a sword. He will not bother with spells or magic. If people do not see his glamour, he will have none.'

Anna said, 'Mikey and me, our dad, he thinks he's so glamorous.'

'What's glamorous?' Mikey tugged at Anna's arm.

'Glamour is a kind of magic,' said the Queen. 'A person believes they have a beauty and attraction that draws others to them. It is not real.'

'Our dad thinks he's special but he isn't, he's nasty.'

Anna stared at Mikey, realised her jaw had fallen open, and closed it.

The Queen sighed. 'Well, it is over. I must ask the snake in my soul to sleep. My sister the Sea Snake will always come if I need her help. We are as one, thanks to you, and to Mikey.' She turned to Kazan and inclined her head. 'Thank you, my soldier.'

Kazan's father dropped to his knees. 'I thank you, my Lady.'

Kazan knelt beside him. 'Queen, my Queen.'

Anna was not distracted. 'How can you make the snake in your soul go to sleep?' She felt the power flare through her body, colours pounding through her blood.

'I must not depend on it.' The Queen shook her head, and red, green and blue lights shimmered in her golden hair. 'And you, Anna, you have the snake in your soul too, Leaf and Stone.'

'Anna's not a snake.' Mikey folded his arms. 'You mustn't say that.'

The Queen placed a hand on his head, very gently, and he stood quite still. 'No, but she has been in our minds. She will need you to help her remember she is Anna.'

'I can do that,' said Mikey.

Much later, lying in bed, Anna wondered if she could get her hair to look the same as the Queen's. She would ask Reima where she bought her hair colours. Mum might be cross – or she might laugh. Dad would hate it.

Chapter Thirty: Saturday

A View from the Scar

*T*hey stood by the Mushroom at the top of Scout Scar. The sky was smudged with layers of cloud and on the horizon, beyond the greeny-gold of the fells, Morecambe Bay sparkled in the sun. Everything was changing colour.

Diego read out the engraving on the plaque. '"The Mushroom four-way shelter was built in 1912 to commemorate the Coronation of King George V. It was refurbished in 2002 by Underbarrow and Bradleyfield Parish Council on the occasion of the Golden Jubilee of his Granddaughter Queen Elizabeth ll." It must have taken a lot of labour to fix this.'

'There are huge cairns on top of some of the high fells. How they got the stones up there I can't imagine.' Tara set Andy down and he ran around the four quarters of the shelter, pretending to be an electric car so they would only know he was there when he crashed into them. That was his version, anyway. Mikey ran with him in case he fell over and banged his nose. 'Actually, I can imagine. Some men like nothing better than giving themselves really hard tasks so they can show off their muscles.'

Diego lifted her off her feet and swung her round. She threw her arms around his neck and kissed him, so gently Anna had to look away. Did Mum ever kiss

Dad like that? Diego and Tara loved each other. She didn't see how the King and Queen could ever have been in love but maybe they had been, at first. Everybody loved the Queen. The King got jealous. He didn't like her being as popular as he was, and then more popular.

'Mum, why do people get jealous?'

Mum wasn't listening. She had pulled a little book out of her bag, opened it and was glancing from the page to the skyline. 'This is a wonderful little book, Tara. Thank you, I think I can see the hills. He's drawn them so well. Look, children, Anna, do you see this diagram? Great Gable, Langdale Pikes, High Raise, Ullscarf – oh, and these must be Ill Bell, High Street, Harter Fell. What do the names mean? What is a Pike? I thought a gable was a kind of roof. Why is a high mountain called High Street? It isn't a street.'

Tara had sent Diego to chase after Andy. She laughed. 'The Romans used it as a road, I believe. It's quite easy to see when you're up there. A couple of centuries ago the locals used it for horse racing.'

'So high? How did the horses get up there?' Anna took the book from Mum and stared at the fine, detailed drawing on the pages.

'Walked, no doubt,' said Tara.

Anna thought of Caval, the noble chet. Would he have enjoyed racing with a rider on his back? He only allowed special people to ride him, she was sure of that. Diego came up behind her with Andy on his shoulders. For no reason she could think of, she said, 'When he goes to school will you put him on the register as Andrea?'

He turned sharp grey eyes towards her. 'Why?'

Mum said, 'Anna, please. That's not polite.'

Diego glanced past Anna at Tara. 'Well, he will be registered correctly but we will say he is to be called Andy.' Tara nodded.

'Yes, but –.' Anna bit her lip. Was it rude to say what she knew would happen?

'You don't like his name?' Tara frowned.

'No, I love his name, I mean, it's, children can be horrible. Even little children can be so unkind.' She had not meant to blurt it out. 'And sometimes teachers aren't always nice.'

'We did wonder. His second name is Marco. Shall we call you Marco instead, my son?' Diego grasped the little boy's fists, clapping them together.

Anna reached for Mum's hand and squeezed it.

'What's the matter, moro mou? You've creased the page. Oh Anna, how careless,' but Mum stroked the hair from Anna's forehead as she took back the little hardback book.

Anna wanted to ask if Dad had ever, ever been gentle with her when she was a baby? Had he ever stroked her hair, or lifted her on to his shoulders? She couldn't imagine it. He was far too interested in his appearance, his cleverness, his total sense of being right about everything – except for the moment when she had grasped his wrist to stop him punching Father Bernard.

'What's wrong?' said Mum, but Anna was walking away to the edge of the Scar to gaze out across the valley at the sunlight winking on the distant sea. The Queen had discovered how to use the power of the snake inside her. Anna didn't know what the power was, but something had flowed through her, stopping Dad from punching Father Bernard.

In the past it had been Mikey who had stood up to Dad. Well, yes, she had told Mr Carey at school about Dad hurting Mum, and then the lawyer Dad had brought, but she hadn't done anything to make Dad recognise himself. No one could make him change, but maybe she could make him listen, properly listen – or she could arrange things so he wouldn't be able to get out of listening.

'What are you thinking about?' Tara arrived beside her on the edge of the escarpment. Below, the land fell steeply away towards the flat Lyth valley. 'Have you seen the snow on the Howgills?' She took Anna's arm and gently twisted her around to see the view behind them. 'Some people call those hills elephant bottoms.

'I suppose they do look like elephants,' said Anna, not concentrating. 'Tara, can I ask your advice?'

Mikey said, 'Mum, can Mark and Nathan come with us next time?'

'I don't know if they have a car, moro mou.'

'Yes they do, they got a big one like Diego's.'

Diego turned towards them. 'More friends? We could plan a picnic. It's getting colder but we could wrap up.'

'I'll ask Abigail and Jake,' said Mum.

Mikey swung on her arm. 'Andy can play with Sam, can't he? He can be like a big brother.'

'Advice about what?' Tara led Anna away from the others.

'Dad.'

Chapter Thirty-one: Tuesday

Snake Rising

On Monday Anna rang Karina to ask if she would help arrange a meeting with Dad. Karina took some persuading but Anna was sure of herself. Tara's questions had made her sharpen her arguments. There was a lot of sighing during the phone call, but eventually Karina said she would call Mrs Dodd, and make sure she was on stand-by, Mum was to stay with Mrs Dodd and Mikey would wait upstairs until he was called.

She herself would be coming. No way could she let Anna and Mikey be alone with Dad.

On Tuesday afternoon, Mrs Dodd caught Anna's shoulder as Mikey bounded across the road towards their house. 'I hope this all works as you wish. Karina says she's sorted things out for you. What about Sofia? What does she say?'

'She was a bit upset. I did go behind her back.'

'I imagine she is very, very worried on your behalf. Still, you have every right to be in touch with the family social worker. Oh, who's that in the car with her?'

She pointed at Karina's small blue car, drawing up outside home.

'It's Roger, oh, that's great. He said he asked for her to be his mentor. See you later, Mrs Dodd.'

'I'm here if you need me.'

Roger wore his usual anorak but beneath it a dark blue suit. His shirt was open-necked. He looked very correct, like a teacher. He grinned and said to Mikey, 'Shake hands?'

'You look funny in those clothes.'

'Mikey –.'

'It's okay, Anna. Mikey, I'm practising. I need a suit today but I won't for every client.'

Karins handed Mikey a small carrier bag. 'I brought biscuits. I know Mrs Dodd gives you home-bakes and I can't compete but these are pretty good. Do you want to get ready?' She glanced at Anna. 'Your father is coming at four-thirty.'

'Have you talked to Mum this afternoon?'

'Let's go inside and get organised. She's apprehensive but she's agreed to trust me.'

Roger said, 'She's waiting for you at Mrs Dodd's? Is that right?' He rubbed his chin. 'You're very brave, Anna.'

'She'll come when Father Bernard arrives.' Anna's heart had started to beat too fast for comfort. She unlocked the door and stepped into the hallway. The house felt cold.

'Let's turn on your electric fire for half an hour, warm up the sitting room,' said Karina.

Mikey came back from the kitchen carrying a large white plate, with biscuits laid out in neat rows. 'I made it look nice.'

'You surely did,' said Roger, taking the plate from him. 'Shall I make tea and juice? I know where everything is.'

Anna took off her coat, dropped her backpack and stood behind the sofa, staring out of the window at the darkening street.

'Okay, lass?' Roger patted her shoulder. She nodded, hoping he would not notice her hands were shaking.

'Sit down for a moment.' Karina sat on the sofa and patted the seat beside her. 'Are you certain about what you want to say to your father?'

'I think so.' She fell silent. 'I just need to go over it in my head.'

Karina said, 'What's the most important thing you want to say?' Her round face was creased and there were grey shadows beneath her eyes. Anna grasped her anxiety and doubt as clearly as if she had spoken out loud.

She wanted to reassure Karina. 'Oh, stuff about listening.' She thought for a moment. 'I need to tell him he can't live my life for me. I'm going to live it for myself.'

'That's a very grown-up statement. We must make sure he pays attention.'

Mikey had finished his biscuit. 'I'm going to play dinosaurs in my bedroom.'

'You'll come down when I ask you?' Anna frowned at him.

He shrugged. 'Whatever.'

Roger's eyebrows wiggled. After Mikey had left the room he said, "They pick up stuff so quickly. *Whatever*. Playground chat.'

Dad had to ring the bell because Karina had dropped the latch. Anna heard him stamp his feet on the doormat, say something sharp, and he flung open the sitting room door so hard it banged against the wall. He almost stepped back when he caught sight of

253

Roger, almost bumped into Karina. His scowl told Anna he was annoyed but she did not care. She knew what she would say.

Karina stood up. 'Please take a seat, Mr Daniels. Roger Grey is one of my trainees. He's sitting in on this interview.'

There was no attempt at shaking hands. Dad wore the leather jacket and white polo-neck sweater and stood in front of the electric fire with hands in pockets, as if this were his house and he could take all the heat for himself.

Karina gave a sideways wink to Anna, one Dad couldn't see, and sat down again. The old sofa wheezed and Anna smothered a laugh as she joined Karina. The wheeze was a relief. Karina patted her hand. 'This interview is at Anna's request.' It seemed to Anna that Dad stopped breathing for a moment.

He rubbed a hand over his mouth. 'She's a child. She can't make demands.'

Karina leaned forward, hands lightly clasped. 'She has every right to make a request. I checked her status with our Children' Services and I must remind you, Mr Daniels, that although Mrs Daniels does not wish to press charges against you for abduction I can report you to the police. I will, if you do not cooperate with Anna.' The lines on Dad's face tightened. 'Over to you, Anna.'

Anna could not face her father from an old mock-leather sofa. She stood up, opposite him, but beyond his reach. She did not think he would try to slap her but she saw the surging rage in the flare of his nostrils, the whitening patches on his face. Roger was close enough to rescue her if she needed it.

And the Snake, but that wouldn't be a good idea ...

'I was thinking, Dad, about all the people I've met since we came to this house, like my grandparents, and Diego and Tara, you've seen them. Teachers at my new school, teachers at St Nick's. Mr Carey's still there. He's still the headteacher. He's the one I told about you hitting Mum and he rang social services.'

Dad shifted his weight from one foot to another. 'Old tales, Anna, why do you repeat them?'

Anna did not look away. Something inside her intensified and it was not fear. 'You know what, Dad, they all have something in common. They're truly interested in Mikey and me.' Dad opened his mouth but she did not wait for him to reply. 'You'll say stuff, like, you had our best interests at heart, but really, what you wanted was for us to be exactly like you. Mum says you were lovely and kind when you first got together but I think you were just putting on an act. If you loved her how could you have kicked her or half-strangled her? We saw that, Mikey and me. Mikey tried to stop you that time when you punched him in the eye. Oh, Mikey – I wasn't expecting you yet.'

Mikey stood in the doorway, holding a dinosaur toy in each hand. Dad stood so still Anna shared his held breath, the tightening muscles in his abdomen but she shook herself free. Roger patted the arm of his chair and Mikey went to lean against it.

Mikey wasn't ready to talk. She guessed he'd got nervous, waiting upstairs on his own. 'Okay, Mikey's turn in a bit. We've met some great dads, haven't we, Mikey? Diego, and Jake, he's at our church. You saw our priest, Father Bernard. I never got why he's called a father when he isn't married, but I see it now.'

Dad's eyes bulged. Anna had never seen someone's eyes bulge before, except Mum's when he had his hands around her neck. She swept on.

'I don't think you know how to be a dad. You're more interested in other people watching you, thinking you're *drop dead gorgeous*. You used to pose in the playground when you were picking us up from school.'

'I picked you up from school because your mother was not competent.' The corners of Dad's jaw flexed.

Anna spread her hands. 'There's another thing, our geography teacher is so good, she gets so excited when somebody does a good project she says, "Oh, I never thought of that before," stuff like that.' Words seemed to explode in Anna's brain. 'She makes people believe they're clever. She's not a bit interested in being clever herself. I think she's brilliant. She looks a bit untidy, she pins her hair up but it keeps coming down. Our teachers are meant to have a dress code and she does her best but nobody could say she looks smart. I don't know what your students think about you when you're teaching them. Do you tell them they have brilliant ideas?'

Dad said, 'You're over-excited. You don't understand what you're saying.' He took a step forward but Anna gestured again, glimpsed the colours flaring in the skin of her wrists as the strength swelled inside her.

'Being a good dad and being a good teacher,' searching for the words she wanted, 'there's stuff in common, like, wanting things to be good for *us*. Not the way *you* think they ought to be but how *we* want them to be. You can't be me, Dad. Only I can be me.'

Something shifted in her father's face. His

eyelids flickered. He could not meet her gaze.

'I got to say it now, Anna.' Mikey was carefully handing his dinosaurs to Roger.

'Okay.' Anna crossed her fingers behind her back and Karina leaned sideways to switch on the standard lamp. New shadows fell across faces. Perhaps it would help Mikey if he couldn't see Dad's expression.

His voice had a high-pitched note. 'You locked me in that car. You said Mum was in a bad bad accident but she wasn't and anyway you hurt her. I don't like you only I don't like not liking you. It makes me feel peculiar in here.' He rubbed his hand against his chest. 'You ought to be a proper dad and you're not. I don't talk to you because – because, it's horrible having a dad who's bad and it makes me so sad so if I don't talk to you I feel like ...' Anna reached for his hand, squeezed it. 'I feel like I'm being bad only it isn't my fault. I'm not the bad one. You're not like a dad.'

'It isn't your fault. You want Mum to be safe.' Anna squared her shoulders.

Dad's face was red. Anna had never seen him so angry but he could not touch her – there were witnesses – and the strength of the Snake was pumping through her arteries. He folded his arms tightly. His nostrils flared and she rubbed her nose, determined not to look the same. 'Well, fine. Now you've finished lecturing me perhaps I can speak. I have no intention of defending myself. I do not need a defence. I am very surprised that apparently educated persons like you, Karina whatever your name is, and you –.' He flung out a hand at Roger, his finger vibrating. 'What's your game? What's your

257

connection with my family?'

The floor began to roll under Anna's feet as the power pulsed in her blood, streamed into every cell. She pulled Mikey closer, spoke in his ear. 'Remember the Queen? She didn't say a spell. We can do this,' and there were voices outside, a key in the latch, the front door opened and footsteps sounded in the hall.

Dad swung round. 'What now?' He ran a finger around the polo neck of his white woollen sweater, tugging it away from his throat, and flicked his ash-blond hair behind his ears.

Mum came into the room, stopped, gazed first at Anna and then at Dad. She had tied her hair into a knot on top of her head. The dark curls fell either side of her face and Anna's heart beat faster than ever. Mum was so beautiful. She was nervous but she was going through with it.

'Good evening, Anthony. Thank you for coming. I know this cannot be comfortable for you.'

Dad began to speak but Father Bernard appeared, wearing his blue sweater. Anna bit her lips the drooping hem of the sweater, and the hole in one elbow. She must not laugh. He didn't seem to mind. 'Hello everyone. Hi Mikey, Anna. You must be Roger. Dave has told me about your charity work together. Good evening, Mr Daniels.'

Dad turned his back.

Karina got to her feet, adjusting her jacket. 'We'll wait outside, Sofia, as we agreed. Roger and I will be in my car if you need us.' Without glancing at Dad, she moved towards the door. 'If only all my clients had your determination, Anna.' She put out a hand to pat Anna's shoulder but stopped short. 'There's something about you.'

Anna could not tell Karina about the Queen, the Sea Snake, the force exploding in her body. It wouldn't last. She needed the power for as long as it took to make Dad accept Mum's right to her own life. She smiled awkwardly at Karina and Roger, giving a little wave of her hand. As he followed Karina, Roger offered Mikey his dinosaurs but Mikey said, 'You can have them if you like. I got lots more.'

'Thank you. I'll take good care of them. They'll come and visit next time we're here.'

The room felt colder once they had left. Mum took Karina's place on the sofa and pointed Father Bernard at the chair Roger had used, but he said, 'Surely Mr Daniels, you'd prefer to sit there? Can you find me something to sit on, Anna?'

'We got stools in our kitchen.' Mikey rushed out of the room.

Dad faced the fire. 'This is farcical. Sofia, what nonsense have you organised?'

'You have to stop talking to Mum as if she's feeble-minded. You said all the time she has mental health problems but she doesn't.' Anna moved closer to Dad and saw his eyes slide sideways, meet her gaze – and he stepped sideways, away from her. She sat on the sofa, next to Mum. Had he glimpsed the Snake within?

Mum stared into her hands, and then at Dad. 'I know you don't believe what I believe, Anthony. I never tried to change your beliefs. I never asked you to join me. In my family faith is strong but I don't take it as something I must follow because I was brought up as a believer. I believe because of what is in my heart.' She laid a hand on her throat, and Anna caught sight of a little silver cross. She'd never noticed it before.

Dad's folded arms tightened. 'Indoctrination. Buying into a state of mind because it's easier to conform.'

To Anna's amazement, Mum laughed. 'Father Bernard doesn't tell us what to believe. We make up our own minds.'

Father Bernard was leaning against the wall. He scratched his ear. 'Mr Daniels, I'm sure you know change comes from within. I can't make anyone change their beliefs or their choices. No doubt you love Sofia and your children and want to protect them –.'

Dad spun round, face contorted and fists clenched. 'You presume to tell me how I feel, you arrogant bastard,' but stopped when Anna planted herself in front of him. Mum stood up, took Anna's hand and held it tight. A rush of strength flowed between them, the same heave of energy Anna knew on Pelm. The floor rolled beneath her feet but nobody else seemed to notice.

'Thank you, sweetheart,' said Mum, lifting Anna's hand and kissing it. 'You have done more than enough.'

Dad shook his head. He looked like someone who'd just woken up from a deep sleep and didn't know where he was.

'Anthony, it's time for you to leave. Anna, Mrs Dodd has made lemon drizzle cake – can you go and ask her to join us? Thank you for coming, Father. Please don't go.'

Everything in the room seemed to rise and fall, and Anna's body floated. Her mind let go. Dad tried to grab her arm and stumbled back, doubling over as if someone had struck him in the stomach. Somehow Mikey arrived, carrying a stool, Father Bernard took it from him, set it down. Then they were in the hallway, and Father Bernard was opening the front door to make sure Dad went out, and on the other side of the road Mrs Dodd's doorway was a rectangle of golden light, and Karina and Roger were leaning on the roof of Karina's car, softly talking about a film Roger saw last night.

Mrs Dodd said, 'Here we are. It's one of my best, this lemon drizzle.' She looked hard at Anna. 'Your eyes are changing colour, did you know? Or didn't I look at them properly before? I thought they were a lovely blue but your irises are almost green.'

Anna said, 'Turquoise? Maybe it's just the light.'

Chapter Thirty-three

Nobody owns us

*D*ad was waiting by the wall, under the tree. Anna stopped dead, heart unexpectedly thumping hard. His face was icy-white, but more shocking was his hair – cut short, as short as hers. And he had started to grow a beard. A fringe of grey stubble edged his chin.

She shifted her rucksack from one shoulder to the other. 'What do you want?'

'Oh, you think I come with demands?'

'You always do.' The words sprang out.

Dad folded his arms. 'You've some nerve, talking back to your father like that.'

'I told you before, Dad, leave us alone. Mum won't take you back.'

'You think this is over? You and Michael are my children.' He tapped his chest and she wondered if he was aiming at his heart.

'You don't own us. Nobody owns us.' Anna half-wanted to look around to see if anyone else was near. She might have been safer. A powerful pulse beat at Dad's throat, black shadows circled his eyes and from the way his weight shifted from foot to foot, she guessed he was balancing on the balls of his feet, like a runner ...or a fighter. 'You can't keep turning up like this. It's stalking.' Her heart was still pounding.

'It isn't over. Tell your mother, tell that interfering fat social worker, that ludicrous priest, it isn't over.'

Anna sighed. Her bag was heavy with homework. 'I'm going home.'

As she moved away, Dad said, 'I have no intention of letting some ridiculous judge tell me what to do. I've taken another legal opinion – King's Counsel, really knows his stuff ...'

The Snake stirred within her. 'Dad, it doesn't matter what some guy tells you, we won't let you ruin Mum's life.' It wasn't strong enough. 'I won't let you.'

'You're only a kid.' His voice was too high.

'You don't know who I am, Dad. Give it up.'

'Never.' It was a hoarse whisper.

She did not tell Mum or Mikey, but Roger came round for a cup of tea and in the kitchen, where she was slicing cake, he said, 'Something bothering you, Anna?'

'Oh, Dad was hanging round again. He says he's getting more legal advice.'

Roger poured milk into a mug. 'We can always go back to the court.'

'He's not going to change his mind. He thinks he owns us.'

'Is this tea the right colour for your mother?'

Anna glanced across, saw Roger's grave expression. 'It's okay.'

'I don't think so. What does your mother say?'

'I haven't told her. Please don't you tell, Roger. He'll keep on having a go at me but he's not going to – well, it's annoying, but he's not going to hurt me.'

Roger had taken a sip of the tea and frowned.

'Damn. This is Sofia's mug. I don't know how you can be sure of that.'

Anna slid a piece of chocolate cake on to a plate. 'Thing is, he still hates looking as if he's not in charge. You know what I mean?'

'Promise you will keep me in touch? You'll tell me?'

'Mum likes this mug too. Yes, I'll text you. I'm not afraid of him, you know. I used to be. Mum still feels sorry for him and in a funny way, so do I, now.'

Roger took a bite of cake. 'You are remarkable, Anna.' He laughed.

Chapter Thirty-four

The Snake Beneath the Skin

*A*nna and Mikey stand side by side at the edge of the lake. The water laps against the sand, and the chiriku swoop over its surface in flashes of yellow and green, orange and sapphire, crimson and purple, calling to one another as they snap at insects too tiny for Anna to see. They make a rainbow in the air – a twirling curve, a video in the sky, with colours merging, separating, bursting apart like fireworks.

'Are we saying goodbye?' Mikey pokes at the sand with a branch he has picked up on the beach.

'I don't know. The Queen will let us know, I suppose.'

'I'm not saying goodbye to Kazan.'

Anna cannot think of how to reply. She doesn't want to say goodbye to Kazan or his family, or this world where creatures are so nearly like the ones they know but different enough to bestir her imagination. Mikey nudges her with a pointed elbow. 'You don't listen to me.'

'Yes I do. I don't want to leave Pelm. Every time we come there seems to be something we are meant to do, and then things change at home.' She traces a pattern in the sand with the toe of her shoe.

'I don't know exactly why we're here now, only Tanda called us.'

Mikey tries to draw the outline of a cat, gives up and smudges it with the sole of his sandal. 'We could bring Mum here.' He turns to her with a toss of his head, his eyes wide and the black curls slightly fuzzy in the moist air. 'She'd like to see Nazan. She'd like everything.'

'Maybe.' Anna thinks about believing in things other people can't see or understand, and it occurs to her that maybe Mum has her own place to visit, her own magical island. Nobody knows what someone else dreams, only what they say about their dreams.

'How true that is.' Anna starts. She has not heard the Queen's approach, not even the swish of her gown. Today the Queen wears flowing green trousers and a kind of yellowy tunic, drawn tight around her waist by a silver belt. 'I still feel your thoughts, Anna. I don't know for how long I will sense your presence but I am glad of it.' Tanda jumps out from behind the Queen and twirls like a kitten, chasing her tails.

Anna drops to her knees, not caring that the sand is wet. The squillkit leaps into her lap. 'Will we have to go away now the King is just ordinary?'

'Ordinary can be wonderful. When I first came to the island to marry him, he was tender and kind. Now, he has bad dreams. He keeps remembering the Shrivelling, the tearing down of trees, the killings.'

Anna says, 'Do you want to help him forget?'

The Queen raises her arm, and a great orzel soars down to perch on her wrist. Its bright blue eyes stare at Anna, stare through her, making her shiver with the strangeness of it. The white crest rises along its back. The Queen says, 'I fly with my creatures, I swim with them. I have promised to sleep at LeafFall, to join the Dream of Root and Branch. I try to share these memories with the King but he cannot grasp them. I did not choose to change, but I chose to act and now I am different.'

She leads them towards the lake. Soon they are knee-deep in cool, clear water. Little fish dart away, their fins catching the sunlight.

Mikey says, 'Are we going paddling?'

'You will soon discover,' says the Queen, but Anna already knows. Her heart races, she glances at her bare arm and sees, beneath the skin, the dance of colours, blue and yellow and green, like the colours of a bruise but cleaner, clearer, filling her with a deep happiness. The great body of water in the lake begins to shift, pressing against her legs, and she knows the Sea Snake is coming close, threading through tunnels linking the lake with her ocean, her vast body arcing through underwater forests.

When her presence swims into Anna's mind, she tells of shafts and caves beneath the island, crystals glinting in the rock walls, the exhilaration of gliding from a salty ocean to a freshwater inland lake.

Mikey drags at the Queen's hand. 'I can't swim properly yet.'

He gasps as the Sea Snake rises above the surface and scoops him on to her back, just behind her head. Anna and the Queen settle behind him, with Tanda perched on Anna's shoulders. The

Queen leans forward, speaks quietly into Anna's ear. 'If you want to return, you will always find a way. You carry us within you now.'

'Will I always hear you?'

'That will depend on how you use the power.'

Anna thinks how Mikey does not want to be the son of a bad father, and he does not want to think badly of Dad. He does not know how to think about Dad. Is she meant to use the power to help Dad change?

'Let it go,' says the Queen. 'Let it go. Let your mother, your father, all the others you know, work out for themselves how to be. Be yourself.' The Sea Snake raises her head and Mikey squeals. 'Take a deep breath. We are going on a journey.'

Anna woke suddenly, blinking against the light streaming in from the landing. Mikey stood in the doorway. 'What's the matter?'

'I had a dream.' He came further into the room.

'It's the middle of the night.' She sat up, yawning, leaning over to squint at the little clock by her bed. Two o'clock. 'Was it a bad dream?'

'It was amazing. There was this ginormous snake.' He spread out his hands. 'We went under the sea and you were there and we could breathe under the sea.'

Anna clasped her knees. 'We swam under the sea?' Mikey rubbed his eyes and she saw he was on the verge of tears. She patted the duvet. 'Did you like the dream?'

He sat heavily on her feet. 'I want to go back. Did you dream about the big snake too?''

She wanted to take his hand but he was too big

to be treated as a small child. 'Yes, I dreamed it too.'

Mikey pulled at his lower lip. 'Did you see Kazan? When we came out of the lake he was waiting for me only you were talking to the Queen. I asked him if he had the Starstone and I could have it again one day. Can he come here?'

Anna caught her breath. She had not seen Kazan. Had Mikey begun to make his own Dream? 'I'm not sure it would be a good idea.'

'People might be nasty about him being green.'

A throb of pain shot through Anna's left wrist and she saw, in the dim yellow light, a change of colour in her skin. 'Do you feel a bit better now?

Mikey said, 'He doesn't have the Starstone. He says it's gone into the air, into the trees and the rocks, it's like everywhere.' He waved a hand. 'Like shrivelling, only different. Sort of the opposite.'

Anna's skin rippled with colour and she felt what Mikey could not explain – how the Queen had sent the Starstone back into the land, the air, the very beginnings of the world.

'What's wrong with your skin? Anna, you look like the Queen only –.' Mikey backed away. 'Have you going to get a snakeskin like the Queen?'

'Of course not.' She breathed deeply, in and out, in and out, counting, sending the Snake – the Queen and the Sea-Snake and the Dream of Leaf and Branch – deep inside. Dad was still around and she would need it. 'We've both changed a bit, being on Pelm. I didn't see Kazan but you did. You are the Keeper of the Starstone here.'

'But it's all gone.' His face twitched. 'There isn't a Starstone any more.'

'I think – I think there is, only we can't see it. Well, I can't see it but maybe you can. Maybe you will, one day.'

'Oh.' Mikey stared at the floor and then directly at Anna. 'Your eyes look different.'

Anna leaned forward. 'So do yours. You've got sort of green flecks.'

'Like Kazan's?

'A bit like Kazan's.'

There was a long silence and then Mikey said, 'Do you think Roger likes my dinosaurs?'

'He's silly if he doesn't. Next time you get out Mrs Dodd's farm we ought to think what the animals would be like on Pelm. We won't tell her. Horses are easy, we've to imagine the two horns for chets. What about cows and sheep? And did I see ducks and geese and hens?'

'There's a huge horse. Mrs Dodd says horses like that are on the beach near us.'

'Maybe Diego and Tara would take us to see them.'

'And Mark and Nathan can come too.'

'Mum will have to ask Abigail. We said before, we'll ask them. Can you sleep now?'

He went back to his room, and Anna was in darkness again. She closed her eyes, reliving the dream of plunging through the ocean on the Sea Snake's back. As she drifted, she dreamed of flying over Scout Scar and Coniston Old Man with an osprey or sparrowhawk.

If the Queen could explore Pelm through the eyes of an orzel, Anna might view her own mountains and lakes with the birds. She could fly across Windermere, skimming the surface, she could ask a blackbird to take her to Derwentwater and Ullswater and maybe, maybe a golden eagle would agree to carry her further, to Crummock and Buttermere, to Ennerdale and Wastwater and all the places she saw on the map but had never visited. She could perch above Scafell Pike and Skiddaw and Blencathra ... if the birds would allow her to see through their eyes.

The golden eagles had gone, for the moment. Maybe Anna could coax them back.

Magical.

Acknowledgments

Thank you to Professor Linda Anderson RSL, poet, and to my fellow writers in the Writers' Rump – novelists, poets, playwrights, award-winners – Anne Banks, Anne Cleasby, Adrian Horn, Des O'Halloran, Caroline Moir, who read and commented in enormous detail, spotting anomalies, making suggestions, offering copious encouragement.